THE ORDINARY BRUJA

MARISOL'S STORY

LAS CERRADORAS
BOOK 1

JOHANNY ORTEGA

Published 2025

Printed in The United States of America

ISBN (paperback): 979-8-9869826-7-0

ISBN (hardback): 979-8-9869826-9-4

E-ISBN: 979-8-9869826-8-7

Library of Congress Control Number: 2025915236

Cover design by Praveen Kumar Chukka.

Imagery used under license from stock photography provided by the designer.

Back cover imagery by Jan Kopřiva

via Pexels. Used under Pexels license.

Map, Family Tree and Character Portraits by Gideon K.

Line editing by Amy Lisane

Copy Editing by Nicholas Carter

Printing by Ingram Lighting Source

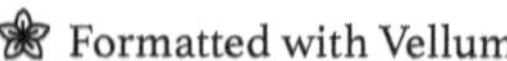 Formatted with Vellum

The most common way people give up their power is by thinking they don't have any.

— ALICE WALKER

FOREWORD

Today

replied to your comment on
post: our
country don't thrive on none of that lol our
culture is a mixture you like it or not. 38m

Reply

replied to your comment on
post: @haveacupofjohanny
you are nothing but a puppet of black
people, look at your likes mostly black
people, you are nothing but a disgrace. 39m

Reply

What Happens

replied to your comment on
post: Dominicans dont give
a fk about nothing and thats the beauty of
our people we dont care about feelings if u r
way too black ur nickname will be
something like that if ur nose is too big
guess what ur nickname will be we just dont
care this thing about dominicans are anti
black is crazy because our national sport is
baseball n our players are black like big
papi, soto our players are black and we fight
against anybody for our people, we love
basketball im 100% sure all dominicans love
jordan, bryant, lebron. embrace the black
side we do embrace it, we live in black
neighborhoods not in white ones prison
is filled with african americans n dominicans
we used to fight for power but things have
changed 11h

Reply

replied to your comment on   post: @haveacupofjohanny @haveacupofjohanny Let's take that same exact logic you just put together right... then why do y'all love being LAMBONASOS!!! to AA's and the black diaspora if all they do is clown you woke tards? Seriously asking though? Why can't y'all just be Dominicans?????????????? Corny ass people man. "BUt tHE SpAniaRds DoN't lIke U" and Blacks do????? 16h

View reply

replied to your comment on post: @haveacupofjohanny maybe you're just annoying? Dominicans get easy citizenship in spain. 15h

Reply

When We

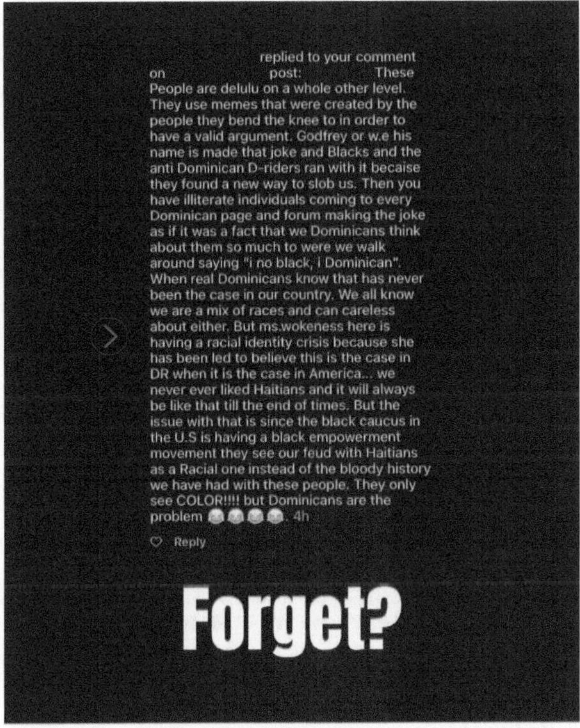

There was a moment I almost walked away from this story. *The Ordinary Bruja* began as a soft exploration—a girl, a little magic, and a whole lot of yearning. But then I spoke a truth online. I said something I'd witnessed for years: that many Dominicans cling to our Spanish ancestry while rejecting the Blackness and indigenous within us. And I shared that, in my lived experience, Spain does not claim us back with that same energy.

What followed was a flood of vitriol. Strangers called me a disgrace. A puppet. Accused me of being confused, annoying, delusional. All because I said we are more than one thing. All because I remembered something many have tried to forget: that we are African, Taino, and yes, European—but we are not just European or the offsprings of our colonizers. We are also the survivors of the ones the colonizers colonized. We are the magic that wouldn't be killed. We are the stories that live in our bones.

That moment was a turning point for me.

Because of that, when I looked at the rewrites for this book, I turned it into a reckoning.

The Ordinary Bruja is about what happens when a girl forgets who she is—because her family was too afraid to tell her. Because fear and shame got passed down like heirlooms. Because when we forget our ancestors, their voices get quieter, until one day, we think the silence is truth.

Marisol's journey is fictional. But the forgetting is real. The shame is real. And the rage I felt—the grief, the ache, the defiance—is all in these pages. This story is not about blame. It's about memory. It's about remembering the whole of who we are.

To everyone who's ever been told to hush, to fit in, to be grateful, to assimilate and to not rock the boat:

You are not too much.

You are not confused.

You are not broken.

You are remembering.

And that is a powerful kind of magic.

— **Johanny Ortega**
Author of *The Ordinary Bruja*

CONTENT WARNING

Heads Up, Babes

The Ordinary Bruja explores ancestral memory, identity reclamation, and the ghosts we carry—some literal, some emotional. Along the way, you'll encounter themes of grief, family estrangement, psychological manipulation, religious trauma, bullying, and the implied presence of generational abuse.

These elements are never graphic or explicit, but they are emotionally and spiritually charged. Please take care of yourself as you read. Pause when you need to, and come back only when you're ready. Your well-being matters more than any page turn.

Con cariño,

Joa

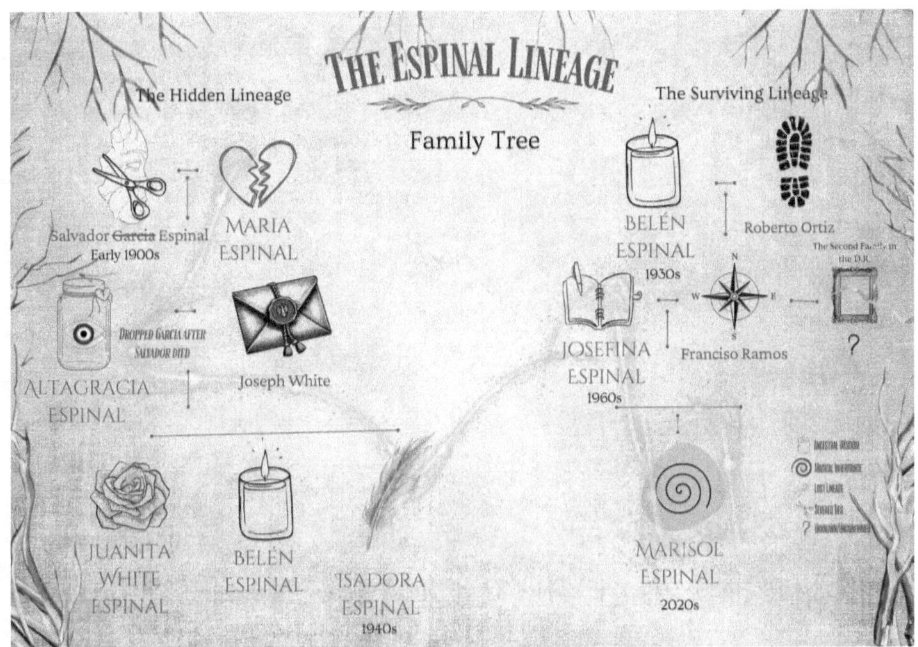
THE ESPINAL LINEAGE
Family Tree
The Hidden Lineage
The Surviving Lineage
Salvador Garcia Espinal
Early 1900s
MARIA ESPINAL
Dropped Garcia after Salvador died
ALTAGRACIA ESPINAL
Joseph White
BELÉN ESPINAL
1930s
Roberto Ortiz
The Second Family in the D.R.
JOSEFINA ESPINAL
1960s
Franciso Ramos
?
JUANITA WHITE ESPINAL
BELÉN ESPINAL
ISADORA ESPINAL
1940s
MARISOL ESPINAL
2020s
Ancestral Wisdom
Magical Inheritance
Lost Lineage
Severed Ties
Unknown/Undiscovered

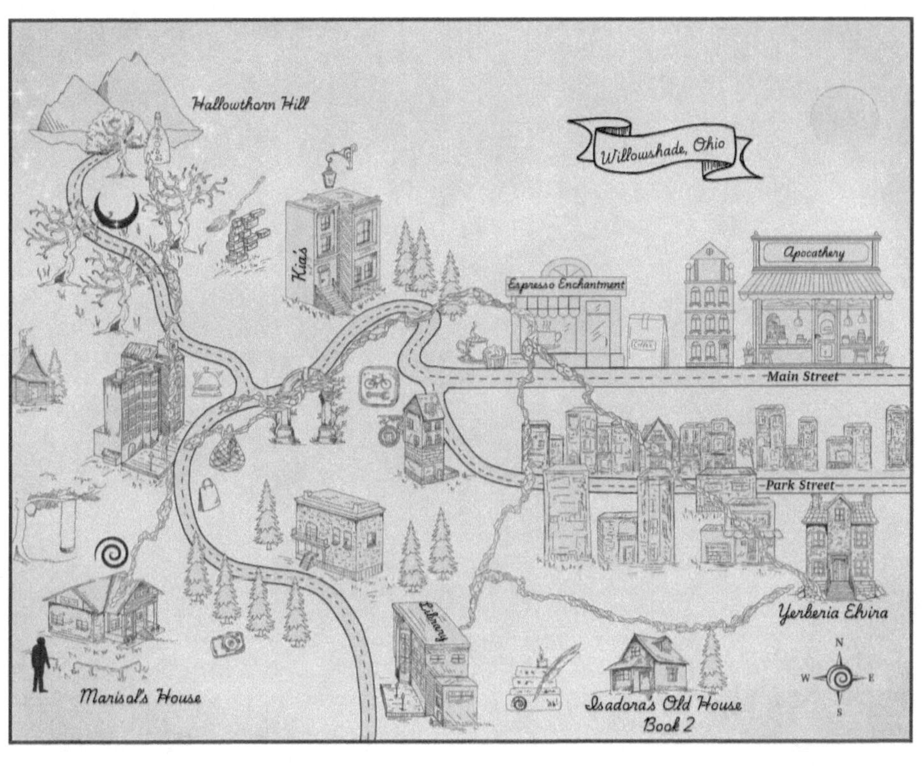

Hallowthorn Hill
Willowshade, Ohio
Kia's
Espresso Enchantment
Apocathery
Main Street
Park Street
Yerberia Elvira
Library
Isadora's Old House
Book 2
Marisol's House
N
W E
S

PROLOGUE
DONDE TODO COMENZÓ (WHERE EVERYTHING BEGAN)

Hallowthorn Hill loomed stubbornly over Willowshade, Ohio. Its roots were tangled with the secrets of the Espinal women, and with the man who had stolen everything from us. I used to climb that hill. It called to me, whispered my name in the rustle of its leaves, hummed it in the ground beneath my feet. At first, I thought it was just my childish imagination. You know, como los muchachitos, like kids who think shadows are monsters.

The hill knows our family. It knows the magic Altagracia buried there. Magic that Salvador Espinal tried to take for himself.

Mi tatarabuelo, Salvador... Ay, Dios. He was a horrible man alive and an even worse ghost. He made his own daughter, mi bisabuela, Altagracia, bury the jar of magic. Said it was to keep her and our family safe. But it was really for his own greed.

Then, when he realized the magic wouldn't open to him, he forced Altagracia to do it, but she had something up her sleeve. Altagracia was not one to mess with, and he fell for it como un bruto, dying right there on the hill.

But death didn't stop him. Oh no. It didn't.

He, too, had something up his sleeve, a way to break the rules and steal the power for himself. But you know what? Magic like ours? It doesn't belong to cowards.

The joke was on him because not even the hill wanted him. It spat him out like gristle, and someone had to bury him somewhere else, not on the hill but close enough that he could still poison it. Even in death, he never really left. He clung to the edges. Because even if he couldn't wield the magic, like the women in the family could, he could still feed off it. Leech it. Mooch it.

And he has for generations.

Let me tell you, magic isn't a harmless fairytale. It's old. Demanding. It wants to be seen, to be known. And it's tired of being buried.

It called Isadora. It called me.

And now, it's waking up again and calling mi pollita.

Mi Marisol.

She doesn't know it yet. If she did, she'd roll her eyes and call it porquerías like she always did when I tried to tell her about our magic. She never wanted to hear about the hill, the jar, or our power. And I get it, now that I am dead. The world told her that magic—our magic—was silly. That her curls were too wild, her body too soft, her imperfect Spanglish bordering on no-sabo too embarrassing. That who she was wasn't enough. So, she has learned to disappear—to not stand out.

But the hill knows better.

And so do I.

Marisol is the one. The hill is calling her like it called me. If she doesn't find the jar—the real jar—and release the magic, Salvador's spirit will keep whispering. Not only that, if the seal fades and mi pollita is not there to receive it, it will wander the world, causing chaos. Salvador will chase it like a dog and poison not just the Espinals but everyone he comes into contact with, leaving them with shame and fear.

And once the magic can't find us anymore—after it has been disconnected from the land, from the Espinal women—it will wither. Our ancestral power will die. And those of us trapped on the hill will either become his image or vanish, leaving nothing but silence where our history once lived.

So, here I am, talking to you.

Help her. Be a witness.

Because when Marisol climbs that hill—because she will—I need you to watch. I need you to watch how she kicks every doubt off her like mud-caked boots on the edge of our porch. I need you to watch how she finds her courage and how she finally finds her voice and roars. Because after she's done, doubt won't have any room to walk in our house anymore. But it won't be easy.

She'll have to face Salvador, his lies, his fear. She'll have to decide if she's ready to embrace every part of herself: the curls, the curves, the culture, the magic.

And that is never easy. Not for her. Not for you. It certainly wasn't for me.

But she's my daughter. An Espinal woman.

She's got this. I know she does.

Ahh... Do you hear that, dear reader?

That's the hill. It heard her grief.

The seal on the jar is fading.

It's calling Marisol.

1

BRUJA EN EL CAFÉ (A WITCH AT THE CAFÉ)

Marisol Espinal's name tag glinted under the harsh café lights, a cruel little mirror. The letters wavered, morphing into something off. God, she hated mirrors. The letters twisted like heat waves on pavement. Her stomach squeezed. Does it say "ordinary"? Heat rose to her neck. She blinked, but the word was still there, pulsing as if alive, refusing to prove her sight wrong.

Right then, the faint scent of cigar smoke drifted past her, starkly out of place amid the café's familiar aroma of espresso and pastries. Marisol glanced around, wondering if someone was smoking inside or lingering too close to the door. She tore her gaze from the nametag. She had always hated mirrors, but this felt different.

Still, she wondered if someone was playing a sick joke on her.

She crossed to the café's large selfie mirror by the corner booth. Eyes followed her, but she didn't care.

Who would play with my name tag? ¿Las tres mojonas? They had been cruel enough in school, and she was sure they still were.

She felt a tug on her sleeve and looked behind her. Her jaw clenched, half expecting to see Delgada or one of her cronies, but it was Kia. Tall, calm, and somehow always exactly where Marisol needed her to be. Her hair was in a high puff, the café's soft light haloing it, and her hoodie hung off one shoulder as if she hadn't noticed or didn't care. Kia never tried too hard, and maybe that's what made her magnetic, steady in a way that made Marisol memorize every line of her face. She smelled faintly of coffee beans and peppermint lotion, always carrying the scent of the café with her, as if it clung to her skin.

"You good, Mari? You've got that faraway look again."

Marisol released a shaky breath. She took a glance at the mirror, just long enough to catch her nametag's glint. The letters seemed to shift.

That is a "B," not an "O," right?

Her stomach twisted again.

"Mari?" Kia called.

Marisol blinked at her reflection. Same old word: Barista. Nothing had changed. It's just exhaustion. Yet the unease gnawed at her stomach.

She turned away from the mirror, silently promising herself not to look at it for the rest of her shift.

"Yeah, I'm okay. Just tired."

Kia nodded, but Marisol could tell she wasn't buying it.

This was why she avoided mirrors. They showed too much.

It had only been ten months since Mami died. The mirror showed that too. Ten months since she had dropped out and come back to the place she promised herself she'd never return to. Gosh. Every time she thought of having come so close only to come home with a diploma-shaped hole filled with student debt, it made her feel like she was walking around with a wet shirt on during winter, and everyone staring at her.

Failure lodged beneath her skin, sour and sharp. It was in this café that she used to dream of becoming someone else, someone better. She was supposed to come back from college extraordinary. Untouchable. She used to imagine walking back to Willowshade, a new version of herself, radiant and success-ful, making the ones who looked down on her scramble for her attention. She'd let them, just so they could feel what they made her feel—dismissal and humiliation.

But that fantasy shattered the moment she returned. She hadn't changed. If anything, things had gotten worse. She'd lost everything. Tears pricked the back of her eyes, and Marisol turned away, unable to think about it any longer, and headed toward the counter.

Behind her, the old-school bell above the door chimed, sharp and familiar, cutting through the noise in her head. Without thinking, Marisol gave a greeting to whoever had walked through the door. "Welcome to Espresso Enchantment."

"Watch out," Kia murmured.

Her best friend's tone raised alarm bells, but it was too late. With a new hazelnut syrup bottle in hand, Marisol turned around. In front of her stood one of her three nightmares in living form: Delgada. Heat rose to the back of her neck all the way up to the tip of her ears. Suddenly, she wondered if the apron showed her chichos.

Delgada was the queen of calorie counting. The girl who indirectly taught her how to hate her body and starve it so it can be worthy of love. She was one of three girls who'd made her life a living hell, and one of the reasons she used to dream of running far away to another state.

Did I manifest her?

Their eyes locked, and for a second—just a second—Delga-da's lips moved before she actually spoke, a sense of déjà vu slipped into Marisol's present.

It was the same smirk. Slow and deliberate, curling at the edges that met her in seventh grade when she walked out to look for the clothes Delgada had hidden. "Café con Leche Curves," Delgada had said that day, and the crowd of girls followed in a chant. It would be years before she could get rid of that echo.

The image vanished when she blinked, but her stomach clenched, letting her know that a part of her was still back there. A hand landed on her back, and she realized her jaw had been so tight her teeth ached.

"You want me to take care of her?" Kia asked.

Marisol looked at Delgada, wrapped in designer leggings, an overpriced jacket, trendy boots, and wore an insincere smile to match. She forced a breath. "Please. I'm not letting her ruin my whole day."

Kia always stood up for Marisol, even before she knew she needed defending. Other friends had vanished when she lost her mother, and her grief became inconvenient. But Kia never disappeared. Even now, she caught her watching Delgada, poised to step in if she tried anything.

"I think it's too late for that," Kia said, popping a muffin onto a tray. Once she finished, she darted toward Marisol and leaned into her ear. "I have a plan. How about I spill hot milk on her shoes? Accidentally, of course."

Marisol squared her shoulders before smirking. "You'd only miss and spill it on my shoes instead. And unlike you, I don't have 'emergency backup boots and outfit in my trunk' energy."

She knew that if anything derailed her badly enough, she would go back home, climb into her mother's bed, and never come out. Marisol wanted so badly to be light instead of weak. To joke, to play things off, to not feel like every nerve in her body was constantly exposed, especially in front of Kia, who had done so much for her since Mami died. Still, a knot of dread wound tight in her middle as she thought about this interaction that she had avoided since she got back. But it was bound to happen, and if one of the mojonas found her, the other one who still lived in Willowshade wouldn't be too far behind. She might as well rip the band-aid.

"You think my aim is that bad?" Kia said, interrupting her mental downward spiral. Her friend arched an inquiring eyebrow, and Marisol raised her own in response.

Kia huffed, feigning offense before adding with a wink, "When I miss, it's on purpose."

Marisol couldn't think of anything else to say. A different kind of heat crept into her cheeks. *Since when did Kia being cute come with...feelings? Romantic ones?* She shook her head hard, shoving the thought away. They were friends. That was all.

Kia leaned her head against Marisol's shoulder. "Don't let her get to you."

And for one quiet second, Marisol's world tilted upright.

"I see you two are still playing footsie," Delgada chirped, interrupting their whispered back-and-forth. She tossed her ponytail like a show pony trained for shade. "Anyway, good morning."

As Kia headed back to get more baked goods, her fingers grazed Marisol's balled fists. "She's not worth it," she murmured.

She was right. Marisol wasn't going to give Delgada the satisfaction of getting under her skin. But looking at her just made things come back. Gosh, she had wanted to be home-schooled so badly. Las tres mojonas—Delgada, Sabia, and Blanca—had made her wish it every single day.

"Oat milk, extra foam. You remember, right?" Delgada asked, her eyes fixed on her phone.

"Of course," Marisol said. She punched in the order, pressing the keys harder than she intended, and cracked a nail.

"Well, that's tragic," Delgada said, finally looking up and not meaning any of it.

Marisol rolled her eyes. *Don't let her get under your skin. Don't let her get under your skin.*

She began working on the order. Out of the corner of her eye, Marisol caught Delgada tugging at the zipper on her designer jacket, fingers fumbling before she glanced around, weary for just a moment. *Is she being self-conscious?*

But then, Delgada caught Marisol's gaze, and she pulled on that smirk Marisol hated. It was like armor covering anything that may have cracked.

"I told Sabia and Blanca you were still here. They don't want to believe me." Her syrupy-sweet, dripping-with-condescension tone cut off whatever kind words Marisol could have said. Delgada snapped a picture, capturing Marisol in the most awkward moment.

"Hey—" Marisol began.

"We are all friends here. Right?" Delgada said, mock-offended. "Plus, this is a nice gig. A nice life. No real responsibilities, just doing whatever you want. You probably dump a ton of syrup in your cup and go full fat, huh? That must be so nice. I say you are winning, Marisol."

Marisol clenched her jaw and slid the syrup bottle out of reach, afraid she might hurl it at the floor or at Delgada. She tore the receipt from the register and handed it to her without a word, her nostrils flaring. She wouldn't give Delgada the reaction she wanted, although her nerves were frayed raw.

The hiss of steam drowned out whatever other jabs Delgada threw. Marisol's breath came short as she nodded along, pretending to listen. She should have known she couldn't start working at the café without seeing Las Mojonas, who still live here. She should have expected this. She should have prepared herself for it.

I should just go home. Tell Mike and Jill I'll start next week.

But no. She couldn't do that. What her mom left wouldn't last long, especially if she didn't supplement it with a job.

"Breathe," Kia murmured as she passed by with a tray of croissants. "You know she lives for that reaction."

The rattle of cups, the suffocating cigar smell, the bell ushering arrivals and exits, Delgada's voice — all of it crashed together inside her skull until it was too much. Marisol's head snapped. Her palm struck the counter.

"Knowing that doesn't make it hurt any less. Okay?" The words burst out, too loud, too raw. She winced the moment she uttered them. They hung in the air between them as dense as a wall. *Why did I do that?*

"You forget." Kia's voice broke. "I know what it's like to be written off."

Kia cut her eyes at Marisol and walked off toward the other end of the counter.

Delgada, savoring the scene, accepted her oat milk latte. She gestured at them both. "Yeah...Good luck with that."

Marisol waited until the bell rang, signaling Delgada's exit. Only then did her shoulders sink and guilt settle in her stomach. Sometimes she forgot that Kia — ever the optimist — had survived parents who tried to pray the gay away.

She opened her mouth to say something — an apology, an 'I understand' — but froze as the acrid smell of tobacco returned. It snaked around her senses. She turned sharply, eyes darting toward the café window. For a brief, heart-stopping moment, a shadow shifted beneath the streetlamp outside, perfectly still, as if watching her.

Then, just as quickly, it vanished. The vision disoriented her, tilting her world. She swayed. *What is happening?*

"Marisol?" Kia was at her side now, her voice edged with alarm. "What's wrong?"

Marisol gripped the counter to steady herself. Kia's hand reached for her lower back, warm and grounding. She swallowed hard. Suddenly, she was cold.

"Mari?" Kia's hands rubbed up and down her back.

"Nothing," she lied. "I guess I'm just—exhausted."

Marisol drew a deep breath, letting the rhythm of Kia's hand calm her.

"You know Mike and Jill don't care if you take a day off. They understand everything is still...fresh."

She shook her head. "I'm okay."

"And I don't believe you, but I'll be right here," Kia said, pointing toward the second register before stepping away.

Marisol turned back to the espresso machine, annoyed with herself, with Delgada, with everything that picked at half-healed scars — and with her mind for making her see things that weren't there.

Gosh, she hated mirrors.

2

MEAN GIRLS, SPANGLISH EDITION (LAS MOJONAS, EDICION SPANGLISH)

Seeing Delgada reopened old wounds. The pinching of her chichos, the gym chant, the cruel DMs—all of it crawled back into her mind like cockroaches scattering in the light. Shame settled under her skin with every memory. How was it fair that her tormentors thrived, their lives effortless and polished, while she fought just to stay upright?

You just have to get through the first week, Marisol told herself as she scrubbed down the tables, muscles aching with each swipe. This was a restart. She'd holed up in her house for almost a year—living off deliveries, doomscrolling on social media, numbing herself with trash TV, and cleaning the house with tears. The weeks ahead had to be easier. At least, she hoped they would be.

Marisol heard Kia humming behind her, the tune low and steady as she worked. She glanced back and caught her friend bent over the espresso machine, tackling the hardest task with all its tiny, finicky parts. Of course, Kia would take it on — patient, methodical, never letting even the most tedious jobs rattle her.

Kia's eyes flicked up, meeting Marisol's. She smiled. *How*

long have I been staring? Heat rushed to her cheeks, and she quickly turned back to wiping the tables, pretending to focus as if she hadn't been staring at all.

An hour went by like that, Marisol cleaning harder than she ever did in her own house, Kia and the rest moving about with ease through each task on the closing checklist. By the time her shift ended, Marisol's entire body ached. Her mind was restless. The sharp tang of smoke and ash clung to her throat, dry and bitter. She knew she'd done Kia wrong. She had seen it in her friend's eyes and realized too late that her own words had cut deep. Marisol knew how much words could hurt—she'd lived it —but she had been so focused on her own pain, she hadn't noticed she'd hurt her best friend.

She wrung her hands as she approached Kia. "Movie at my place?"

"Sure." Kia rearranged a stack of cups, then glanced carefully at her. "Hey, are you really okay? Delgada always rattles you, and I know that was not you back there."

"I'll be fine." Marisol hesitated before forcing a smile. She thought about Delgada. "It's like seeing her brings all of it back."

It's not only the pain she carried from their meanness. It was also that, back then, she had her mom, grandma, and Kia. Tears welled in her eyes when she looked up at Kia. She was all she had left.

Kia walked around the counter.

"I'm fine." Marisol dried her eyes with the back of her sleeves. Her voice was thick with emotion. "You know me. I always bounce back."

Kia's expression softened. "Yeah...but you don't always have to bounce back alone, Mari."

Marisol pushed back on the lump that settled on her throat. She nodded. Kia squeezed her shoulder. Marisol found comfort from the closeness and warmth there, but she bit back every word that came close to her tongue. Everything sounded horrible in her head. A beat passed before Kia returned to her tasks.

Marisol watched her move confidently behind the counter. Kia was thriving, on her way to becoming a manager. She hadn't let her past define her. And Marisol? She wasn't even at square one; she was closer to a negative five.

As she wiped the counter, a cold draft brushed past, rustling loose napkins. Goosebumps prickled her arms. She glanced around the empty café. The door was shut. Maybe a window was open. But it wasn't the cold air that unsettled her. It was the smell that came with it—pungent and invasive.

"Okay, that's enough. Whoever's smoking needs to stop. It's gross and I'm nauseous. Who's been smoking?"

"No one." Kia and the two other workers with them looked around, puzzled. "Why?"

"You don't smell that?"

Kia stepped closer, sniffing the air around her dramatically. The other two laughed good-naturedly before returning to their duties.

"Careful. I ran out of the house without deodorant today," Marisol joked weakly.

Kia rolled her eyes. "Oh, stop. You always smell good. But seriously, I don't smell anything."

"Maybe I'm just imagining it," Marisol muttered, the chill down her spine intensifying.

"Maybe..." Kia shrugged and moved away to finish her closing duties.

By the time Marisol stepped outside, it was nearly eight, and fatigue pressed down on her like lead. Above, a winter full moon hovered, casting skeletal shadows across the pavement. The air smelled of chimney smoke and oversalted sidewalks — small-town winter scents that blanketed everything in stillness. Main Street looked like a Pinterest board come to life, all quaint signs and storefronts. The houses beyond lined up like they'd shared the same designer. But if anyone walked to her family's home, they'd see a very different Willowshade.

The Espinal estate had once been grand, but as the years passed and family died, it seemed to wither too. Paint peeled from its walls, the mailbox leaned crooked, and the porch complained with every gust of wind. In the back, the family cemetery sagged into itself, headstones eroded to anonymity. And above it all, within the estate's perimeter, loomed the hill —brooding and watchful.

From here, Hallowthorn Hill shouldn't have been so prominent. Buildings blocked it, distance dulled it. But it dominated her vision, dark and unyielding, as though it had shifted closer, demanding attention. Marisol hated that hill as much as she feared it. She hated the way people treated it like a hiking trail, as if it wasn't private land steeped in a silence that was never empty.

Every shadow it cast whispered warnings her mother once gave her. Legends she'd dismissed as fairy tales pressed against her memory. Even its silhouette made her pause. She often wondered why it stirred her this way. But she never held to that for long. At least, not until now.

Lately, escaping the hill seemed impossible. It appeared in her dreams, in reflections, in murmurs at the edge of thought. Tonight, it loomed larger. Close. Watching. Waiting.

3

SHHH, EL HILL IS SPEAKING (CALLATE, LA COLINA ESTA HABLANDO)

An icy wind picked up and slipped through the gaps in Marisol's coat. She pulled her key fob from her pocket, her finger hovering over the alarm button—just in case. The cold sank deep into her bones, and as her eyes adjusted to the night, she spotted her car parked at the back of the parking lot. But the figure she'd seen earlier—the one under the streetlamp across the street—was back, lingering in the corner of her vision, watching her, staring.

I'm going crazy.

Grief was relentlessly persistent. It was always seeping in, trapping her like a hamster running endlessly on a wheel, making her see and feel things that couldn't possibly be real.

"Marisoool," the wind murmured, carrying the scent of damp earth along with it.

She jerked her head sharply toward the hill. The man's silhouette shifted subtly, then vanished.

No, she thought, her heart racing, *it's just exhaustion.*

Yet something pressed against her back, cold and insistent, as if the hill itself leaned into her ear. A second voice rose from the same darkness, sharp and commanding: *"Don't look away."*

Marisol sprinted toward her car, nearly slipping on the icy pavement. The hill seemed closer now. Impossibly close and alive, its twisted, frost-covered trees bending forward like limbs reaching for her. Their knotted roots, half covered in snow and dirt, were like dirty boots walking her way. Its slope was hunched, as if weary.

She reached for the car door handle, but panic made her fingers clumsy, and she pressed the key fob too many times, locking the doors instead.

"Marisoool."

The keys slipped from her trembling hand, clattering loudly against the pavement.

"Leave me alone!" Marisol yelled, quickly scanning the empty lot, suddenly self-conscious. She scooped up her keys and managed to unlock the car, nearly tumbling inside as she scrambled onto the seat. She slammed the door and punched the lock button, breathing heavily as she counted the rapid beats of her heart.

"What the hell was that?" Marisol whispered, peering anxiously at the hill as if it would give her the answer. Yet it remained in its place, ominous and unchanged, and she wondered who the voices belonged to and if one of them belonged to the creep she had caught staring at her.

Her warm breath fogged up the windows, prompting her to start the car and blast the heater. Cold air flowed before warmth slowly replaced it, easing her shivers and calming her nerves.

"What did Mami always say about that hill?" Marisol asked herself, her voice quivering.

～

THE MEMORY CAME SWIFTLY, clear and vivid.

She was eight years old, sitting cross-legged on the living room floor. Her mother was gently combing through Marisol's curls, her fingers skillfully weaving them into tight braids. It was late, and the wind outside howled against the windows.

"Eso no es una colina normal, Marisol," her mother had said. "That hill watches us. It waits."

"Waits for what?" Marisol asked, wincing slightly as her mother tugged on a knot.

"For the Espinal women. For those who must awaken and listen to its call."

Marisol rolled her eyes, squirming impatiently. "Yeah, right, Mami. You're just telling stories to scare me into going to sleep early."

Her mother laughed softly, shaking her head. "Maybe. Pero las historias son como recuerdos, mi niña. Stories are how we remember. Someday you'll understand."

A SUDDEN HIGH-PITCHED SCRAPE—METAL against glass—snapped Marisol from her memory. She froze, eyes widening in horror as words appeared slowly on the fogged-up windshield: "*La colina nos llama.*" The hill calls to us.

Her blood turned to ice in her veins. There were no fingers, no hands, no visible source, yet something had written those words.

"Nope, I'm out of here," Marisol muttered fiercely. She shifted into drive and pressed the accelerator hard, desperate to escape. Suddenly, the radio blasted to life, nearly deafening her. Static crackled, sharp and chaotic. Then, a voice cut through.

"*...Mari—sol...*"

Her name, warped and thin, slipped through the speakers

like a whisper tangled in static. Marisol gasped, her hand jerking on the wheel before she managed to steady it and gun the car out of the parking lot. But her mind, spinning with thoughts she couldn't even begin to make sense of, pulled her focus off the road. Instead of turning left, she veered right.

"Goddammit!"

Her tires skidded dangerously on a hidden patch of ice, and she gripped the wheel tightly, fighting to regain control of the car. The car lurched sharply before she steadied it just inches from entering the obscure side of Main Street. She began to sweat underneath her jacket. She had been avoiding this end for months, ever since her return to Willowshade.

Breathing hard, Marisol carefully guided the car down the familiar row of shops, her attention caught by the glowing herb store. Its front window was crowded with hanging bunches of eucalyptus and dried lavender, the glass fogged just enough to obscure what was inside. A hand-painted wooden sign that read 'Yerbería Elvira' in weathered script hung crookedly above the door.

Marisol could see Doña Elvira standing calmly behind the window, gazing at her with unmistakable concern. Her chest tightened. This had once been Mami's sanctuary—until COVID took her away. The thought made the anger that simmered right beneath her grief vibrate under her skin. *How had Elvira stayed healthy throughout the entire pandemic, yet couldn't keep Mami safe?* Irrational, maybe, but the thought clung to her anyway. Kia had always pulled Marisol back from the edge, saved her from herself more than once. Why hadn't Elvira done the same for Mami?

"Why am I like this?" she said to herself, gripping the wheel so tightly that her knuckles turned white.

But she couldn't come up with an answer. Marisol eased on the accelerator, desperate to escape. Yet the ice forced her car into a crawl, moving forward like a procession passing something she'd rather not face.

Marisol used to love this side of Main Street—the forgotten shops, untouched by forced cheer. It was quieter here, with less traffic. A mural stretched across the bricks. It was one of her favorite places in Willowshade. But it wasn't because of the mural as a whole. It was the brown woman with a broom, caught mid-sweep, her gaze fixed on everything and nothing at once. That was what caught Marisol's attention.

The woman with a broom reminded Marisol of the shops themselves—unassuming, uncurated, real. Living in the mural's margins, just as these shops lived in the town's. But regardless of how much she loved it, Marisol couldn't risk running into Elvira.

Still, curiosity pricked her. Before passing the row of shops completely, Marisol looked at the place she had been avoiding, like the mirrors she couldn't face, and held her breath.

Doña Elvira stood vigilantly behind the window, her gaze unwavering, and for one fleeting moment, she saw someone else beside her. *Mami?* She was smiling softly, her eyes gentle and forgiving, as if she had forgiven Doña Elvira.

Marisol blinked hard. *No—she's not here. She's gone.* Tears stung her eyes, and she braked sharply. Still, hope played her for a fool. She glanced again, only to find Doña Elvira and the reflection of her own car in the shop's window. Heat rushed to her cheeks. *Mami isn't here. Get a hold of yourself. God, what are you even thinking?*

Static crackled through the radio, and Marisol jumped in her seat. Before she could hear the creepy voice again, she reached for the knob and turned her radio off.

"Nope."

She pressed further down on the gas, urging her car forward through the wintry conditions. But deep down,

Marisol remembered something else her mother had said about the hill.

It was patient. Waiting.

And sooner or later, an Espinal woman would have to climb it.

4

CALOR DE MEMORIA (THE WARMTH OF MEMORY)

It was nearly ten when Marisol heard the tires of Kia's car crunch against her icy driveway. She grabbed her jacket, opened the door, and waited for Kia to come up the steps.

The porch light flickered, casting long shadows on the weather-worn steps. From where she stood, Marisol eyed the Virginia creeper clinging to the banister. It was leafless now but still wrapped tight around the house, refusing to let go. Old. Stubborn. Unmoved by winter's silence. The paint on the doorframe had chipped away in slow, persistent patches. The mailbox tilted to one side, her family's last name barely hanging on in fading letters.

The Espinal home wasn't one of those cute historic houses in Willowshade, with matching shutters and manicured hedges. It didn't photograph well. Then again, it didn't try to.

But standing here now, with the cold air curling around her ankles and memory tugging at her ribs, she felt it. Her mother's presence still lived inside the walls. The corners still held warmth. The house hadn't forgotten her.

Marisol leaned back against the front door, suddenly struck by the stillness inside the four-bedroom house. It had once been full of life, with Mamà Belén humming in the kitchen, Mami and her dad talking over each other in the living room, the TV blaring just as loudly, Kia's laughter spilling into every corner.

Her grandfather had died in a car accident years before Mamà Belén passed away from natural causes, and something in her grandmother dimmed after her husband's death. The loud, spirited woman who used to dance while stirring her café stopped dancing altogether. When she passed, she did so quietly, the kind of quiet that felt like surrender. Marisol liked to believe she was just happy to be with grandpa again.

Now, in her family's absence, the house felt too big and hollow. It felt more like a haunted castle than a home.

Kia stepped out of the car and walked toward her, a familiar smile on her face.

"Hey," Kia said warmly.

"Hi, you," Marisol replied before opening the door to let Kia inside.

When Kia entered, she pulled Marisol into a hug, her perfume wrapping around them both—warm, grounding, safe.

The strap of Kia's bag slipped from her shoulder and brushed against Marisol's side. It was the same bag that had stayed here the first weeks after her mother's death, when Kia slept over every night, helping Marisol through grief she didn't know how to survive alone.

She noticed Kia's eyes scan the space immediately—the neatly stacked dishes, the folded throw blankets on the couch —and caught the slight lift of her brows and the gentle curve of her smile. Kia didn't say anything immediately, but Marisol saw the quiet approval in her friend's expression.

"I've been trying to keep the place up," Marisol admitted sheepishly, shrugging as if it wasn't a big deal.

Kia grinned, setting her bag down by the stairs and moving

toward the bathroom to wash her hands. "I see that. And you even clean your hair out of the shower drain?"

Marisol rolled her eyes, a small laugh escaping. "Don't push it."

Kia chuckled softly. "Okay. Okay. But, I'm proud of you, Mari. You know, you didn't have to push me away. You could've let me help."

Marisol's smile faltered. Guilt crept back into her chest. "You practically live here, Kia. You know you're always welcome. I just thought maybe you wanted your own space, some privacy. Plus, I'm grown."

Marisol didn't know exactly where her complex and shame came from. Maybe it started with her pre-Kia friendships, the ones that labeled her as high-maintenance or needy, before slowly drifting away until they eventually ghosted her altogether. Since then, she'd carried a quiet guilt whenever she leaned on someone too much, always afraid her needs would make people leave. Kia had never given her a single reason to think that. Still, the fear clung to her anyway, stubborn and familiar.

Kia shook her head, her eyes warm but firm. "What space?" Before Marisol could reply, Kia pulled her into a bear hug so tight Marisol thought she'd run out of air. When Kia finally let go, her expression softened. "I stayed because I wanted to. I left because I thought you needed it. But the truth is, I missed being here, too."

Marisol swallowed thickly, emotions clogging her throat. She missed Kia. She missed the way her presence made everything feel bearable. It had been close to a year since Mami died, but the house still smelled like her. Still felt like her. Some days, that was a comfort; other days, it made Marisol want to scream. "I missed you being here, too," she finally admitted. "But you deserved your privacy, too. And you deserve a friend that doesn't drag you down."

Kia reached out and nudged Marisol's shoulder, playful at first. "Privacy is so overrated, and I deserve you."

Marisol's breath caught in her throat at the contact, the warmth lingering longer than it should.

"Besides," Kia added quickly, as if to smooth over the moment, "it feels like home here."

Kia moved into the kitchen with practiced ease, heading straight to the pantry for popcorn kernels. The kitchen, spacious but worn from years of cooking and laughter, still carried faint aromas of coffee, spices, and something comforting Marisol could never quite put her finger on; maybe it was just memories.

Kia turned on the stove and started melting the butter. Soon, the scent of freshly popping kernels filled the air, warm and buttery, instantly making the house feel alive again.

Kia glanced at the four chairs surrounding the kitchen island. "Remember when your mom sat us both right there?"

Marisol furrowed her brows, trying to recall.

"Come on, freshman year? The rumble?"

Marisol covered her face with her hand, laughter bubbling up uncontrollably as the memory rushed back. "Oh my God, yes."

"You know your mom was serious if she came out with her dubi still wrapped and no makeup on," Kia said, chuckling.

"It was supposed to be a fun dare," Marisol said, laughing and shaking her head. "But you almost threw hands with Delgada. Who does that?"

"She started it, Mari! And I was gonna finish it. Until your mom came out preaching about the dangers of the hill, shaming everyone for being there. What did she call them? Feral cats? She was definitely trying to scare them off your property."

"Yeah. Everyone uses the hill like it's public property." Marisol sighed.

"But then talk crap about it and your family," Kia said, her voice softening with sympathy. "Now you know that's high-level petty behavior."

Marisol nodded, her laughter fading into quiet reflection.

"You know? I thought your mom was going to kick me out for good," Kia confessed quietly. "I thought she was going to say 'she's never allowed here again.'"

Marisol shook her head. "No. Are you kidding me? Mami loved you, Kia. She used to call you her hija postiza." Her voice lowered as she slipped into her mother's cadence. "'Go get my other daughter, Mari. Dinner's ready.'" The words came fuller, lilting, just like her mother's, like the voice that used to call them to the table with love wrapped in every word.

She laughed softly, almost to herself. "And I'd say, 'Mami, Kia doesn't even live here.'"

Marisol shifted her voice once again, this time into something more playful and teasing. "'Well, maybe she should.'" Her inflection curled into her mother's favorite kind of sass, the kind laced with affection and certainty.

Marisol paused, the warmth of nostalgia softening her insides. For a moment, she just held the memory of her mother's familiar voice full of love.

Then, her smile softened, giving way to the memory she'd truly been circling all along. Unlike the dare-turned-almost-rumble, this moment wasn't filled with laughter. It was filled with something deeper. Wisdom. The kind she hadn't understood back then.

Marisol glanced toward the kitchen doorway, and for a moment, she could almost see her mother standing there, equal parts love and lecture written into the lines of her face.

With the weight of the memory returning, her voice lowered. "She looked right at you and said, 'Kia, tienes un corazón de oro. You protect the ones you love so fiercely.'"

Kia nodded with a faint smile, tugging at the corner of her mouth.

Then, Marisol's voice dipped, imitating the precise seriousness her mother reserved for truths she wanted etched into memory. "Then she turned to me, all serious, and said, 'But you, Mari—you need to learn that one day, when I'm not here, and maybe Kia isn't either, you'll have to fight your own battles. Y entonces, ¿qué tu vas a hacer?'"

She rolled her eyes, but there was no bite behind it. Just ache.

Marisol shook her head fondly, her eyes glassy with emotion. "She was always dropping those '¿Y cuando yo me muera?' bombs casually. Like, okay, Mami, thanks for the existential dread."

Marisol's throat tightened at the realness of it. Kia gave her a gentle, understanding smile, but stayed quiet. Mami had a knack for dramatic lessons, constantly reminding Marisol of a future without her, a future Marisol had never wanted to imagine. Yet, here she was, living that very future. Maybe her mom had been right all along, preparing her for this moment, knowing someday she'd have no choice but to stand on her own.

Kia's eyes glistened as she reached across the island, squeezing Marisol's hand, anchoring her with muted, steady reassurance. "It's okay. No one knew. There was no way of knowing. But I'm here. And... I've basically lived here more than I ever lived in that other house. So, yeah. Your mom was right. You're stuck with me. And I'm not going anywhere."

Marisol let out a soft laugh. She nodded, and a tender silence settled between them. The kitchen felt thick with memory, like every surface had soaked in her mother's warmth and refused to let it fade.

Marisol parted her lips, wanting to say what she'd never put into words—that she felt safe with Kia, that it meant everything when she stayed. But the fear pressed just as strong: if she even acknowledged the feelings growing inside her, she might ruin everything between them. So, no words came. Instead, she squeezed Kia's hand and met her gaze, praying her eyes didn't betray her.

"I've always loved it here," Kia said softly. "Especially when your mom told her stories."

Marisol smiled, though something fluttered in her chest, small and insistent, a feeling she couldn't name. At first, it felt like nostalgia, the comfort of every late night they'd ever shared. But the longer she held Kia's gaze, the more it shifted—warmth curling into want, safety tipping into something sharper. The way Kia's eyes softened in the dim kitchen light made Marisol ache to lean closer, to ask the question she couldn't form.

Don't make it weird, she warned herself, shifting slightly. *She's just your best friend. That's all.*

But still, her pulse betrayed her. To get her mind off thinking about impossible things, Marisol veered the conversation in another direction. "Mami and her stories. I think she watched 'Practical Magic' way too much. She was always lighting candles, whispering secrets to the air. Ay, Mami...I think she started believing it."

"So, you don't believe it?" Kia asked.

Marisol blinked. The question caught her off guard. Kia had always respected her mom deeply, but she also had clear boundaries when it came to anything witchy. Fiction was fine. 'Practical Magic'? Sure. But real rituals and spiritual practices? No. Kia kept her distance.

Marisol had always understood that. But maybe this wasn't about belief. Maybe Kia was just missing her, too.

"Maybe all that magic stuff...was just Mami's way of keeping us connected," Marisol murmured.

Kia nodded. "It always made things feel...whimsical. I've always appreciated that."

Marisol's breath snagged in her throat as she met Kia's gaze, warmth settling deep between them. They carried their bowls of popcorn into the living room. They then sank onto the old couch, its cushions worn smooth by years of family gatherings.

"So," Marisol said, grabbing the remote, "what are we watching?"

"Practical Magic," Kia said without hesitation, flashing a teasing grin.

Marisol and Kia burst into laughter so loud and for so long that it took them several minutes to even start the movie. They needed that laugh. The heaviness of their shared memories lifted, if only a little.

Marisol leaned back, letting Kia's comforting presence soothe away the lingering shadows at least for tonight. As the familiar scenes unfolded on the screen, a rare sense of peace settled over her, grounding her in the warmth of friendship and memory. But as the movie played on, a quiet unease slowly crept back into her chest. The gentle laughter and easy conversation couldn't erase the whispers from earlier, or the feeling that something was shifting, pulling her toward a truth she'd always dismissed.

"Hey, Kia?" Marisol said softly, almost hesitant to break the moment.

"Yeah?" Kia glanced over.

"When—" Marisol paused, the words catching on her tongue. It was a dumb question. She knew that. But since Kia had asked, the question had lodged in her throat like a stone she couldn't swallow.

She didn't even know what kind of answer she was looking for.

If Kia said yes, did that mean it was okay for Marisol to believe it, too?

If she said no...then what? Did they just go back to pretending it was all porquerías?

She turned and looked at Kia, voice quieter now. "You asked if I believed the things Mami believed. But...do you?"

Kia let out a breath and shook her head, firm but not unkind. "No. Oh no, Mari. You know I don't mess with that stuff." Her voice softened, eyes dipping briefly. "And I don't think I ever will." She hesitated, then added with quiet honesty, "Not because of you. Just...because of how I was raised. What my parents did to me wasn't right, and I don't believe God hates me for being who I am. But I do believe in Him. All that other stuff is not good. It's not God. You know?"

Not good? Was she trying to say evil without hurting my feelings? The thought left a bitter taste in Marisol's mouth. She didn't think she was evil, and neither were her mother or grandmother.

Kia's voice fell even softer, almost a whisper. "But if anyone could've made me believe...it would've been your mom."

Marisol swallowed hard and turned back to the screen. Her thoughts drifted, carried by whispered warnings, shadowed hills, and secrets that seemed to be buried deep in her blood.

5

HUÉRFANA CON WI-FI (AN ORPHAN WITH WI-FI)

The next morning, Marisol sat cross-legged on her bed. The mattress still dipped in the same place her mother always used to sit, brushing out Marisol's curls. The floral comforter—sun-faded and pilled at the edges—smelled faintly of Vicks and rosewater. Her mother's scent refused to leave, no matter how many times Marisol washed the sheets.

Marisol hadn't changed the curtains either—pale green with tiny, embroidered birds that her mother said reminded her of La Vega. Now they just looked like little ghosts frozen in flight. A rosary hung on the doorknob, dull with dust, still tied in the loose knot her mother made the day she swore she'd start praying again.

Everything in the room remained untouched, as if it were waiting for her mother to come back and pick up where she left off. The silence wasn't peaceful. It pressed against Marisol like a second skin, itchy and suffocating. She held her phone as though it were a lifeline, the only thing keeping the unwanted memories at bay. Its soft blue glow lit her face as she doom-scrolled mindlessly through her feed. The warmth from last night's movie marathon with Kia had faded, replaced by a quiet emptiness. She sighed softly, already missing Kia's easy laughter and the way her presence effortlessly chased away the shadows.

Dance challenges, makeup tutorials, and bursts of laughter blurred together. Perfect faces. Perfect bodies. Perfect lives. A familiar heaviness pressed against her chest, shortening her breath. Each video was a stinging reminder of the life she wasn't living.

Then, on a swipe, she found Blanca's pin-straight hair cascading effortlessly down her shoulders with the type of silkiness Marisol's curls stubbornly defied. Her makeup was flawless, her voice sugary yet sharp. Marisol stopped.

"Y'all ever notice how some people just butcher Spanish?" Blanca's voice rang sharp and sweet. "If you don't know it, just don't. It gives no-sabo energy."

Jokes and agreement poured in from the comments.

@CulturaReal21: OMG yes!

@LatinaLite88: Stick to English. It's less cringe.

Shame crawled up Marisol's skin. She hovered over the keypad, typing: What about the ones who didn't grow up speaking Spanish at home? Some of us are still holding on to what little we have left. Her hands shook. She deleted the message. What was the point? Blanca's empire would drown her out in seconds.

Maybe she needed a social media detox. She'd heard somewhere it helped with anxiety. Perhaps without the constant images of perfection, her mind wouldn't spiral each time she saw her reflection.

Marisol tossed her phone onto the corner pile of clothes she had taken off the night before, as if her phone had burned her. A sudden waft of cigar smoke curled into the room.

Marisol froze, her chest tightening as the scent seeped into her lungs. Goosebumps rose along her arms. She glanced around —nothing but empty space, yet the smoke lingered, thick and suffocating.

Blanca's voice spilled again, louder, clearer. A new video.

"Burning rue or ruda, as some of you call it, doesn't make you spiritual. That's smoke, not spirit." She tilted her head in faux sympathy. "There's a girl here—I won't name names. But she's broken. Una huérfana con Wi-Fi. No foundation. No direction."

Marisol's throat closed. Heat flooded her chest. She picked up her phone.

Then, Blanca reached off-camera and lifted a rosary into frame.

Marisol flinched so hard she nearly dropped the phone she had just picked up. *A goddamn rosary. As if Blanca wasn't the devil herself.*

"You can wrap your crystals in Dominican folklore all you want. But if your family's cursed? Maybe it's not magic. Maybe it's just consequences."

Tears blurred Marisol's vision. She hadn't even realized she was crying until one slipped down her screen. What if Blanca was right? What if she was paying for something she didn't even understand?

And then—her grandmother's voice, steady and sure, cut through the storm, so clear it felt conjured by longing alone.

"Mija, el idioma no te define. Tu corazón lo hace."

Marisol's breath caught at the realness of it. Her pulse steadied. The tears still fell, but now they shimmered with a sense of recognition. This wasn't the menacing voice from the hill, heavy and strange. This was different. Familiar. Comforting. Her grandmother's voice. The kind she could trust. The kind she could answer.

"But Mamá," she whispered, broken, "what if my heart isn't enough?"

Silence swelled around her, thick and still. Only the faint scent of cigar smoke remained, curling into the corners of the room like an answer she didn't want to hear.

6

—————

MIRA BIEN, MARI (MARI, LOOK REAL GOOD)

Blanca's voice had lodged itself deep in Marisol's mind, like an echo trapped in a cave. Cold. Isolating. A place where every emotion bounced back louder, heavier, and harder to escape.

Suddenly, she was fourteen again. Back in the cafeteria, the air thick with mystery meat and overcooked fries. She leaned toward Kia, carefully sounding out the word corazón. Before Kia could repeat it, Blanca's voice sliced through the noise, sharp and dripping with ridicule.

"Really, Marisol? You're teaching her Spanish? You barely know it yourself." Blanca tossed her glossy hair, her voice loud enough to turn heads. "It's pronounced corazón, not whatever sad Spanglish you made up."

Heat flamed across Marisol's cheeks, humiliation cinching her throat. But Kia stood instantly. Her gaze locked on Blanca.

"Must be nice, talking all that mess from your high horse," she shot back. "Not everyone gets summers in Spain with expensive tutors. Besides," Kia said, her voice dropping into a casual jab, "I like Marisol's way better. That S sounding like a Z? Makes you sound ztupid."

Laughter rippled across the table. Marisol stared at her tray, grateful but still aching. She'd always envied Blanca's polished Spanish, bought with tutors and summer trips to the so-called motherland. Meanwhile, her mother had wanted to teach her —had even started, with songs and cuentos—until the meeting.

A speech therapist once told Josefina that if she kept Spanish at home, Marisol would "fall behind." With her father gone most of the time, there was no balance—no parent for Spanish, no parent for English, the language the counselor insisted she needed to master outside the home. Josefina didn't have the authority of an expert, so she folded. English crept in until it replaced every Spanish word, not just outside but inside their walls.

Marisol carried that resentment for years, all the way to her mother's death. But grief does strange things—it makes you revisit old memories, re-examine the feelings you pinned to the person who's gone.

She realized she had been angry at the wrong person. Instead of raging at a system so biased it erased her language, she'd blamed her mother. And while her father drained their savings on a second family, her Spanish drained away too. What remained were cracks, and the shame of knowing she'd been a shit daughter.

Before she spiraled further, a warmth she couldn't place wrapped around her bones, pushing back the coldness guilt had left behind. Then, something brushed her ear, and a voice pierced her consciousness.

"Ábrelo."

Marisol stiffened, eyes darting around the room. Her pulse quickened. She looked down, startled to find her hand gripping the drawer handle on her nightstand. As if burned, she yanked her fingers back. But the voice came again—this time insistent, impossible to ignore.

"Ábrelo."

She gasped. The presence was undeniable. Still, she hesitated. She had always told herself she didn't believe in this kind of thing—no matter how much Mami and Mamá Belén had insisted the otherworldly was real. But lately...she wasn't so sure. If spirits did exist, then some had to be dangerous, just like people. *Which type of spirit was speaking to her now? Telling her to open it.*

Her mind went back to the guilt that had knotted in her stomach—the shame of her forgotten language—and then to the strange warmth that had eased it before the voice appeared. That comfort wasn't what evil felt like. It had brought peace, not dread.

Slowly, reluctantly, Marisol reached for the drawer again and slid it open. The creak filled the silence. Inside was a chaotic jumble—old receipts, tangled earbuds, random pens. And beneath it all, half-buried, lay something she had never seen before: an old spiral notebook, its cover faded to a weary pinkish gray, its edges frayed from use. A sticker peeled at one corner, its design long worn away. Across the front, in familiar handwriting, were two words that made her breath hitch:

Josefina Espinal.

Her fingers trembled as she pulled it free. Flipping through the pages, she found hurried notes in English and Spanish. Some names she recognized, others had been scratched out so viciously the ink tore the paper. One in particular had ripped nearly through the page, but the faint curve of an E remained at the beginning. Marisol frowned. She couldn't think of anyone in the family whose name started that way.

In the margins, strange symbols twisted across the page: A spiral intersected by three lines. Her heart skipped. She remembered her mother doodling the same shapes absent-mindedly during phone calls, weaving them into bedtime stories she'd tried so hard to forget.

An uneasy curiosity pulled at her.

Before she could second-guess herself, Marisol grabbed her phone from the nightstand and opened the search browser.

She hesitated, thumb hovering over the keypad, then quickly typed into the search bar: "Taino symbols spiral with lines meaning"

Results flooded the screen. Ancient symbols from the Dominican Republic, references to Taino mythology, and cultural traditions. Marisol scrolled through the results rapidly until one made her pause, causing her breath to freeze in her chest.

"The Taino Coquí Spiral: Symbol of Ancestral Guidance and Protection."

Her pulse quickened. She clicked the link, eyes darting across explanations about the indigenous Taino people. The spiral symbolized cycles of life, rebirth, and ancestral connections. The three intersecting lines represented past, present, and future, ancestral guidance spanning generations, offering protection and wisdom.

Every word deepened the chill crawling down her spine. Terms like "ancestral rituals," "spiritual protection," and "legacy" jumped out at her, heightening her unease. Her mother had known all of this. Had her mother been trying to understand, or maybe harness, something ancient? Something rooted in the Dominican Republic? In their shared heritage?

Why didn't Mami ever mention any of this? Or had she tried, and I didn't listen?

Marisol swallowed thickly, turning another page in the notebook. More symbols, accompanied by her mother's hurried notes.

Poder ancestral.

Llamada.

Hallowthorn Hill.

Protección.

Her fingertip traced an intricate drawing of Hallowthorn Hill. Swirling lines at the base resembled roots or smoke, curling upward as if alive. Nausea rose sharply within her.

With shaking hands, she typed again: "Hallowthorn Hill Willowshade Ohio Dominican history."

Local legends and articles surfaced immediately, revealing unexpected Dominican connections:

"Dominican Settlers and Their Secret Histories'

"Hallowthorn Hill and Espinal Family Legends"

"Ancient Rituals and Modern Mysteries: Dominican Magic in Ohio"

Her pulse thundered in her ear; she clicked through the link quickly.

"...Salvador Espinal, originally from La Vega, Dominican Republic, settled in Willowshade in the early 1900s. Known locally as a cigar aficionado with a penchant for Taino rituals, he mysteriously died on Hallowthorn Hill..."

Marisol dropped the phone onto her bed, its glowing screen illuminating her horrified expression. An icy chill coursed through her veins.

"Mami...what were you doing?" she murmured into the empty room.

No answer came. Only a heavy, haunting silence, pierced by the faint but unmistakable scent of cigar smoke. The warmth that had guided her was gone. What lingered now was cold, invasive, and nothing like her grandmother's voice. Fear clamped around her chest. Something else had entered the space. Something that did not bring comfort. Something that had been waiting for her to open that door, and would not be easy to shut out.

7

———

LATTES CON FANTASMAS (LATTES WITH GHOSTS)

The familiar chime of the Espresso Enchantment's door snapped Marisol sharply from her thoughts, sending her pulse skittering. She forced herself to smile, though strings of anxiety weighed heavily on her. Today, everything felt off. Her skin prickled as if being brushed by phantom fingers, and a persistent buzz filled her ears.

As she busied herself with the espresso machine, steaming milk, and pulling shots, she tried to let the repetitive motions soothe her frayed nerves. But her mind kept drifting to the night before. The strange articles, Salvador Espinal's mysterious death, and the Dominican connection she'd never known about. How had her mother kept all of this hidden from her?

A sharp tapping on the counter made Marisol jump. When she looked up, one of the regulars stood there with her tween daughter, both giving her that polite-but-wary expression that said she'd taken too long with their order.

"Is this oat milk or almond? I asked for almond."

Marisol blinked. She could've sworn she'd followed the order through. Her hands hesitated over the cartons of milk. *Which one did I pick?*

The scent of cigar smoke curled through the air again, making her wonder if she had lost her mind and her ability to make coffee.

Kia stepped in smoothly. "Oat for the other drink, ma'am. Yours is almond. Promise."

The woman huffed but nodded, muttering something underneath her breath as she took her drinks and left.

"I got you," Kia murmured.

Marisol's fingers still trembled. The scent lingered too long, sharp and out of place. Was it just her nerves playing tricks again? No. She knew what she'd read, what she'd seen in the notebook, what she'd researched, what she'd felt. And if all of it was true, then there was another world out there, watching her, putting her under a microscope. The thought terrified her. It was bad enough when the living stared and whispered. If the dead did the same? No. She couldn't let herself believe that. She wouldn't.

"Hey, you okay?" Kia asked softly, motioning her to the back.

Marisol followed Kia while the other barista moved to the cash register.

In the back, Kia's eyes shifted between Marisol and the spot she'd been staring at in a daze. She had seen her staring at the hill. "You've been quiet all morning. Did you stress yourself out on your day off?"

Espresso Enchantment never really ran on a strict schedule. One of the perks of a small town café was that shifts blurred between whoever showed up. But one of the curses of a small town was that everyone knew everything. Marisol was sure the owners had brought her in out of pity after her mom died, so she never asked for more and felt guilty when her performance fell short of her coworkers'.

Marisol plastered on another brittle smile. "Yeah—no, I'm just tired. Didn't sleep well again."

It wasn't exactly a lie. Sleep had eluded her, replaced by swirling shadows and her mother's voice murmuring cryptic warnings she couldn't understand: *"Nunca ignores la llamada. Never ignore the call."*

Kia sighed, concern creasing her brows. "I'm about to send you some sleep hygiene pins—"

"No, nope. I'm fine. Just stayed up scrolling all night."

"You mean doom-scrolling."

Marisol nodded sheepishly.

"Mari, just call me instead. It's better than absorbing all that mess. You know 99.99% of that stuff is fake, right?"

"Yeah...I know," Marisol admitted, sighing deeply. But then her eyes drifted involuntarily back toward the direction of the hill. Her grip on the counter tightened until her knuckles turned white. She swore something was moving on the other side of the door, as if the hill was growing taller.

"Mari?" Kia's voice sharpened with alarm. "You're pale. Wait here."

Kia ran off to the front and quickly returned with a steaming cup, dunking a tea bag repeatedly to speed its steeping. Marisol took the cup gratefully, sipping slowly, warmth chasing the chill from her fingers. Kia rested a steadying hand on her shoulder, grounding her.

"I mean it," Kia added firmly. "You're not the only one who knows how to make tea or coffee here. Go breathe or scream into the muffins if you need to. I'll cover you."

Marisol laughed softly. "Don't tempt me."

"One day, Mari, I will teach you how to actually take a break. How to let go before you crash and burn. Like emotionally intelligent people do."

Kia squeezed Marisol's arms, and something about her touch made Marisol feel...mushy. Not weak, not broken, just soft. Open.

Was this what Kia meant by relaxing? Because it wasn't

relaxing. If anything, it was amping up something else. Something Marisol would rather shove deep in the back of her mind and leave it there.

Their eyes met—brief, yet full of something—and for a split second, Marisol wondered if both of them felt the same thing. But Kia's voice broke through that thought. "I know you're not fine. I can tell. If you need me to hang after work—"

Marisol shook her head quickly. She rubbed the arm Kia had just touched, as if she could erase the feelings it had awakened. She hated how much she wanted to say yes, so she said nothing at all.

"Fair. Just...tell me when you're ready to not be fine alone, okay?"

Marisol swallowed hard. "That's an annoyingly sweet thing to say."

"I know." Kia winked playfully. "But you love me for it."

Marisol shook her head, even as every part of her betrayed the lie. She loved Kia for more than her playfulness, more than her smile, and that scared her, too.

"Hey." Kia nudged Marisol with her elbow, breaking the lingering tension. "Remember Ashley with the snake tattoo? From sophomore year?"

Marisol raised an eyebrow. "The one who brought tarot cards to gym class?"

"Yeah, she said I had chaotic energy. My aura was apparently 'hostile but protective.'"

Marisol snorted. "She wasn't wrong."

"True. But yours was worse. She told you your third eye was too tired to open."

"She also claimed I carried generational guilt on my lower back," Marisol added.

"Wasn't she squatting while saying that?"

They burst into laughter, a warm moment breaking through the anxiety.

When the laughter faded, Kia's eyes turned serious. "You've always had this energy, Mari. Like...you carry things you never say. Sometimes people take advantage of it, but I see it. I've always seen it."

Marisol's throat tightened. "Kia..."

"I'm not good at this soft stuff," Kia added hastily. Her eyes turned to Marisol's hands before turning back to Marisol herself. "But I'm not going anywhere, okay?"

Marisol opened her mouth, but no words came. She didn't want Kia to go anywhere. Not now, not ever, but now she wasn't sure it was just because she needed a friend. And that scared her.

How had she gone from loving Kia as a friend to wondering if it was something more?

What kind of person second-guessed a bond like that in the middle of grief and unraveling?

She bit the inside of her cheek, mentally kicking herself.

God, she was a mess.

She felt Kia glance over again and quickly looked away—not because she didn't want to reassure her, but because she wasn't sure her face wouldn't give away the real reason she wanted her to stay. She was losing her mind. She might have a dangerous ancestor on her hands and an entire other world pressing in on her. She didn't have the space to think about feelings and relationships. In the middle of this chaos, if she even tried, she'd only make things worse—and risk destroying the one relationship she couldn't afford to lose.

8

LEGACY IN AISLE SEVEN (EL PATRIMONIO EN EL PASILLO SIETE)

Marisol hugged her coat tighter as she crossed the parking lot. She reserved the first half of her off day for running errands. The traffic was better, and she had the whole day to do as she pleased. The Valley Market parking lot stretched wide under a pale winter sky, with scattered rows of cars that had seen better days and salt-crusted trucks glinting dull in the weak sun. Slush crunched under Marisol's boots as she crossed toward the entrance, the chill biting through her coat no matter how tightly she wrapped it. The wind carried the smell of gasoline and fryer grease from the burger place next door. She passed a shopping cart with one broken wheel listed against a snowbank, the front half buried as if it had given up halfway to the return rack.

Marisol kept her gaze down, weaving between cars, but the number of them parked here and now, along with the sound of voices near the entrance, told her that others had the same idea —to take advantage of the slower traffic to shop. A pair of older women huddled together, bundled in hats, gloves, and scarves, with their reusable bags. They laughed, breath fogging the air, then lowered their voices into the kind of pointed hush Marisol recognized too well.

She looked up and caught their eyes on her. Shoving her hands into her pockets, she picked up her pace, boots crunching over the half-ice, half-slush on the ground.

But before she reached the sliding doors, she saw it.

The bus stop bench outside Valley Market had a new face plastered across it: Sabia, glossy and confident, arms folded in a blazer, her smile polished to perfection. Bold letters declared: Born to Lead. Jimenez & Jimenez.

Marisol's step faltered. Her fists clenched tight in her pockets, and before she knew it, she clicked her tongue against the roof of her mouth and rolled her eyes.

One of the women noticed. Her friend followed her gaze and said, louder than necessary, "That girl's going places."

Marisol didn't have to look up to know they weren't talking about her but about one of the Tres Mojonas—Sabia, beaming down from the bench ad.

"Sharp like her father," one woman added. "Isn't she? What a great example of what a girl—"

"A Migrant, Margaret," her friend cut in, voice clipped. "The term is migrant."

Their eyes slid past Marisol as if she were invisible. Normally, she would've let it go. She was not a Sabia or a Tres Mojonas apologist. But not today. Today, the audacity was too much. Born here, raised here—Sabia's family had roots in the same soil as hers. And yet, they reduced her to a word used for birds.

"She's American," Marisol said, stepping closer to the circle.

The women glanced at her. One of them sniffed. "Not with that last name."

Her friend hushed her quickly, but the words hung heavy in the cold air.

"Last time I checked," Marisol said, her voice steady, "if you're born here, you're from here."

The women looked right through her, their silence, deliberate.

Marisol stared back, but she wasn't going to change their minds right then and there. Anger simmered inside of her. *Let it go, Marisol. It's not worth it.*

She shook her head, gave them one more glance, and pushed through the doors into Valley Market. Inside, she grabbed a cart and moved into the cereal aisle, willing to let the experience outside be. But the fluorescent light pressed at her temples. The exchange had drained her, and she felt a migraine rising.

Marisol didn't want to believe people couldn't change. After all, Mamá Belén—old as she was—had accepted Marisol when she came out, even when others her grandmother's age muttered that bi's were just "confused." If her grandmother could see her clearly, then why couldn't these women? Why did these viejitas refuse to see the humanity in people born here, shoot, and even those not born here? A human was a human, was a human.

Marisol let out a breath and pulled out her grocery list. She was here to do her groceries and go home. But her thoughts were knotted—Sabia's glossy bench ad, the women's intolerance, and now the whispers threading back into her head.

And then, as if she had conjured it, a conversation reached her. Had she been the last person in Willowshade to see the bench ad? It seemed everyone in the store was talking about it.

"Even before she joined her dad's firm, she had internships lined up," one voice said.

"She should do some mentoring," another chimed in.

"I know someone who could use her wise counseling," added a third.

Her grip tightened on the cart. Sabia's name floated everywhere, drowning her, and she couldn't help but compare herself to the overachieving mean girl on the bench ad.

A pair of teens shuffled past in pajama bottoms, eyes glued to their phones, following their mom's cart. But the voices didn't stop.

Failure.

You're a failure.

Failure.

Marisol's head snapped up. "Excuse me?"

The two girls turned, startled.

"What did you say?" Marisol asked, her voice sharper than she intended.

"Uh…" one stammered, confused.

Their mother wheeled back into the aisle. "What's going on?"

"I'm asking if your daughters said something to me," Marisol said, heat rushing to her face. The words sounded foolish even as they left her mouth.

The woman glanced at her daughters. They shook their heads, wide-eyed.

"They have nothing to say to you," the mother said flatly. She turned to her daughters and steered them away. "Stay close."

They disappeared into the next aisle, leaving Marisol alone.

Her chin lifted, but her hands trembled against the cart handle. Tears burned in her eyes, making her lip quiver. As soon as the aisle emptied, she bent forward, pressing her forehead into her fists. *Am I losing it?*

A soft rattle caught her attention. Marisol's head snapped as a pyramid of canned tomatoes trembled, then gave way, clattering across the linoleum until one bumped her boot and stilled. Marisol stumbled back, heart hammering. She hadn't touched them. No one had.

People passing at the end of the aisle slowed to stare. Heat surged up her neck into her cheeks.

And that's when she felt it. A pair of eyes on her.

Doña Elvira stood at the far side of the aisle, gaze fixed, unreadable.

Marisol's throat closed. She turned sharply, brushing past. "Excuse me," she muttered, refusing to meet her eyes. She didn't need Elvira's gaze pinning her down, too. She didn't know when or if she would ever be able to talk to her mom's best friend. But now was certainly not the time.

When she was far away, she scrounged her list in her fist and shoved it back in her pocket. Grocery shopping would have to wait. She had soup at home, and there was always Espresso Enchantment. As she hurried toward the exit, more voices rose behind her.

"The Espinals. Dangerous people," a man muttered.

"From what I heard, they left the worst one back on their island."

"What could be worse than these?"

"We must pray for her soul," another said.

"Elvira and that Espinal girl together? Nothing good ever comes from that. Probably why her mother died. There's only one God."

Tears pricked her eyes. She abandoned her empty cart by the door, already drained. It wasn't even ten o'clock, and she felt like she'd climbed Hallowthorn Hill three times.

Then, a sharper voice cut through, dripping with certainty: "Some say Elvira and the Espinal clan brought all those deaths during COVID."

"Jesus saves," another breathless voice added as the doors slid shut behind her.

The words clung to her skin like smoke, heavier than the toppled cans on the linoleum floor.

As she crossed the lot toward her car, Marisol thought bitterly: *I should have just let the judgmental viejas be.*

9

EL PELIGRO TE SIGUE (DANGER FOLLOWS YOU)

The next day, Marisol texted Kia a lie.

Marisol: I'm having horrible cramps.

Kia: So that's why you were acting funky when I called you?

Marisol: 😫

Kia: Bet. Got that Midol ready... Once I'm out.

Kia: Hey want me to bring you chicken noodle? I cooked some. Like really cooked not that can stuff you have.

Marisol: You shouldn't be making fun of the 🥲

Kia: Fine, but I can drop it off once Tony and I close.

Shame curled inside Marisol. The reason Kia was closing

was because she had called in sick. But she couldn't do it. She couldn't make herself get up from her bed and face the same people she had seen at Valley Market yesterday. Just imagining it made her stomach twist into knots.

> Marisol: You are too good to me

> Kia: Always. You know that.

She closed her messages. When the screen went black, her reflection stared back—but behind her face, in the dark glass, the hill hovered like a ghost pressing closer. And something else. She spun around.

Nothing.

Backing up, her foot caught on something, and she fell, landing hard. Beside where she fell, she noticed her mother's open notebook, only she didn't remember leaving it there. Suddenly, the notebook's pages began fluttering open before landing on a page with a message:

El peligro te sigue.

Danger follows you.

Be careful...

Marisol darted to the other side of the room. The space felt too quiet now, the air thick and heavy.

Is the notebook possessed?

"Nope. Nope, and nope," she whispered sharply, cutting off that terrifying thought before it took root. Desperation drove her movements as she lunged forward, grabbed the notebook, and threw it back into her drawer, slamming it shut. She scrambled onto the bed, pulling the blankets and comforter tightly around her, eyes clenched shut against whatever might be watching. The hill may be patient, but she was stubborn, and she refused to give in or get curious.

The following two days were lapses of sleeping and wakeful moments that felt as if Marisol was still sleeping. It was as if she walked on clouds. Marisol called in sick again and slept in her own bedroom, unsure as to how safe it was to be so close to her mother's notebook.

She would have been no good at Espresso Enchantment, she reasoned. Her mind was buzzing with haunting voices. Not even pacing the house eased the anxiety that felt like ants crawling underneath her skin.

Yet beyond the lack of sleep, it was the lie that didn't settle well with Marisol. Her mother had been really sick and died of COVID. Here she was, lying about being sick to hide from a supernatural notebook and the people who talk shit about her and her family. She rubbed her arms, feeling chilly once again. She passed a window and, through the crack in the curtain, saw it.

She couldn't lie to herself; she was also hiding from a hill. From the creeping dread that maybe, just maybe, her sanity had frayed beyond repair. If Mami knew, she would be so disappointed.

Unable to calm her nerves, Marisol headed towards the door. She caught sight of the small altar there. A silent shrine that had remained untouched since her mother's death. A half-way-burned black candle stood at its center, its wick cold and dark, but the wax had warped strangely, twisted into an unsettling shape she had never seen before. *Had it gotten that hot during the summer?* A chill prickled her spine as she noticed the small bowl of dried herbs next to it, their brittle leaves coated in dust, lifeless and forgotten. *Had they always looked so decayed?*

Marisol grabbed her jacket off the hook before stepping outside. Yet something strange happened once she had crossed her door. It was as if the world shifted beneath her feet. The familiar landscape blurred slightly at its edges, colors muted and unnatural, as though she had crossed an invisible boundary. She forced herself forward, the frozen earth crunching under her shoes, but the sound reverberated oddly, too loud and near. She glanced up, breath hitching—the hill looked so close, impossibly tall and dark, trees lining its path like sentinels, their branches twisted sharply, clawing at the gray sky.

Her fingers tingled as if they had frozen and then unfrozen. This wasn't right. None of this felt real.

A gust of wind surged around her, bringing the unmistakable acrid scent of cigar smoke. Before she could react, the wind solidified into pale, translucent vines that whipped around her wrists, tightening painfully. She struggled, panic surging, but her movements slowed as if trapped underwater.

"Come closer," a distorted voice hissed, its echo resonating through her bones.

"No!" Marisol shouted. But for some reason, her voice was muffled as if something or someone was trying to keep her from screaming.

Her heels scraped across the frozen dirt as the vines dragged her up the hill. Her sweater snagged and tore. The cold bit sharply at her exposed flesh. She twisted frantically, desperate to break free, but the vines held her fast.

At the hill's crest, horror paralyzed her. Her mother was there, bound tightly to one of the twisted, blackened trees, its branches themselves wrapping around her limbs like living shackles. Marisol choked up, a sob caught in her throat.

"Mami!" she cried, her voice cracking with desperation.

Her mother's wide, terrified eyes found hers, pleading silently for help as unseen hands moved in the shadows around her, whispers swirling like a storm. A shadowy figure stepped forward, shrouded in darkness, except for the sharp glow of a cigar revealing his presence. Its scent was thick, rich, and smoky, and clung around her like a warning. Her breath caught. And then, just at the edge of the shadow, he appeared.

A man stood still beneath the hill's long shadow, his presence unmistakable. His features were striking, sharp in a way that suggested beauty once softened them, but now every angle felt deliberate. Dangerous. His salt-and-pepper curls framed a face carved by quiet arrogance, and his gaze—deep-set and unreadable—carried the kind of stillness that unsettled. Not cold. Not empty. Just...watching.

He wore a crisp, pale chacabana, which was immaculate despite the wind. Its delicate embroidery caught the faint light. That and the cigars were the only Dominican things about her ancestor.

Yet there was no kindness in his expression. Only the suggestion of a smile, the kind that flickered just before something burned.

"Salvador," Marisol whispered. The smoke curled around him, thick and sinister, enveloping her mother. Branches twisted tighter around her mother's limbs, binding her harshly to the tree. Salvador leaned closer to her mother, his voice a low, menacing murmur Marisol could barely make out.

"*You dared reclaim what was never yours,*" he whispered coldly.

Her mother shook her head, frantic tears streaming silently down her face.

"*For your audacity. For thinking you were owed something sacred, you'll watch what happens when women forget their place.*"

From deep within the hill, another voice emerged, soft yet urgent, carried gently on rustling leaves. It sounded like the one who told her not to look away when she ran off from the parking lot that night. *"Marisol,"* it pleaded softly, desperately, *"this is why we called you. You must help us."*

Marisol's breath hitched in confusion, her heart pounding painfully. Whom could she trust? The ancestor tormenting her mother, or the pleading whispers of a voice with unknown intentions?

"Leave her alone!" Marisol finally managed to shout, her voice hoarse. Her throat felt raw, her struggles futile against her restraints.

The figure straightened slowly, turning his head toward her, features still hidden in shadow. *"Or what, Marisol? You're nothing special. Just an ordinary girl who could hide in wallpaper, and no one would even know. You can't survive without someone else guiding your every step. You don't deserve this power. You don't even deserve to live."*

Marisol flinched as the words echoed painfully within her, doubt seeping deep into her bones. She's always felt safe blending in. Standing out brought attention she didn't need. What was wrong with that? And why did she feel some sort of way when he said it aloud?

"Watch closely," Salvador's distorted voice commanded, forcing her gaze back to her mother. *"Witness the cost of your misguided courage."*

"No!" Marisol screamed as a sharp, gnarled root surged from beneath the tree, driving mercilessly into her mother's eye. A silent scream tore across her mother's face, agony etched deep into her features.

Marisol's vision blurred with tears and helpless rage as the scent of cigar smoke overwhelmed her.

"Mami, please, tell me what I need to do," she sobbed, desperate to reach her mother somehow.

The root withdrew violently, then plunged into her mother's other eye. Red streaks poured down her mother's face, her struggles weakened into tremors of despair.

"Stop it!" Marisol begged, her voice breaking with raw anguish. "Please, stop!"

But Salvador turned toward her once more, its presence filled with cruel, cold triumph. Marisol's heart shattered as her mother's suffering echoed silently through the twisted trees, leaving her vulnerable, helpless beneath the oppressive gaze of the man she now knew to be the descendant she'd read about online: the cigar aficionado who died on this very hill.

10

BRAVA AUNQUE TEMBLANDO (BRAVE EVEN WHEN TREMBLING)

Marisol bolted upright, breath ragged, shirt clinging to clammy skin. Her eyes darted around the room, searching for proof that it had only been a dream. The smell of rosewater and Vicks still clung to the sheets—familiar, grounding—but her mother's scream still echoed in her head.

She was home. Awake. Yet everything still felt wrong. Rubbing her temples, she tried to ease the pounding ache. She pulled the curtain aside. The just-risen winter sun made the hill look less menacing, but deep in her gut, she knew the danger remained. The dream had only confirmed it.

Drawn to her mother's room, she opened the drawer where she'd shoved the notebook. The thought of what she may find scared her. She knew the deeper she went down this rabbit hole, the harder it would be to climb back to anything resembling normal. But she couldn't think of that now.

Dreams were real. They were messages. Before she stopped following her mother's brujería, she used to have them too. They were doorways into glimpses of what had happened or what would happen. The hard part was discerning which one.

Even in the cramped drawer, the notebook's pages fluttered as if moved by an invisible hand. Trembling, she pulled it free. The moment she touched it, the movement stilled.

"What do you want?" she muttered, voice catching with fear.

No answer. She flipped through the pages, searching for something she'd missed. At first, nothing new—familiar sketches of the hill, roots tangled ominously. Then, on the final page, words appeared, bold and urgent in cursive:

Vas a perderla.

Marisol gasped. You will lose her, someone had written. Raw panic invaded every inch of her being. Her vision blurred. She riffled back through the notebook, fingers trembling.

But who?

Kia? That made no sense. How could something she didn't even believe in attack her? Disbelief was armor. So, Kia was the safest of them all. And yet, Marisol's mind raced, colliding with impossible thoughts, scanning through the list of women and femmes she cared about. Except for Kia, they were all gone.

No. That wasn't true. One lived here, in Willowshade. Elvira. For all her resentment, love didn't switch off. Once, Doña Elvira had been like a second mother. Walking past her in the grocery store as though she were a stranger had hurt in a way Marisol didn't want to admit. Elvira still held a place in her heart.

But what if it wasn't only the living at risk? Her mother and grandmother had prayed countless times for peace for the dead, warning that souls could suffer too. What if the warning meant them?

"Mami, Mamá Belén," Marisol whispered, the last fog of sleep leaving her body.

She dragged her hands over her face, hoping to scrub the anxiety away. It thrummed through her anyway. She paced the hallway, desperate to outrun the nightmare—the terrified face of her mother, the silent screams, the shadowed roots plunging mercilessly. Her chest heaved. She needed answers.

In the kitchen, she filled a glass of water, sipping slowly, afraid she might choke if she swallowed too quickly. Voices from childhood echoed in the room—her mother's stories about Hallowthorn Hill, tales she'd dismissed as fairy tales. Only now they felt real, stripped of whimsy, painted with desperation. Her mother hadn't been fanciful; she'd been trapped.

Back in her mother's room, the notebook lay still. The hill loomed outside her window, dark and watchful. Even the sun seemed reluctant to touch it. She'd sworn never to climb it, but now she knew her mother was there, afraid, being tortured. She needed to do something.

She couldn't lose her again. But the thought of asking Elvira for help hollowed her out. The ache in her stomach deepened. She needed help and not just from anyone, but from the one person she'd brushed past yesterday like a stranger. And now she would have to ask for what she'd pretended she didn't need.

Still, Elvira was the only one who could help. The knowledge others dismissed as superstition was exactly what her mother had trusted. If anyone could guide her, it was Elvira.

An hour later, Marisol drove into town, parking quietly near the herb shop. Snow clouds dimmed the sky, casting the street in washed-out gray. Her breath fogged the air as she pulled her coat tighter. The familiar storefront of Elvira's herb shop glowed softly beneath the apartment upstairs.

Above, a light shone in the window like a beacon. Her heart pulled toward it, toward the wisdom she both longed for and feared. She climbed the side stairs to the apartment door.

Standing in front of Elvira's, Marisol lifted her hand—then froze. A bitter taste, like leather and ash, spread across her tongue. Her mother had trusted this woman and spent countless hours at her side until she fell ill. Could she? Could Marisol open herself up to someone who may have hurt her mother? Or at the very least had been neglectful and selfish enough to not check on her best friend and let her die?

Love and resentment tangled, sharp with grief inside of her.

The hallway carpets smelled faintly of acrid smoke. She lifted her sweater to cover her nose. She needed help. But could she ask it from the woman who might've let her mother walk into danger alone?

She drew her hand back. She couldn't gamble on trust she didn't have. Quietly, carefully, she slipped out of the building, avoiding the parts of the floor that might betray her.

Outside, she turned onto Main Street. The mural stretched across the visitor's center wall: Willowshade's history in warm earth tones and pastel skies. Children chasing butterflies. Settlers smiling with baskets of grain. And near the edge, a brown woman with a broom, eyes cast down.

Almost part of the scene. Almost.

Marisol looked away. Just a mural. Just paint. Her family's story had never been the kind worth painting.

She walked on. Antique lampposts lined the cobblestone sidewalks, their iron frames twisting like branches. Across the street, the white-owned apothecary boasted "Handcrafted Herbal Remedies," crystals glittering in the window. Next door, a bookstore offered tarot readings, as indicated by faded signs. *Holistic when they did it, superstitious when Elvira did.* Even though Marisol didn't care much about her mother's best friend, Willowshade's hypocrisy burned.

Yet even in the cozy, curated magic of Willowshade's town center, Marisol felt like the woman in the mural—an outsider, broom in hand, staring into a life not hers. Her gaze drifted toward Espresso Enchantment. She thought of Kia. As much as she loved her, she could never ask Kia to step into this danger. She was safe, not believing, and she needed to stay that way.

11

LA DUDA QUE CRECE EN LA OSCURIDAD (DOUBT THAT GROWS IN THE DARK)

Marisol walked back to her car, unlocking it manually to avoid attention. Casting one last longing look toward the once comforting glow of Elvira's shop, she got in.

She felt utterly alone, except for the gentle hum of Main Street waking up around her. The faint clatter of shop doors opening, distant laughter drifting on the morning breeze, and the subtle warmth spilling from inviting storefront windows only intensified her sense of isolation. The cheerful storefronts, hanging plants, and handmade signs belonged to another world. They couldn't touch the ache pressing down on her. Yet deep within, beneath that persistent ache, a stubborn resolve hardened.

It wasn't just the hill calling to her now. It was Salvador. His presence had invaded her life, twisted her dreams into nightmares, and cruelly tormented her mother's soul. Her mother's silent scream still echoed vividly through her mind, painfully fresh and undeniably real. Marisol couldn't afford to delay and self-soothe. She had to be brave.

"Ponte brava," Mamá Belén had said fiercely when Marisol had run home crying one afternoon, crushed under the girlies' relentless bullying. "They only torment you because you let them. Muéstrales quién tú eres, mija. Nunca bajes la cabeza ante nadie."

Mamá Belén always spun everything around, like it was up to Marisol to fix the world crashing down on her, like she could somehow stop assholes from being assholes, when some people were just shitty, full stop.

Back then, her grandmother's advice had felt impossible. How was she supposed to stand tall when Las Tres Mojonas' laughter echoed in her ears, tearing her down word by cruel word?

But Mamá Belén had kneeled in front of her, gently wiping the tears from her cheeks, eyes sharp and unwavering.

"Tu fuerza viene de aquí," she'd said, pressing her hand firmly over Marisol's heart.

"Your strength is always inside you, mi niña. But you have to claim it."

And in a way...it kind of worked.

The bullying didn't magically stop. Shoot, it still happened now. Delgada, with her compliment-hiding-insults, 'I say you are winning, Marisol' when she clearly is not. Blanca talking crap about her online, and even Sabia mocking her through the bench ad, showing her everything she wasn't. No, they hadn't really stopped. Las tres mojonas had just graduated to adult versions of it, and Marisol had learned to swallow it without choking. But she had also learned something important: miserable people always looked for company.

So, maybe Mamá Belén was right. Maybe she could do something. Maybe she could bluff Salvador. Pretend to be stronger than she felt. It had worked on the girlies—why not an ancestor with control issues?

If Salvador were the well-to-do businessman she read about, he would react to strategy and bargaining. She had taken enough business classes not to finish a degree, but to know enough about how to negotiate.

Stake your position. Don't show fear. Hold the line. Boom.

She just needed to see the hill up close and confront whatever it was before it sank deeper into her life.

But doubt tugged at her.

That's not going to work.

Marisol pushed the thought away.

She walked quickly, got in her car, and drove home.

Once inside the house, her movements were hurried yet deliberate. She tugged off her sturdy boots; their worn soles told of years pacing through uncertainty. But she didn't take off her coat. Instead, she pulled it tighter around her, feeling its comforting weight as armor—fragile protection against an enemy whose threats whispered invisibly through cigar smoke and shadow.

She hesitated at the small altar shelf. The half-burned black candle sat straight and solid, unlike the warped nightmare version from her dream.

Good. She exhaled shakily, relieved that reality still held firm here. But doubt prickled at the edges of her thoughts again. *Was reality truly so secure? Or has Salvador already begun reshaping my world?*

Beside the candle lay a bowl of dried herbs, their fragrance long faded, remnants of protection she'd ignored too long. Near the back sat a smooth river stone etched faintly with a spiral. One, her mother had often rubbed gently between her fingers whenever storms gathered or shadows stretched too long. Marisol picked it up carefully; its cool weight grounded her briefly against the storm brewing inside her. She felt a gentle tug deep within her chest, an echo of her mother's touch, a whisper of memory and strength beyond words.

"I never believed you," she whispered, shame coloring her voice. "I thought it was all just stories and superstition. But Salvador was real all along, wasn't he? You tried to protect me. You tried to warn me."

She slipped the stone into her coat pocket, its presence a steady reassurance, a promise.

Her gaze drifted back toward the altar, and she gave a respectful nod. "I promise," she said quietly, her voice strengthening with each syllable, "I'll come back. I'll relight your candle, refresh your herbs, and face everything I've ignored."

Outside, the wind stirred sharply.

"This has to work," Marisol whispered as she walked toward the entryway.

The click-clack of branches accompanied by the swoosh of wind snaking through the trees was an orchestra anticipating her arrival. "I can do this."

If the dream were true, Salvador had claimed the hill. She was going to him to negotiate. She was going to his turf because that was better than inviting him here. Marisol squared her shoulders, trying to feel good about her decision. She would go to him. She will convince this businessman to see reason. She swallowed, but her throat was dry.

Marisol grabbed a cup and took a sip of water before putting her boots back on. Her feet moved almost without her permission, carrying her steadily toward Hallowthorn Hill. With each step, its dark silhouette loomed larger, pressing heavily on her spirit, yet she did not falter. A powerful force pulled her forward. It was something deeper than fear, stronger than loneliness. She would confront this malicious ancestor and free her mother.

Yet as she neared the hill, a quiet uncertainty flickered within her, without Kia. Without Doña Elvira. "Naciste sola," Mamá Belén used to say, and she was right. She would face this alone. She would show Salvador and this hill that she refused to run and hide. She would be brave—even if bravery felt tenuous, even if her resolve trembled with every step.

She had no idea what waited for her at the summit, or if courage alone would be enough. But she had to try. She owed it to her mother, to Mamá Belén, and most importantly to herself.

12

LAS VOCES DEL HILL (THE VOICES IN THE HILL)

Marisol stood at the base of Hallowthorn Hill, her feet sunk into the soft, damp earth. It didn't give. It was as though something beneath the surface had been waiting for her weight. The scent of decayed leaves was thick in the air. The cold wind sliced against her skin, sharp and biting, carrying with it a faint, metallic taste that lingered on her tongue. The trees loomed overhead, their gnarled branches twisting like skeletal fingers, creaking as they swayed, adding to the gothic symphony playing all around her.

She took a breath, trying to calm her nerves, but it was anything but calming. Cold air burned her lungs.

"This was a good decision," she said to herself through gritted teeth. Yet, every part of herself screamed at her to turn around, to go home, to lock the door and pretend the hill didn't exist.

But she couldn't. Not after that vision. Not after seeing her mother on this hill, reaching to the sky, terrified and alone.

She stepped forward.

The ground shifted beneath her boots, hard, cold, and

unyielding. As if the hill had changed its mind. As if it said, 'No, I don't want you to come further.'

Well, what is it?

But Marisol stopped herself from questioning the innate landmark. *What if it answers back?*

Yet, the hill gave no answer. Instead, the wind stopped. Just like that, the symphony ceased, and everything went silent. The branches that had been rattling moments before had gone eerily still. No creaking. No rustling leaves. Just—silence. Deep and suffocating.

The back of her neck prickled. The hairs on her arms stood up. Something shifted in the air; it was subtle but undeniable. This had the same energy as the girlies. Incessantly talking about her but stopping when she was within earshot. The hill had been waiting for her, had been talking about her. And now that she was here, it was ready. It had been preparing for this, and it wasn't going to let her go.

She clenched her fists. Her nails bit into her palms. She was here for her mother. She was going to save her. And yes, she knew her mother had died. She was not delusional. But she couldn't shake the feeling that her spirit was suffering. Why else would she be having those dreams? Why else would her mother appear on this hill, terrified and alone?

Marisol hadn't bought into the mystical stuff Mami and Mamá Belén used to talk about, but maybe there was a smidge of truth to it. Maybe that's why her mother's spirit was trapped here, waiting for Marisol to save her. And if there was even the slightest chance that her theory was correct, even though Marisol's body rejected the idea, this was where she needed to be, at least for now. And once she finished, she would never come back to this hill again, and everything would go back to normal.

She let out a quick breath filled with tension and questions.

She watched white fog curl in the frigid air in front of her. This was it.

She had to move. If she didn't, she never would.

"Move," she admonished herself.

Marisol took her first step. The hill watched her, its shadow stretched long and dark. The trees bent as if craning their necks to get a better look at her.

She shivered, pulling her coat tighter, but never taking her eyes off the path winding upward. It seemed steeper than she remembered, the trees closer, their branches knotted and tangled, blocking out the sky. A cold breeze snaked around her ankles, winding up her legs, curling around her waist, her chest, her neck. It felt like fingers, cold and skeletal, brushing against her skin.

Marisol's throat tightened and her stomach twisted. She took another step, then another, forcing herself to keep moving, to keep climbing. The air grew colder, the wind picked up again, this time stronger, murmuring words she couldn't understand. Her name drifted through the trees, soft and faint.

"Look, there she is."

"Ya llegó."

"Ahi esta la muchacha."

The voices murmured all around her.

She shook her head, trying to clear it. It was just the wind. Just the trees creaking in the cold. It wasn't real.

The shadows moved at the edges of her vision, flickering between the trees, twisting and curling as they pushed against the wind. Marisol's heart skipped a beat; her steps faltered. She looked around, but the shadows were gone.

A whisper slithered through the air, oily and deliberate, curling around her ears like a serpent coiling to strike, threading into her thoughts with a cruel intimacy that reeked of Salvador. Then, the unmistakable scent of a freshly lit cigar emerged. She coughed as the smoke clung to the back of her throat.

"She's already gone."

Marisol clenched her fists. That voice—low, invasive, slick with cruelty—was unmistakable. This was that ancestor. He was not a memory. Not a dream. He was here, and watching.

"You let her die."

Her breath hitched. The words echoed in her own voice, but the layer beneath was imperceptibly his. Like a foul undertone laced into her thoughts, warping them—this blending unnerved her. It was as if he were already inside her head, using her own voice to break her down. The scent of cigar suffocated her.

Salvador laughed low and raspy.

She felt dirty, invaded. *He was influencing me–influencing me to be the worst version of myself.* Unable to take the echo, Marisol squeezed her head between her hands.

"Get out of my head," she said, but even that sounded wrong, like he was repeating her words back to her as she said them.

She forced herself to keep climbing. Her footsteps crunched against the frozen earth. She was afraid to think, afraid to speak, worried that even a stray thought might summon that twisted echo of her voice now fused with his. The air grew colder, the shadows darker, stretching long and thin across the path. The hill loomed above her, its tangled roots bulging from the ground like knuckles. The trees along the path bent lower, their branches curling downward, twisted and gnarled, fingers reaching out to touch her.

Marisol remembered the nightmare she had of being trapped in these same branches, and she shivered. Her breath caught in her throat, heart thudding in her tight chest. She wanted to run, to turn around and leave, but her feet kept moving, carrying her forward, closer to the top.

A flash of light caught her eye, bright and sudden, blinding her. She blinked, but her vision didn't clear. She continued to blink and scrub at her eyes and then—

Her mother was there.

Josefina Espinal stood at the top of the hill.

Her hair, dark and thick like Marisol's, blew wildly in the wind. Her high cheekbones and full lips were unmistakably Espinal, though now they were drained of color. Her face, usually defiant and dazzling, was pale and terrified, exactly like it had been in Marisol's dream. Gone was the bold, radiant makeup that was always part of her face. Her blouse hung crookedly on her shoulders, and her long skirt looked faded and wrinkled, unlike anything her mother would've allowed herself to be seen in. She looked like a shadow of the woman Marisol remembered—the glamorous, commanding presence who never left the house without full makeup or heels that clicked with purpose. It was as if the hill had stripped her of every layer of pride and poise she'd once possessed.

"Mami!" Marisol shouted, and for a second—just one second—she was five years old, lost in a store, spotting her mother, reaching for her safety net.

She ran toward her. "Mami."

Her mother didn't move. She stood still—too still—her eyes wide and hollow, lips moving soundlessly, forming words Marisol couldn't hear.

Marisol reached out, but her fingers brushed the air, as if her mother was being moved by an invisible force further and further away from her, like a sickening mirage. Her mother's body flickered like a glitch in a video. Her face twisted with fear. A shadow moved behind her, dark and twisted, wrapping around her, pulling her backward.

"No!" Marisol screamed, stumbling forward, grasping at empty air.

Her mother's eyes met hers. Wild. Desperate. Her mouth formed one final word. *"Ayúdame."*

Help me.

The shadow curled around her mother, dragging her down, into the earth, into the darkness. Marisol took off running again, but her foot caught on a root, and she fell, hitting the ground hard.

"Mami, wait!" Marisol screamed, desperately reaching out to her. But her mother was gone. Cold seeped into her bones. Pain shot up her leg. Her hands, scraped against the frozen earth, now bleeding. She looked up again, hoping to see her.

The hill was empty. Only the trees remained, dark and twisted, with shadows curling around them like smoke.

The wind howled, low and mournful, as if it too mourned her mother's sudden disappearance. Marisol's chest tightened. Her breath hitched as she tried to fight back tears.

Her mother is here. Her mother is trapped. Her mother needs her.

But the shadows drew closer. They had been watching and waiting.

The ground shifted beneath her. The earth rumbled as roots curled towards her, reaching for her like cold, skeletal hands. She scrambled, but she couldn't get up fast enough. It was as if the soil was trying to swallow her. One rotten branch slithered low, trying to grab her, to take her.

"No!"

Marisol tried to jerk away, but she was tethered. One branch wrapped itself around her ankle. Another came up to her waist. It barely brushed the pocket of her coat before recoiling. It jerked back as if burned, hissing before the branch gripping her ankle retreated too. Soon, every branch recoiled off of her and into the shadows. Marisol sat up. Her breath came short. She didn't know what had just happened, but she was relieved. She scrambled to her feet.

"Get out," Salvador said, his voice ragged with frustration.

Marisol wondered, just for a breath, why he sounded so furious. Why had his voice stopped echoing in her head?

Why had the branches done what they did? Why hadn't he pulled her into the shadows like her mother?

But, she didn't have time to dwell on these questions, and she definitely didn't have the mental capacity to do it right then and there. But she knew he had been ready to drag her down, to twist her fear into submission, and something had stopped him. Something that wasn't supposed to be there.

She looked around, her heart pounding, fearful that something else would jump at her. And when she knew it was safe to move, Marisol backed her away towards the trail.

Right then, a whisper echoed through the air, low and cold, laced with anger. *"Stay away, Ordinary Bruja."* It carried Salvador's rot—bitter, resentful, pulsing with his fury.

Then, another whisper rose. This one was softer, layered, like many voices speaking in unity. *"No...come back."*

The forest itself seemed to sigh with it. This voice didn't carry malice. It carried longing. Desperation. A plea. Hallowthorn Hill was calling to her not to harm her, but because it needed her?

"You learned how to protect yourself."

Marisol's blood ran cold. She froze, caught between Salvador's push and the Hill's pull.

"I learned to protect myself?" Marisol shook her head at the ridiculousness of that comment.

The ground shook, causing her to move. "I don't have time for this. Not here."

Whatever she still needed to understand—how to protect herself, how to save her mother—she wouldn't figure it out standing here, exposed. She was better off doing it away from Salvador's reach. And as if her ancestor knew her intention, a branch jetted out in her direction.

"Oh no, you don't," Marisol said breathlessly before dodging the branch and running down the trail.

She was out of breath by the time she got home. Marisol's phone buzzed with notifications. She glanced at the reception bars, then at the screen: a text from Kia, and a voice message from an unsaved number.

Her thumb hovered. She debated pressing play. She only saved numbers from people she trusted. If it wasn't saved, chances were she didn't want to hear it, and she needed to get inside.

At the door, she tugged off her boots, letting them fall where they landed. She shrugged out of her coat and dropped it to the floor, too tired to care. Then, she shot a quick reply to Kia before setting the phone on the dining table.

She began to pace. Her mother was still out there, trapped on that hill, and the thought cracked something inside her. As the adrenaline drained, tears welled and spilled hot down her cheeks.

What had she even been thinking? That some evil ancestor would just listen to her? That a pebble in her pocket would be enough to face whatever lived on that hill? She wasn't prepared.

Not really. She needed a plan—something real, not just panic, desperation, and the flimsy hope that stubbornness plus a few leftover lessons from business classes could carry her through.

The screen blinked.

Another voice message.

Her stomach tightened. Five new messages.

Maybe it was her aunt, the one who hadn't reached out since before her mother died. She pressed play on the latest.

A voice. Faint. Distorted.

"You are so ordinary..."

"What?" Marisol's breath hitched. She played the others.

"Ordinary."

"Ordinary."

"Ordinary."

The word crawled under her skin, etched itself into her bones, a curse injected straight into her blood.

Marisol hurled the phone against the wall.

But the voice lingered, echoing inside her skull.

13

GRIEF Y RESENTIMIENTO (PENA AND RESENTMENT)

It had been three days since Marisol fled the hill. Her chest still burned with failure and shame. Three days of barely sleeping, of staring at the altar pebble and trying to make sense of what had happened. When she returned it to the altar, it had been warm to the touch, almost glowing. She had stood there, frozen, the heat of it still warming her palm as if it were a living thing that pulsed with blood. Was the pulse a warning? An acceptance? A connection? She didn't know.

And because she didn't know, she hadn't gone back to the hill. She needed answers. But her doubts were thick, tangled in her chest like overgrown vines.

And now, here she was.

"Hey, Marisol," a passerby said.

She smiled and nodded, then froze. Kia had been checking in—texting, stopping by—because she thought Marisol was sick, not standing here outside Espresso Enchantment. She shifted quickly out of the way and whispered a quick prayer that the woman heading inside wouldn't mention seeing her.

Kia didn't do supernatural—not the real kind—and Marisol respected that, wanted her to stay that way, even. With everything unraveling, Kia's disbelief kept her safe. Marisol clung to that, grateful. Still, it left her walking a fragile line: offering only the truths Kia could handle, careful not to sound like she'd lost her mind. Because if Kia looked at her the way everyone else in Willowshade did, she'd shatter. Better to hold back, keep the chaos tucked away until she could face it with someone who did believe. Someone who lived and worked on the shadowy side of Main Street. Someone she'd been avoiding.

Her eyes drifted to the Yerbería Elvira down the street. The air was cold, sharp, and biting against her skin, the sun barely warming the frosted pavement. She hugged her coat tighter, her fingers numb, her thoughts circling the vision she'd seen on the hill. Her mother's pale and terrified face haunted her; the memory of that desperate cry echoed through her mind.

Marisol hadn't slept. Every time she closed her eyes, she saw shadows curling around her mother, pulling her down into the earth. Every attempt to forget only brought it rushing back —the broken echo of the woman she remembered, whispers tangling around her like vines, one pleading, one rotted, and the pebble pulsing in her pocket.

Her own voice threaded through her head, warped by Salvador's, cruel and foreign. She remembered the branches shrinking when it touched the pocket where the pebble had been, and then the pebble itself—warm, glowing, alive, fire against those vines. And always, the acrid taste of her ancestor's presence. Marisol stopped short. A chill ran through her. That smell—it was the same as the one she'd noticed inside Doña Elvira's building. She had written it off as stale smoke trapped in the carpet, but the only one who lived there was Elvira. Maybe some customers had wandered through the wrong entrance, but not enough to taint the place with that stench. Elvira didn't smoke, and the things she burned—ruda, albahaca, rosemary—smelled nothing like it.

None of it made sense. But she questioned every rationalization she had had, wondering if she had made the right call. She replayed that moment again and again in her mind, unable to shake it.

Marisol shivered, the frost sinking into her bones. She glanced toward the herb shop. The windows were dark, the faint silhouettes of dried herbs swaying behind the glass. A blurred figure moved inside—Doña Elvira's shape, ghostly through the frost.

Her chest tightened. Salvador had tricked her, steered her away from help. She pressed into the awning, hidden from view. Yet, deep inside, resentment simmered. Salvador had not planted that there. Once, Elvira had been like a second mother. Her own mother had trusted her with everything, especially matters like these. Elvira was supposed to be the wise one, the protector. So, why hadn't she stopped her? Why hadn't she kept Mami safe?

Marisol remembered the charms hanging in Elvira's home, the warded windows, the quiet rituals woven into every corner. Elvira knew how to protect herself, both spiritually and physically. Why would she let her best friend walk out into the world without protection?

They had always worked together. Mami trusted Elvira with everything, especially matters of brujería. Elvira was the seer, the one who claimed to sense what others couldn't. If anyone should have recognized danger, it was her. And yet, Mami still ended up unprotected and vulnerable, while Elvira survived.

How did that happen?

It was easy to tell herself Elvira had failed, had withheld the very gifts that might have saved her mother. But Marisol knew Elvira wasn't the only problem. There had been no vaccine then, no answers—just death moving through Black and Brown neighborhoods like the reaper himself, taking people in waves while the world looked away.

And Marisol? She was the most guilty of all. She hadn't

come home. She'd quarantined at her roommate's family estate in California—spacious, filtered air, strong Wi-Fi, the luxury of pretending she was someone else, someone untouchable. Until the hospital called. Until her so-called friend vanished with the words, "Poor people's problems are too heavy. I have to protect my peace."

Elvira vanished too, after Mami died. Was it guilt that silenced her? Or shame? She left messages Marisol never answered, casseroles she never touched. Not because she was drowning in grief, but because betrayal cut deeper than that.

Marisol had seen the wards, the charms, the calm, practiced power Elvira carried. She couldn't forgive her for surviving when her mother hadn't. In Marisol's mind, if Elvira had truly used her gifts, Mami would have survived COVID like she did.

Maybe it was irrational. Maybe no one could have stopped it. But grief didn't care about reason. And neither did betrayal. Still, it was easier to avoid her, to pretend the silence between them didn't ache. But the vision—the memory she replayed— wouldn't let her rest. And Marisol was running out of places to look. She had no one else to turn to.

The internet was a mess of clashing spells, contradictory advice, and half-baked witchcraft threads that could take weeks to sort through, if she even believed half of them. But Elvira... for all her faults, wouldn't scoff at talks of spirits or curses. Wouldn't flinch at the idea of an evil ancestor haunting a hill. Even if Marisol didn't fully trust her, she knew the woman had a gift, some kind of wisdom that was grounded in something real.

If Elvira seemed trustworthy enough, if she responded like someone who knew, someone who would not sabotage Marisol, someone who could help her tackle this with more than just instinct and fear, then Marisol would trust her with this. At least, until she gave her a reason not to.

Her feet moved before she could think, because if she

thought about it, she wouldn't go. So, Marisol grabbed the handle, and pulled the door open.

The bell chimed, welcoming her into Yerberia Elvira. It hadn't changed. Same hanging herbs. Same quiet watchfulness. Same feeling of stepping into a story no one else had bothered to write down.

The air was warm, heavy with the scent of incense. The dim light cast shadows across the wooden shelves lined with glass jars. Marisol's throat thickened as memories flooded back. Saturday mornings with Mami, laughing as they browsed through the shelves, their fingers brushing over the jars, the air thick with the scent of hierbabuena and lavender.

She swallowed hard; her eyes stung. She had been here so many times, but it felt different now. Colder. Emptier.

Doña Elvira emerged from the back room, her dark eyes widening in surprise. Marisol's breath caught. She looked older and more frail than she had that day at Valley Market. Now, her shoulders were hunched, and deep lines were etched around her mouth and eyes. She hadn't noticed then how her once-thick curls were thinned, shortened, and streaked with silver—though still frizzing at the edges from years spent surrounded by smoke and incense. This woman had been so familiar, yet here she was, with a heavy weariness Marisol hadn't seen before.

Doña Elvira had been lively, energetic, always moving with purpose and grace. Always smiling. But today, her smile was faint, brittle at the corners, as if it might shatter if she moved too quickly. Marisol's chest tightened with guilt. How long had it been since she'd really looked at her? She had been so consumed by her own grief, her own pain, that she hadn't even seen Doña Elvira's.

"Marisol," Doña Elvira said in almost a whisper.

Marisol tucked a curl behind her ear. If it hadn't been for what happened, she wouldn't be here right now. Yet, she forced herself to meet Doña Elvira's gaze, while her temple throbbed with grief, shame, and uncertainty. She came in filled with doubts, so she couldn't lead with vulnerability or be completely open. Not yet. Not before she knew she could trust this woman.

"Yeah. I…" She smoothed the front of her jacket. "I just came to pick something up."

Doña Elvira's face softened, her eyes darkening with something Marisol couldn't name—something that looked like recognition, as if she saw a piece of herself in her.

"I know, Mija." Elvira's voice was soft but grounded. "Grief doesn't just sit on your chest. It burrows in your bones. Doesn't it?"

Marisol's breath hitched. She fought back tears. But she couldn't afford to fall apart. Not yet. Not before she was sure. This was her moment to watch, to listen, to test. She cleared her throat, forcing her voice to be steady as she studied Elvira, not for comfort but for signs. If Elvira downplayed—if she dismissed—what Marisol was about to say, then she'd know. She'd known what Mamá Belén had told her many times was true, that she was all alone in this.

"I… I've been having nightmares. About Mami. About…the hill."

"The hill." Doña Elvira's voice dropped, low and steady, carrying a weight Marisol hadn't heard before. She said those two words, as if confirming something long buried. But Elvira's eyes didn't narrow in disbelief; instead, they searched Marisol's face, cautious but open. "Tell me what you saw, mija. If you're ready to hear it, I'll tell you what I know."

Marisol's stomach twisted. She didn't want to talk about it. Didn't want to admit how scared she was, how lost she felt. But this was the moment. The test. She kept her voice even, careful not to reveal too much. "I saw her there. On the hill. She looked…so scared."

Doña Elvira's expression darkened, her eyes shadowed with

a look that seemed like anger. "Did she speak to you?" she asked, her voice low and measured.

Marisol's heart pounded. She nodded slowly. "She didn't say much. Only 'Ayudame.'"

Elvira didn't ask anything else. Instead, she nodded, her eyes scanning the room as though expecting something to reveal itself. When her gaze connected with Marisol's, she said, "Salvador."

But as soon as she said it, Elvira's hand flew to her mouth; horror flashed across her face. It was as if the word were a stone, and it thudded on the floor.

"He's not supposed to be acknowledged," Elvira said quickly, her voice low and tense. "Josefina believed speaking his name gave him more power. She told me once, near the end, that he was part of your bloodline, an ancestor who wronged his own daughter, who twisted the family's magic for himself. But she never uncovered the full story. She barely had time to piece it together before she...before she got sick."

Marisol stiffened at hearing her mother spoken of so plainly, with that same weight of unfinished stories and fading memory. It hit harder than she expected. The image of Mami's terrified face on the hill surged up again, clawing at her throat. For a moment, she wanted to leave, to walk out of the shop and pretend she had never come. But she clenched her jaw. She couldn't turn away. Not now. Not when some part of her already knew that the truth would only come if she stayed.

Doña Elvira finally met her eyes. "It means the things buried there—secrets, spirits, old grief—they don't rest. It's like a purgatory he created. But something stirred. Maybe your grief called to it. And now it's watching. Calling back."

Vile rose up Marisol's throat. She swallowed before she could speak. "I saw my mother. She was suffering, Doña Elvira."

Elvira's body tensed. Her hand reached out to steady herself on the counter as if a particular realization had just sunk in.

Marisol watched as her mother's best friend put her hand over her heart and closed her eyes. Then, her lips parted and moved as if she was searching for words that wouldn't come. When she finally spoke, it was barely above a murmur but raw and shaken. "Josefina is trapped there. He trapped her. Who knows who else he's trapped...and now he's calling you."

A chill ran down Marisol's spine.

"Why?" she asked. "What does he get from all of this?"

Elvira moved slowly, setting the herbs down with quiet reverence. "Your power."

Marisol blinked. "I don't have any powers. I'm beyond ordinary. I'm mid at best."

Elvira let out a weak laugh. "If you were, he wouldn't be in your thoughts."

Marisol's brows rose in shock. *How does she know he's in my head?*

"He knows who you are," Elvira said, her voice quieter now. "He knows your love. Your doubt. Your guilt. And he's going to use all of it. He twists things. Makes you lose yourself in your worst thoughts."

Marisol's body went cold. A sharp, internal chill made her limbs feel heavy. She had been right. It was him. Every time she smelled that cigar, it had been him near her, and those were the times when she had been at her worst. Marisol rubbed the back of her neck. A ringing filled her ears, blurring the edges of the moment.

"But there were other voices too," she said hoarsely. "Not just his voice."

"Other voices?" Elvira blinked, taken aback by this information. "Like I said, he could have trapped others there. But what did the other voices say?"

"To stay." Marisol stuck her finger in her ear and shook it, trying to ease the ringing there. Ever since all of this started, it was as if tension had hitched a permanent ride inside of her.

"Which was confusing because Salvador told me to leave, and I know it's him because it feels different."

Elvira paced. She raised her hands to the sky as if in prayer before saying, "Ahí, madre, dame la información que necesito."

Mother, give me the information I need, she'd said.

Doña Elvira paced some more before looking at Marisol square in the eyes again. "Bad people don't get better after they die. If anything, they become worse, and of what little your mom told me about Salvador, he was not a good man. He wasn't just a controlling father; he was a horrible human being. So, his spirit grew into something sinister. I'm sure what he's doing to your mother's spirit, he has done to others."

A sob slipped from Marisol's lips. She bit down hard, trying to keep it together. "I don't know. I don't know what to do."

Doña Elvira's gaze was steady. She reached for Marisol and held her hand as if she knew how much she needed her constant presence. "Your mom was trying to clear your path. I remember that. She knew he'd call you one day. That's why she wanted to finish it. She thought if she did it, it would save you from him."

Marisol's world spun. Mami had tried to save her and failed. If her mother couldn't defeat the monster on the hill, what chance did she have?

"I-I don't know," Marisol said, unable to meet Elvira's gaze any longer. "If Mami couldn't do it—"

"But she knew you could, Mija. That she told me. Your mother had faith in you, and so do I."

Marisol swallowed, feeling the weight of expectations on her shoulders. She licked her lips. "Mami, she had a notebook. I just found it. It has doodles and notes..."

"I know it's a lot to take in. But knowing who you are facing and what they are capable of helps in being prepared, Mija, and if your mom had some notes in that notebook... Is the notebook about this?"

Tears stung Marisol's eyes. She nodded.

"Then you must read it through. Read it all. I can help if you would like," Elvira said carefully.

Marisol wanted so badly to hold herself together like a perfectly wrapped box. Still, she was busting out of the wrapping. Her hands shook. Doña Elvira pulled her into an embrace. One that reminded her so much of her mother. Of the hugs that used to feel like a cocoon, like a recharging of sorts. But this was different. It felt like a hug before going into a battle she didn't know she would come back alive from.

"It's okay, Mija. I am here."

And that she believed.

Marisol nodded. She couldn't trust her voice right now. She couldn't trust that it wouldn't break and give her away. But at least she was not by herself. At least she had this woman. This wise woman, who was once a second mom and now a trusted person to help her through this.

Doña Elvira hadn't hesitated, hadn't tried to twist her words. She had been open about what she knew. Marisol knew she could trust her.

14

YOU WERE CHOSEN, MIJA (TU ESTÁS ELEGIDA, MIJA)

Marisol sat curled up in the farthest corner of her room, tucked between the dresser and the wall with the curtains drawn tight. She shut her curtains, pushed her desk against the flaps to keep any unruly wind from flapping it open. She knew it was irrational, yet she thought that if she could see the hill, Salvador and any other monsters on the hill could see her too.

Her mother's notebook lay open on her lap. The pages had become familiar, the ink faded in some places, smudged in others where her mother had pressed too hard or paused too long. The room was dim, lit only by the glow of her desk lamp. The pebble had been prickling at the edge of her thoughts ever since she came back from the hill, like a splinter of energy she couldn't ignore.

When she returned from Doña Elvira's, she'd grabbed the pebble from the altar by the front door without thinking. It had been calling to her in its own quiet way. She'd been holding it, studying it, trying to understand why it had reacted the way it did—why it had grown warm, protective. She remembered seeing the same spiral etched in her mother's notebook.

Her laptop sat open beside her, its screen casting pale light across her comforter. She scrolled through her browser history, searching for what she had once dismissed: spirals in folklore, spirals in magic, protection symbols, ancient glyphs.

There were patterns, sure, but nothing definitive. Some cultures saw spirals as symbols of rebirth, cycles, or the soul's journey. Others believed they were portals or traps for spirits, depending on how they were used. One site mentioned the spiral as a memory anchor. That made something in her chest twist.

She opened a saved PDF—downloaded during her first search but never touched until now. She had become so overwhelmed that she hadn't had the energy to read it or even glance at it. It had a rough diagram, very similar to the one carved into the pebble. Her heart began to quicken. Underneath the sketch, someone had typed: "Used to bind energy. Also used to unbind it." The note mentioned Taino cosmology. It talked about how spirals represent cycles of time, birth, and spiritual movement between worlds. In Dominican folk rituals, similar patterns were sometimes used in protection work. Elders believed the spiral could trap harmful entities, confusing them within its eternal loops, like catching a predator in a maze with no exit. It wasn't just symbolic; it was a kind of spiritual defense, passed down through gestures, chants, and carvings. A ward etched into stone.

She chewed the inside of her cheek. What did her mother know about this? Did she find the pebble, or was it given to her? And why had it reacted only when Marisol was on the hill?

She reached over and picked it up. It was cool to the touch. She held it in her palm and closed her eyes.

And almost immediately, her breath slowed.

The hum of her laptop faded. The flickering light calmed. The sounds of the world softened.

The pebble grew warm.

A breeze passed through the room, though she had made sure her window was shut. It brushed over her skin—not cold but charged like it came from somewhere that didn't belong to this side of the world. Marisol's body stayed perfectly still, even as her mind traveled.

She saw trees.

Swaying. Not menacing this time. Reaching, not grabbing, not controlling. Inviting.

Then, a voice, faint and distant. Not her mother's. Not Salvador's.

"You're close."

Marisol snapped her eyes open. *Who had said that?*

The room was still again. Her laptop screen had gone black.

She looked down at the pebble in her hand.

It was warm.

She exhaled, slow and shaky, and set the pebble down on her nightstand. Then, almost instinctively, she reached for her phone. She saw a text from Kia letting her know she was going to stop by later. Marisol had told her earlier it was okay, and Kia was now reminding her.

> Marisol: I'm not going anywhere

Kia tagged her message with a heart, which made Marisol's own skip.

She shook her head and went into her contacts. She needed to call Doña Elvira.

She answered on the second ring as if she knew she would receive this call. "Marisol?"

"Hi," Marisol said, surprised by how relieved she was to hear Elvira's voice. "I know I just left your shop, and I'm sorry for calling again so soon. I...I need to ask you something. It's about the pebble. The one I took from the altar. I didn't mention it earlier, I know. I wasn't sure what it was at first."

Marisol picked at the nonexistent lint on her sleeve. She'd been so focused on testing Elvira that she kept it to herself. She wasn't about to admit that out loud—not yet. Things between them were still too fragile.

"What about it, Mija?"

Marisol glanced at it, still pulsing with faint warmth. "I didn't mean to take it, not really. It felt...important somehow. It still does. And when I got home, it started to glow. Like it recognized something."

"Describe the altar it came from," Elvira said gently.

Marisol did, down to the way the items had been arranged, the dried herbs, the candle, and the pebble.

When she finished, Elvira sighed. "That altar... Your mother built it using some things I gave her. Every item meant something. Protection. Strength. Ancestral connection. But that pebble... I'm not sure, Mija. I don't remember giving that to your mother. But everything else on that altar, yes."

She squeezed her eyes shut. "So, it's real. All of it? All of this?"

"I'm afraid so, Marisol, and you are going to have to believe it. Truly believe it to do something about it," Elvira said. "Your mom was clearing a path for you, and she knew your instincts and your strength would get you through."

Marisol let out a whimper before opening her eyes. Strength and instincts. Are these the same strengths and instincts that led me to drop out of school? Run from the hill? From everything that seems insurmountable?

"I don't think I have any. Or at least they don't work. My strength and instincts just make me fumble everything I do."

"Don't do that," Doña Elvira said. "Don't doubt yourself. You'll only make it easier for him."

She knew that Salvador's presence brought out the worst in

her, but she had been doing this before she smelled any cigar nearby. She's been inadequate all on her own. "It feels too true to be a doubt."

Elvira was quiet for a beat. "And how do you know it is true? You're so full of fear and doubt, you can't see clearly. What if, when you finally let that doubt go, you could see the truth? Finally, see what you're capable of."

Marisol blinked. The words hit deeper than she expected. She imagined herself taking doubt off her body as if it were a sweater. Her thoughts slowed. She was lighter and for the first time in days, something in her chest began to uncoil.

Suddenly exhausted, she asked, "What do I do?"

"It won't be easy, what you will need to do," Elvira said, her voice more certain now. "But now that you have told me all of this, I think you need stronger protection. I'm going to walk you through a warding ritual that's been in my family for generations. Keep the pebble close while you do it. Whatever it is, it's helping you. It chose you for a reason. It knows who you are, even if you don't yet."

Marisol grabbed a pen, ready to write. Her hands no longer shook.

15

PROTECTION CON SAL Y FE (PROTECCIÓN WITH SALT AND FAITH)

Later that night, Marisol had gone over the instructions Doña Elvira had given her three times already. She had everything she needed. She could do this. But she wouldn't be reckless. She would not set herself up by having dark corners, Salvador and other spirits could crawl into. No. She had to make sure nothing hid in the gaps, in the spaces that stayed dark.

Marisol turned on every light in the house. Every overhead bulb, lamp, and nightlight. The old house hummed with brightness. Flipping every light switch was a spell on its own. It was a warning that no one could hide in the shadows. She was in control here.

She looked around. This was Mamá Belén's home before it was her mother's and now hers. A legacy passed down like a tale wrapped in drywall and creaking wood. It was hers to protect.

But before she began, she needed to text Kia. Kia hadn't stopped by yet, and the last thing Marisol wanted was her knocking in the middle of a protection spell.

> Marisol: Going for a walk in a bit. If I call,
> pick up.

It was vague. It was a lie. But she wasn't going to tell Kia she was cooking a spell. That would've sounded ridiculous, or worse, unhinged. And she couldn't risk scaring Kia away. The text was enough. Just enough to plant a thread of caution in case things turned sour. In case she needed someone—like Kia. Steady, dependable Kia. The only person whose name brought a strange ache to her chest. One she didn't know how to name. Marisol rechecked her phone. Battery full. Volume on high. Just in case.

Then, she laid the items Elvira had told her to gather across her floor: salt, the black candle that had twisted in her nightmare but stood steady in the light of day, a small bowl of water, and the pebble. Her breath came slow and measured. She sat within a circle of salt, the candle burning low to her left, the bowl of water at her right, and the pebble directly in front of her.

She recited the words Elvira had given her, her voice low but steady. With each phrase, she touched the pebble lightly, like activating a switch. It didn't glow at first, but the air around her thickened with charge.

When she reached the final words of the chant, the flame flickered sideways, against the still air. The bowl trembled. The pebble pulsed with heat.

Then, an audible pop, like the sound of a bubble bursting. The flame shot straight up. Her bedroom light flickered off.

A silhouette moved just at the edge of the circle.

Marisol froze.

It slithered up the far wall, stretching unnaturally long, like a smear of ink bleeding across old paint. Its edges wavered as if trying to take shape, grasping at something solid, but it never quite settled. It moved like it had purpose. Like it needed to run. Like it didn't want to be seen. Like it was scared.

Marisol's gaze darted as she attempted to catch every movement. It climbed toward the ceiling. It hovered, coiled in the corner like a spider deciding whether to drop and take its chances on the floor. Then, just as quickly, it recoiled, slipping inside the cracks on the wall.

Gone.

Marisol's breath caught. Her instincts screamed to end it, to blow out the candle and run. But she stayed. The salt had held. The circle remained unbroken.

She pressed her fingers against the pebble. It was warm again.

"Okay." She rubbed her arms, rocking herself. "Okay."

She blinked, still stunned. If someone had told her even a week ago that she'd be sitting cross-legged in a salt circle, whispering protection chants with a candle and a rock, she would've laughed, called it una de esas porquerías, Mami was always doing. But here she was.

And it had worked.

She felt a flicker of something unfamiliar, like pride. Not the loud kind, not the kind she had to talk herself into. This was quiet and real. She'd followed her instincts, trusted herself, and for once, it hadn't ended in disaster.

For the first time, it didn't feel like she was helpless. It felt like she had drawn a line, and whatever was out there knew not to cross it.

Her phone buzzed a few minutes later.

Kia.

Marisol hesitated for half a second before answering. Her mind was all over the place.

"You good?" Kia's voice came through sharply. "You send me a cryptic text at night like we don't live in a town where the streetlights flicker for fun. I was two seconds from calling your tia."

The mention of her tia stirred more than humor. It stirred the hollow silence her mother's family left behind. A single denied money request turned into an estrangement that spanned decades.

"It was just a walk," Marisol said, willing her voice to stay steady. Here she was alone, estranged from family that had pulled away, voluntarily apart from her friend she needed to protect, trying to do something her mother didn't finish. Suddenly, the heaviness that lived on her chest came back again.

Kia's agitated voice broke through her thoughts. "At night? Alone? Mari, Willowshade may have zero crime, but that doesn't mean you tempt it. You are worrying me. I was running late, but I am coming over now."

"No. No. Don't do that. I just...needed a break from the house. I've been cooped up for a while now."

There was a beat of silence on the other end.

"Go on FaceTime," Kia said, voice dropping, less irritated now, more concerned.

Marisol looked around before facing the camera. She wanted Kia to see only her and not anything else.

"Wow, it's so bright," Kia said. "You are going to run up your electricity bill."

"I was looking for something, and you know how dark it gets in here."

"Okay. Look, it's hectic over here. In like an hour I'll be done—"

"Kia, go home. Rest. You are already doing a lot, especially since I've been...sick. Just rest. Please. You'll make me feel horrible if you come over here instead."

Kia shook her head slowly. Her eyes narrowed. She opened her mouth to say something.

"Please," Marisol said before Kia could say anything else.

Kia rolled her eyes. "Fine. Tomorrow, then."

Marisol stared at the pebble still warm in her hand. "Take your time. I'll be fine."

She wasn't. Not really. But how could she explain it? If she wanted Kia safe, and if she didn't want to sound like she'd lost her mind, she had to keep it quiet, just between her and Doña Elvira.

"Okay," Kia said before her gaze turned serious. "Don't go getting mysterious on me. That's my job."

Marisol smiled, stepping away from the ritual space. She propped her phone against a shelf and linked her pinkies together. "Promise."

They hung up, but the guilt lingered. Marisol hated holding back. Yet if Kia believed her, truly believed her, it wouldn't just be too much; it would open the door for him. That was the danger. And beneath it all sat her oldest fear: that letting someone see the truth meant losing them, one way or another.

16

ENTRE MOJONAS Y MONSTERS (BETWEEN MEAN GIRLS AND MONTROS)

Marisol stood at the base of Hallowthorn Hill the next morning. Each outward sigh met the winter air, blooming into a faint cloud of vapor. Dawn hadn't fully broken; the sky was still a bruised gray, and frost crackled beneath her boots. A pair of white-tail deer lingered near the treeline, heads lifting at her presence before bounding silently into the woods. Somewhere far above, a squirrel scurried—a sound far too ordinary for a hill that seemed to be holding its breath.

The air was dense with waiting. Marisol moved as if tiptoeing around a sleeper. She adjusted her bag over her shoulder, its weight grounding her. Today, she hadn't been pulled here. She had chosen to come.

And the hill knew it.

Still, she couldn't bring herself to climb while darkness blanketed everything. No. That would have been reckless. She waited until daylight, until at least a sliver of sun was strong enough to pierce the night. Even so, the choice steadied her. A quiet certainty grew beneath her skin, vitalizing her steps.

Whatever the hill held, she was going to face it. But only in daylight.

The growing light warmed her shoulders like a quiet reassurance. Then, she saw it: a tree that looked less like a tree and more like a fortress. Massive buttress roots fanned out like walls, and its trunk rose thick and gray, armored with conical thorns. Unlike the other trees stripped bare by winter, this one remained full, its leaves dark and wide, catching what little light broke through the clouds. For a moment, what had felt dense and watchful turned sacred.

She hadn't noticed it the first time she climbed. Then, she'd rushed along the shorter path, unaware of what the hill had been showing her.

But today she lingered, letting the sun stretch over the earth.

Her steps slowed when she reached the tree. Its trunk rose pale and smooth, the bark warm under her hand. A faint vibration thrummed beneath her palm, so steady it almost felt like a heartbeat. Marisol tilted her head, admiring the strange stillness of it.

She pulled out her phone, snapped a picture, and made a note to look it up later. She wanted to know what kind of tree it was, how something could feel so alive and yet so alone at the same time.

She lingered for a few moments before beginning to move toward the hill's landing.

Then, she heard it: voices drifting down. Light. Careless. Punctuated by laughter.

Her stomach knotted. She knew those voices.

Delgada's laugh sliced through the air, smug and sharp. Blanca's followed, pitched loud, as if she wanted it on record. Marisol froze, every nerve bracing. She should turn back. But she couldn't. Not now.

"She just tries so hard," Delgada said. "Honestly? It's giving flop era."

"She's back with the witchcraft thing again, huh?" Blanca said. "As if that fixes generational mediocrity. That shop should have closed a long time ago."

"A loser and a devil worshiper," Delgada said.

"Which one is which?" Blanca replied.

Cackle followed.

Anger surged hot and blinding. Her nails dug half-moons into her palms. Her ears rang. Not with noise, but pressure, as though her body was holding something in with nowhere to go.

Her chest rose sharply. Once. Twice.

They spoke of a practice that had been sacred to her mother, to her grandmother. Something that was helping her now fight spirits, none of which they could ever see, because they didn't believe in them and didn't care about anything other than themselves. And Doña Elvira's shop was her life. How could they talk about it as if it were disposable? They had no idea what it meant to fight for something sacred. And still, they laughed. Marisol had had enough.

"Don't say her name," Marisol said, voice low, close to her belly. She was an animal waiting to pounce. In her mind, she had grown teeth as big as a beast and shredded the skin off their bones in agonizing, slow strokes. Their screams rang in her ears, and without knowing, a smile crept up Marisol's face.

"Are you going to snap?" Blanca asked. There was fear in her voice.

Behind her, Sabia murmured something about calling the police. Marisol turned to look at her and snapped out of the vision that had surged her with...joy. She put distance between herself and them. Sabia was back. Las Tres Mojonas were back together again.

Sabia leaned toward Blanca and whispered something in her ear. Marisol blinked. She wanted the vision of shredded skin, snapped bones, and blood to leave her mind. That was not her. That was not what she wanted. As much as she hated them, she didn't want to inflict harm. She only wanted them to stop.

She pushed a curl away from her eye and breathed out. "Don't say her name."

Blanca's eyes flickered with fear. Her tone was placating. "We're just trying to help elevate you. I could help you gain some exposure. Be smart about it."

Marisol stepped closer, fists tight at her sides, keeping whatever beast had awakened inside of her leashed. "You think I need your coaching? Your pity?"

The pebble burned warm in her pocket, and she remembered what she was here to do and what influential force was nearby, probably within reach. If he could reach her at Espresso Enchantment, he could get her here. Rage had flooded through her as easily as water flowing around rocks in a stream. Had Salvador planted those thoughts in her mind? Or had years of careless cruelty been the seeds that created these visions and feelings?

It didn't matter. She refuted them. She refuted the gore and the joy that came from them. She would not mirror Las Tres Mojonas. She would stand her ground, but she would not become what they were.

Silence stretched taut. Finally, Sabia looked away and put her phone in her pocket as if she had decided not to call the police. The other two followed her.

Marisol didn't need to say more. Blanca looked back, and Marisol met her gaze, unflinching. Let her keep her platforms and filters. Marisol had had enough of giving them her silence and her time.

She lifted her eyes to the hill. Tangled roots veined the earth, waiting. That was where her energy belonged. She had to save her mom.

The air grew colder as she climbed, the shadows stretched long, and the tree limbs bent low, watching. She kept her head high, shoulders stiff, unwilling to let them see her hesitation. Above, the sky dimmed behind a thick gray haze. It was as if darkness prevailed here, no matter how much the sun shone. Frost covered the roots, making the ground slick and treacherous. The scent of old leaves and smoke filled the air.

She clutched the bundle of herbs she had put together with Doña Elvira's instructions. The old woman had told her not to wait too long, not to let fear build. She asked Marisol if she wanted her to come with her. But Marisol had said no. She needed to do this alone. If Elvira came, she'd lean on her, wait for her to explain everything, for her to step in when things got too hard.

And Marisol couldn't afford to do that anymore. Salvador was wrong. She wasn't helpless. She could do things on her own, even if she were scared. She didn't need someone holding her hand every step of the way. Instead, she needed to see who she could be without leaning on someone else to translate the magic for her.

She'd tied the twine herself and handed it off to Doña Elvira for inspection that very afternoon. Elvira turned it around and nodded. "This is good," she had said.

A ripple of pride fluttered through her chest when she heard those words. Afterward, while still holding the bundle, Elvira began praying over it. Marisol didn't understand anything she said. But then, just like now, she had inhaled the faint scent of ruda and hierbabuena. It calmed her. Now, as she went up the hill, she called to the herbs so they could do it again.

But they didn't.

Silhouettes flickered at the edges of her vision. They moved, curling and twisting against the wind. She didn't look at them. She didn't listen to the murmurs chasing her up the hill.

The air pressed heavily against her ribs, her lungs straining. Her vision blurred, the edges of the world tilting. The trees groaned, their limbs contorting once again, like grasping fingers. Beneath her boots, the ground shifted and roots bulged, wrapping around her feet. This was unreal, but all too real at once.

A voice snaked through the air, low and distant, tinged with something almost...familiar. The cigar smell followed.

"Stay away."

Marisol gasped. She knew that voice. Her father. The man who taught her how to lace her shoes and then unraveled their family with the same hands. "Papi...?"

Her father appeared. His figure wavered, mouth moving, but no sound came out. His gaze—dark, empty, and hollow—broke a silent scream inside of her.

Marisol looked around, knowing Salvador was here, every-where in this damned hill. Her hands trembled with rage and fear. "I demand you release my parents."

"You demand?" Salvador's voice dripped with condescension.

Her father's form moved like a glitch from where Marisol had seen it to behind Salvador. A blade-like root rose from the earth. Hate glimmered in Salvador's eyes, and with a flicker of his hand, the root slashed across her father's throat.

"Papi!"

Marisol stumbled back, a guttural cry ripping from her mouth.

"The powerless don't get to demand, little girl," Salvador's disembodied voice said.

Marisol pulled her bundle. The smoke crawling toward her recoiled. "Let him and my mother go. Let them rest."

"They are mine, Marisol. You and your little herbs can't control the dead."

Marisol walked toward her father, swinging her bundle in front of her.

"At least you are protected," Salvador said, his words turning into a sinister laugh.

The more she tried to reach her father, the farther away he seemed to go. She watched, frozen, as his form distanced itself away from her. Blood bloomed against her father's shirt, but no cry escaped his lips. Only silence. It was as if the hill swallowed the sound, stealing her father's agony.

"No. No!"

A different voice curled through the air, sharp as broken glass. *"Efigenia remembers. And she wants what was denied to her..."*

The shadows twisted around her father's feet, dragging him down into the earth, into the darkness.

A cold sweat prickled across her skin.

Her father had sold their land, had abandoned them, and gone to the Dominican Republic for a life they didn't know existed. He died on a different soil.

And yet, he had ended up here.

Trapped.

Like Mami.

Like her?

She clenched her fists, nails cutting into her palms. The hill had shown her Mami. Now it was showing him. Her father. Betrayer. An absent ghost, even when he had been alive. Her mind spun. This wasn't just about her survival.

Her lips parted, but no sound came. She had cast spells, tied twine, and braced herself against Salvador. But what about them? The ones already trapped? Her mother. Her father. Maybe even ancestors she had never known. She had been fighting only half the battle.

Her cheeks flushed with shame. She wanted to run, hide her head underneath her pillow. She looked around. Her father was gone, but the air was still dense. She couldn't see Salvador, but she knew he was still here.

The ground rippled, having swallowed her father as it had her mother. Stillness followed.

"Stay away..."

Her vision tunneled, the world narrowed. She pressed a hand to her chest, as if to cage her hammering heart. Salvador had been waiting. She had sensed it in the smoke, in the way the shadows shifted like they knew her name. Now, she could no longer deny it. This wasn't about protecting herself. It was about facing him, so she could protect the others. All the ones stuck here.

And she still didn't know how to fight him.

17

EL DOLOR DE PAPI Y MAMI (MOM AND DAD'S PAIN)

A whole day had passed since she'd seen her father's torture, since she simmered in her inadequacy. Marisol sat cross-legged on the floor of her mother's room, sunlight leaking thinly through the curtains and striping a rug in pale gold. Dust floated heavy in the air, each particle glowing and falling as if time itself had slowed. She'd thought about it again and again, let it rot in her gut, but never spoke it aloud.

The images of her father screaming as the hill swallowed him whole pricked her eyes until the tears finally slipped free. She climbed into her mother's bed and curled up into a ball. The silence pressed heavily around her. She needed to tell someone what she saw. She needed to let go of this weight.

Marisol drove toward Doña Elvira's shop, her palms slick against the steering wheel. Outside her window, life in Willowshade ticked on like it always did. An elderly couple packed away Christmas decorations that had clung to their porch too long. A young man laughed into his phone as he crossed Main without a care for being run over. People moved through the morning as if nothing had happened—as if the hill at the edge of town didn't carry a monster inside it. A creature holding her parents hostage, warping spirits, threatening to twist them into reflections of himself.

She had felt it—the pull. How it crept into her. How, for one terrible second, it almost felt good.

Marisol shook her head. *No. Don't think about that. You are not like him.*

Still, a chill ran through her. How many others had he seduced the same way? She hated to imagine her mother or father falling under his influence, becoming capable of cruelty that wasn't theirs. But if he was torturing them, it meant they hadn't given in. Not yet.

"You can't control the dead," he had said.

Her throat tightened. She thought of her parents, her nightmare. Those haunting eyes. Her mother's ravaged face. The way the light had disappeared behind them.

Could a spirit be broken? She knew the answer. She had seen it for herself—her parents broken on the hill.

She pressed her key fob, shutting her car before walking into the shop. Doña Elvira stepped out from behind the counter, slow and grounded, her eyes scanning Marisol's face.

"Mija," she murmured, setting down a bundle of rosemary. "¿Qué pasó?"

Marisol froze. Words stacked in her chest, restless and unformed.

"Tell me," Elvira said, squeezing her cold hand.

The words tumbled out, jagged and bitter. "My...father is there now on the hill. He's being tortured by Salvador, like Mami. But I...I was protected."

She stared at the floor.

"And you haven't slept," Elvira said gently, cupping her face.

Marisol jerked away, raw and frayed. "You're hiding something from me."

Her voice trembled as her hand lifted toward Elvira's neck. But seeing what she was doing, she stopped herself.

But it had been too late. Doña Elvira took a step back and stared at her with a flicker of fear in her eyes.

Marisol shoved her hands in her pockets. "Please. There has to be more to this, and you know it."

Elvira gently lowered her hand.

"I've told you what your mother shared with me. All of it." Her tone was calm, but her hands shook. "You remind me of your mother during that time. You need to calm down. Sit, Mija. Tell me what you saw so we can figure it out together."

Marisol sat on the chair in front of the counter while Elvira stood on the other side of it. The word *together* scraped against Marisol's pride. Tears burned her eyes once more. "Mamá Belén used to say one is born alone. I can't depend on you. On anyone. He's right. I can't do anything on my own."

Elvira's eyebrow lifted. "*He?* I hope that man is not the one you mean. Whatever you do, do not listen to him, Marisol. That is dangerous."

Her mother's friend turned around and reached inside a box in one of her shelves. She drew out a bundle of hierbabuena and lit it. The sharp, earthy scent bloomed instantly, the smoke curling around them, steadying Marisol's pulse.

"Your grandmother wasn't wrong," Elvira said, her voice cool. "But then you're born into a community. And whether you like it or not, I'm part of yours."

The words caught in Marisol's throat. Her mind began to clear. She rocked herself gently. "Don't let him win. Don't let him win," she repeated.

"That's right, Mija. Don't let him win. Don't let him in. Close your eyes."

She did. Cool branches brushed her arms, a staccato rhythm chasing heat from her skin. Then, a spritz: citrus cut through the air, chased by clove and lavender. Florida Water. Its clean, old-fashioned scent soaked her lashes.

"Déjala," Elvira murmured, striking her with leaves in practiced rhythm. "Déjala. She's not yours to have. Open your eyes."

It was as if a cloud had lifted. Layers of anxiety still pressed heavily, but without the fog of confusion.

Elvira wasn't wrong, but she wasn't entirely correct either. Mamá Belén's wisdom still resonated. She wouldn't argue now. She needed Elvira's guidance, even if accepting it meant trust.

Her shoulders fell. Exhaustion hit her like a wave. Fear made suspicion too easy, even against those who loved her. Salvador's face flashed in her mind, twisting her stomach. He had tried.

"He's hurting my family, and I don't even know how to stop him," she whispered, anger lacing her words. "Why am I getting it so wrong? Nothing I do is right. Nothing."

"Your mother unraveled like this. You must be careful, Mija," Elvira said gently. "Josefina had never been angry or violent. But right before—"

She stopped leaving the rest unsaid, the weight of it heavy in the air.

Marisol's chest clenched. *Right before she died.* For a moment, she braced herself, daring Elvira to twist the knife. Then, she saw it: The sadness in Elvira's eyes, the way her mouth pressed shut. It wasn't cruelty. It was grief.

Marisol's shoulders sagged. "It's okay. You can say it."

"Before she died...I think she had started going up to the hill again. She was exhausted and moody. And one day..." Her hand brushed her own neck, a protective reflex.

Marisol gasped. For a breath, she'd wanted to grab her, to demand she tell her more. But she didn't. She had made Doña Elvira feel unsafe around her.

Her jaw tightened. "Mami looked like I do now before she died?"

Elvira nodded solemnly. "Yes, Mija. Like you."

Marisol gulped. *Had she completely lost it?* "Is it too late?"

"No." Elvira shook her head vigorously. "It wasn't the same then. By the time I finally saw her, her aura had already been polluted."

The unspoken question burned in Marisol: *Why didn't you help her?* She shoved it down.

"This time it will be different," Elvira said firmly. "You will come to me. I will come to you. I will make sure he doesn't take over your mind."

Marisol stared at her hands as if they belonged to someone else. She had been so angry, she'd reached for Elvira. She had been so furious that she had wanted to be a creature that could tear the tres mojonas apart limb by limb. *If she had hurt Elvira... If she had hurt Delgada and them...* She pressed her hands under her thighs, trapping them there.

"Mami said he was strict with his daughter," Marisol said once she'd steadied her voice. "Controlling. But she never said he was...evil. Not like this."

Elvira looked away, busying herself with a counter rag. "Your mother was clearing the path for you. I told you that it can mean many things. Energies. Wounds. People. The parts of history we try to bury."

"So, she knew he was *that* evil?"

Elvira nodded slowly. "It's why she wanted to take him away from the hill, to finish whatever she had started, because she didn't want you to come so close to such a being."

Marisol gripped her head between her hands.

"But not because she didn't think you couldn't do it. Your mom was doing what every mom does: take the hardest things away from their child."

The weight of it pressed Marisol down. She needed to finish what her mother had started.

"Tell me, why is my dad there? Papi didn't even die here. He died in the D.R."

Elvira's face scrunched with distaste. She snorted. "Your father was no angel."

"I know. He deserves judgment. But I don't want him to suffer, just like I don't want Mami to suffer."

"You're right. I'm the one who's wrong. I'm so sorry Mija. I need to remind myself that empathy should be given, even to those who wronged us. It's just what he did to your mother—never mind." Elvira cleared her throat. Her voice dipped. "It isn't right that he's there. I think your dad knew about the Espinal magic. I think that scared him, and he ran toward something that is 'normal.' But the only reason a spirit will find themselves in a place other than what grounded them while alive will be a yearning big enough to uproot them somewhere else."

Marisol's mouth tightened. Her father had left before Salvador began whispering to her mother. But what if the whispers came earlier? What if leaving was planted, watered, and allowed to bear fruit? What if he realized he had done wrong and wanted to do right and come back?

He had been a bad husband, a worse father. That was true. But truth didn't stop the ache of wondering if he had once been different—before the hill, before the silence, before he disappeared. Maybe he hadn't only failed them. Maybe he had been the first to fall.

The thought unsettled her. She didn't want to excuse him. She didn't want to forgive him. And yet, beneath the anger, there was still a part of her that longed for him to have fought harder, to have chosen them. That longing shamed her almost as much as her resentment. But no matter how she felt about her father, she didn't want him to suffer.

Her throat ached, and she reached for her phone on

instinct, needing a distraction. The photo of the strange tree on the hill filled her screen. She turned it toward Doña Elvira.

"Your mom used to walk by it. That's a ceiba tree," Elvira said without hesitation. "It's a tree in the Dominican Republic, a symbol of resistance. I'm not sure if your family brought it here. I never asked Josefina. But that one is different because it grows in this climate, and winter doesn't affect it."

Marisol nodded, wondering if that's why she felt a sense of something being alive in that tree, because her mom used to walk by it.

"Just like that Ceiba tree, your family..." Elvira began, her voice pulling Marisol back. "Well, your family's history is complicated. I used to tell your mother, 'How can you say someone robbed you of your magic when you gave it all away?'"

Marisol blinked. "What do you mean?"

"The story your mother told you. About *El Apagón*. Remember?"

18

EL APAGÓN DE WILLOWSHADE (THE WILLOWSHADE BLACKOUT)

A memory unspooled, gentle as cinnamon and rosewater. She was seven, sitting cross-legged on the kitchen tile while Mami stirred a bubbling pot of sancocho.

"¿Tú sabes por qué le dicen El Apagón de Willowshade?" her mother asked, swaying with the ladle.

Marisol shook her head, curls bouncing.

"Porque la tierra misma dijo ya basta. Because the earth itself said enough." Mami tapped the spoon twice against the pot before spinning with a grin. "¡Pa! Se apagaron las luces. Se apagó el radio. Se apagó to' lo que hacía bulla." Boom! The lights went out. The radio silenced. Everything stilled.

She clapped twice—clap, clap—and Marisol joined, giggling. Together they sang:

"Cuando Altagracia enterró el poder,

La tierra gritó, el cielo tembló,

Y todo Willowshade se apagó."

When Altagracia buried the power,

The earth screamed, the sky shook,

And all of Willowshade went dark.

They clapped again, chanting their secret rhythm: *¡El Apagón de Willowshade!*

The clap still echoed in her head when Elvira's voice broke through. "So, do you remember?"

"A little. I remember a song."

Doña Elvira chuckled. "Ahi, Josefina, always turning things into songs and stories. Your mother was a great storyteller. She could hold anyone rapt, all eyes on her. She was a very special person, Mija."

Marisol nodded, her throat becoming thick with loss.

Elvira's voice dropped with reverence as she continued. "Tu Tatarabuela, Altagracia... She buried the jar that night. The one filled with your ancestral magic. Some say it came from a ciguapa, passed down to extend her line. Whether that's true or not, the power was passed from Espinal woman to Espinal woman since that day."

Marisol's breath caught. Her mother's songs, her stories. Tales she had dismissed as legend. But they were real. Her history. Her lineage.

"The magic was so strong," Elvira continued. "You could shape things with thought alone. Some would call it the power of God. And when Altagracia buried it to appease Salvador, the earth rejected it. The soil split open. Trees groaned. People said lightning ripped across a clear sky. Every house in Willowshade lost power. They called it The Blackout, which is what your mom referred to as *El Apagón*. The whole town went dark. No lights. No radios. Nothing."

Marisol's pulse raced. "And no one questioned it?"

Elvira snorted. "Are you kidding? People were furious. Your family would've been wiped out if Salvador hadn't reasoned with the mob—claiming Spanish blood and European civility, twisting the story. He kept most at bay, but whispers spread. Some called your family cursed."

"They still say that now."

"Claro que sí, Mija. But your great-grandmother didn't answer to anyone. She was bold. Maybe she did it to protect her daughters. But around Salvador, she grew small, strategic. She knew what he was capable of. She knew he would come for the jar. This town has been talking about your family since the beginning."

Marisol's gut burned hotter, fed by the truth. "But why bury it? Why not use it against him?"

"No one knows," Elvira said. "Rumors whispered that Salvador harmed children. Families hush such things. Silence twists the mind, and that same mind reasons in ways that no one understands. Maybe burying the magic was her way of fighting back. Ni pa' ti. No pa' mi. Not for you. Not for me. You know?"

Vomit rose in Marisol's throat. Salvador had been a monster in life, and he seemed to have gotten worse in death.

"But there's something special about your power. It only resides in the women of your family, and that didn't sit right with him. He even abandoned his surname to claim Espinal, as if a name could buy him your ancestral power, and many people spoke about that as well. But Altagracia was clever."

Marisol leaned closer. Elvira sat, grunting as she pulled a chair forward.

"Your mother once told me Altagracia knew his true intentions all along and strategized to protect her daughters. But back then, a girl belonged to her father first, then her husband. Never herself."

Marisol swallowed hard. "So, she gave it up? Just like that?"

"Don't judge yesterday with today's eyes. Altagracia was young, in a new country, with no language or rights. Her father was the wall between her and the world. She had no choice but to obey. But she obeyed in her own way."

Marisol stood from the chair and began to pace. She didn't like where this was going.

"When the soil rejected your ancestral power, your mother said Altagracia did something else. Some believe she knew exactly what she was doing. She bonded it to the hill *con una promesa*, with a promise; a prayer. So no one could have it. Not her. Not him."

Marisol stopped cold. "Hallowthorn Hill?"

Elvira nodded. "Your mother found out that the promesa was that only another Espinal woman could open the jar and take what is rightfully hers."

Marisol spun. *Obedience? Or rebellion disguised as obedience?* "And...he found it?"

Elvira's face twisted. "Of course. That was *his* plan. But when he found it, he couldn't open it. The seal wouldn't break." She paused. "So, he forced *her* to open it for him."

Marisol gasped. "And now he has our power?"

"Not exactly." Elvira's voice lowered. "Your tatarabuela played him. Lo vaciló. At least that's what Josefina thought. She believed Altagracia opened something else, something that killed him. Right there on that hill."

Her eyes glinted, sharp despite her frailty.

"A good decoy isn't empty, niña. It leaks just enough to keep a monster busy and hides what matters behind its echo. That's how your tatarabuela outsmarted him."

Marisol's heart thundered. "And now he's trapped?"

Elvira nodded.

"Then why didn't she take the magic back?"

"Every action has a cost, Mija. No one knows what price she paid. That knowledge died with her, and your mother didn't get that far, before..." Elvira trailed off.

Marisol walked toward her and held her hand, squeezing them, willing her last bit of strength into Elvira's trembling hands.

Elvira's eyes brimmed with tears. Her voice softened to a whisper. "Your tataratatarabuelo Salvador is trapped on that hill. Waiting. Watching. Pulling Espinal's souls toward him so he doesn't suffer alone. And now..." Her eyes locked on Marisol's. "He thinks you might be the key. The one to undo what Altagracia began."

The weight of it crushed her. The hill. The dreams. The whispers. Her mother's warnings. All of it pressing at once, too heavy to bear, too loud to silence. She lowered her head to the counter, resting against the cool wood. Elvira's hands settled gently on her crown.

"Your mom may have known more. More that she didn't get to share with me. Have you gone through her things?"

Marisol shook her head.

"Then you must, Mija. I know it's tough, but you will need to."

The touch sparked a memory: Her mother's fingers parting her hair, weaving braids with care, stories folded into every twist. Her chest ached. But under it, something stirred—not comfort, not yet, but the echo of a promise. One that belonged to her now. *I need to find out more.*

19

EMOTIONAL SUPPORT WITH A SIDE OF DEMONIZED MSG (APOYO EMOCIONAL CON UN LADO DE MSG DEMONIZADO)

Marisol sat on the couch, fingers pressed to her temple as if she could hold back the static throbbing behind her eyes. The echo of El Apagón, the truth about Altagracia, the weight of her parents on the hill. All of it churned in her head. She had invited Kia over, but at first, she wasn't sure she could look her in the eye without splintering. But when the doorbell rang, Marisol pushed herself up, grateful for the distraction, thankful for anything that might quiet the war inside her mind.

"Delivery!" Kia said, running past Marisol in a blur. The scent of crispy egg rolls and fried rice—enough to make her stomach growl before her mind caught up—drifted around her. The greasy perfume of sesame oil wrapped around Marisol like a hug and a slap at once. It was warm, chaotic, and impossible to ignore. It was comfort food, and for someone who hadn't felt comfort in days, this was so necessary.

"Did someone order emotional support with a side of socially demonized MSG?" Kia called out as she arrayed the cartons on the table. And just like that, Marisol stopped debating and followed Kia to the kitchen.

Marisol sat in front of the orange chicken. If Kia only knew just how true her joke was. She needed all the support she could get. She inhaled deeply.

"This never gets old." Marisol popped a piece of orange candied chicken in her mouth before Kia set a plate in front of her.

"So...what happened yesterday? You talking to Elvira again?" Kia asked, her voice casual, but Marisol could hear the tension beneath it.

Marisol wanted to tell her. Wanted to spill every terrifying detail, the voices, Salvador, what she had found out. It would all be so easy if she just told her. But it wouldn't be easy on Kia. Their fingers touched as both tried to go for the lo mein.

"Sorry," said Kia. "Go."

"No, you go," Marisol replied.

"Jeez, you go. You look like you haven't eaten in days."

"You bought it," Marisol replied.

"But I'm at your house," Kia said.

"So," Marisol replied.

Kia huffed. "Fine."

Marisol exhaled, forcing a small, weary smile. "Yes. It was nice talking to someone who knew Mami so well. I think I just needed a break. I couldn't talk to her so soon."

"Because she reminded you of your mom?" Kia asked.

Marisol nodded. She didn't want to tell her about the grudge she felt. The one that still lingered, even though she trusts Elvira and knows she wouldn't have done anything on purpose to harm her mother. Still, an illogical part of her couldn't let go of the fact that Doña Elvira survived while her mother didn't. But speaking about it with Kia would mean she would have to explain through magical reasoning, and Kia needed to stay, not believing in any of it.

Marisol swallowed hard, remembering Papi on the hill. His

face twisted in pain, slowly unraveling her. Her mother as well. But she will hold on to that, too.

It was better this way.

So, Marisol nodded, her guilt twisting into something she could almost ignore. "I don't think I'm all the way there. I think I need some more time. I know it's been almost a year—"

Kia put her hand over Marisol's. "Hold up. Grief doesn't carry a watch. You lost your mom, Marisol. That's horrible, and it can be two years, three years, ten years, and if you are still not okay, that's totally normal. Don't ever excuse how you feel because of timing."

The sharp edges in Kia's voice told Marisol she was serious. Marisol licked her lips. Wanting more from Kia felt selfish, dangerous even. Kia was the one steady thing she had, the one person she could trust. How could she gamble that on a desire she wasn't even sure she had the right to feel?

Kia studied her, eyes searching. Marisol wondered if she could see past the lie—that she needed more time not just to face her mother's things, but for reasons she couldn't risk saying aloud.

"I'll talk to Tony. Plus, it's not like the schedule is set in stone. Whoever comes, works. I'll make sure you stay on the roster. He owes me," Kia said. "Do you want help with your mom's stuff? I mean, I know that's something you've been putting off and probably for a good reason, and I fully support you in that, Mari—"

"Yeah, well. Probably about time, right?"

"You don't have to be strong with me." The pad of Kia's thumb traced her knuckles, and the jolt that shot up Marisol's arm was sharper than she could hide. Her body betrayed her every time.

Marisol pulled her hand back.

"Okay," Kia said, voice low. "Then I'm staying."

Marisol blinked. She tried to swallow, but her mouth had gone dry. "You... don't have to."

Kia smirked. "Yeah, but I want to. You don't have to do this alone."

A lump formed in Marisol's throat. The butterflies that never leave when Kia is around fluttered higher now, sharper. Her heart always outran itself when they were mere inches apart, beating off-rhythm like it didn't know the rules.

But they were friends. Had always been friends. Will always be friends. And that was too precious a thing for Marisol to risk.

Besides, her parents were literally being tortured on a cursed hill. What the hell was she even thinking?

She almost told Kia no, that she'd be fine on her own. But she tucked the words behind her teeth. Even if it was only like this, even if they never crossed that imaginary line, she wanted Kia close.

"Alright," she murmured. "Thanks."

The next morning, the door to her mother's closet creaked open as Marisol pushed it. The scent of old Ralph Lauren Blue still lingered. Everything was still in its place. Her clothes hung neatly, jewelry lay out on the dresser, and her makeup organizer sat right where she'd left it.

A single tube of crimson lipstick sat uncapped. It was the last shade her mother wore. Now it was so dry that it had darkened and lost its shine. Marisol feared that if she touched it, it would shatter, just like every memory she'd left too long untouched.

She graced the top of her mother's dresser, remembering how she used to joke during COVID about loving face masks because they kept everyone safe, but hating them because they ruined her lipstick. "I can't even look cute anymore, mi pollita."

And in those rare FaceTime calls, when the lipstick stayed hidden, her eyes had changed. The soft makeup she used to favor had become sharper, more pronounced. It was as if Mami had decided that she would look cute even with the mask on. Marisol hadn't had that much conversation back then. She would nod and laugh along with her mother's jokes, never getting around to asking her what made her go bold in her eyes. What her favorite cosmetic brand was. How she was feeling.

And now, it was too late.

Her shoulders slumped beneath the weight of every unsaid thing.

Marisol felt Kia behind her. She wanted to turn around. Wanted to crumble into her arms, let Kia hold her the way she had before. But it had been almost a year—Almost eleven months now—and the grief still felt as sharp as a bite. When would it dull? Would it ever?

But, she didn't have time to wade through it. She couldn't afford the luxury of unraveling. Not with her parents trapped on the hill, not when she still didn't understand the consequence Altagracia had passed down like a curse.

She didn't have the luxury of sadness.

Kia's voice broke the silence, gentle but pointed. "You sleep here now. So...where are your things?"

Marisol flinched. She hadn't expected that question. Her arms folded tightly over her chest as if to keep the answer at bay. But she knew Kia didn't mean any harm. She didn't mean to push her into a version she wasn't ready for. That while she didn't have the luxury to unravel and grieve slowly, she would do something to honor this loss.

"In my room," she said, her voice low. "I didn't want to move her things. It felt like... I'd be erasing her."

Kia didn't say anything. She nodded, slow and soft. Her usual humorous sharpness melted into something gentler.

"Besides the boxes in her closet, it's like Josefina could walk back in any second," Kia said, understanding it all.

Marisol stared at the space around her, unfocused as images of her mom ran through her mind. "Yeah..."

She felt Kia's hand on her back. A tremble pulsed through her like lightning running across the skies before they opened to let out the rain.

"I understand," whispered Kia.

"Thank you." Marisol stepped inside her mom's closet and began pulling out some of the decorative boxes her mother used to store random things, as well as the boxes she had packed before becoming overwhelmed.

After her second trip to the closet, Marisol looked behind her, expecting to see Kia, but she wasn't there. Instead, Kia was standing in front of the bed. She stepped out of the closet to stand beside her friend, wondering what she saw.

"The dip's still here," Kia said, patting the mattress. "She'd sit right here and yell at us. At first, I didn't believe she was yelling from over here. She sounded so close."

"I told you," Marisol said, remembering the exact moment Kia had that realization. Willowshade Middle had just released grades, and she hadn't shown her mom the copy that came in the mail. Everything would've been fine if not for that one 'F' in gym. Lucky for Kia, she'd come home with her that day to work on a project. She'd never heard Josefina's full voice before. That is, until curiosity pulled her out of the kitchen.

"I remember walking past her room," Kia said, shaking her head. "God, I swear the woman had a loudspeaker in her pocket."

"No, just Dominican," Marisol muttered, a smile dragging across her lips, remembering how alive this house had felt when her mom was here. Their eyes met, and for a second, the weight between them lifted. They laughed, briefly and breathlessly, but genuinely. The kind of laugh that acknowledged the truth behind the joke, and the ache beneath it.

Then, silence.

Marisol's shoulders dropped, her voice quiet. "I couldn't bring myself to change anything, you know? I even tried to box some things. Got kind of far but then—I didn't want to move her out to make space for me."

Kia's voice softened. "Mari...you don't have to explain."

Another beat of silence fell between them. Then, Kia placed a hand on her back, light and steady. "Okay. Then we won't be going through her stuff today. We're just...being with her things. You lead. I follow."

Marisol nodded, swallowing past the lump in her throat.

Together, they moved quietly around the room. Marisol's fingers skimmed the hem of a shirt she had borrowed long ago from her mother, the fabric soft and worn with time. Her mother's laughter echoed faintly in her memory.

She saw her now. Standing at the vanity, drying her hair upside down, talking to Marisol through the scream of her blow dryer like they had all the time in the world. Her purse sat open on the dresser. Her hair was dry now. It was a halo of curls that framed her face and went down the middle of her back. She pulled the lipstick out of her purse. The familiar tube of crimson red in hand. She'd speak mid-application, smacking her lips with practiced flair before using her pinkie to fix the color that had dared slip beyond the lines.

Marisol sighed. She felt Kia's hand on her back, grounding her in the present. Marisol nodded. She pulled three more boxes out of the closet and lined them up beside the others. Gently, they laid the contents on the floor. Revealing purses, makeup, heels, jewelry, receipts, blouses, jeans, all the things that made Josefina who she was.

They walked through them, pulling out those they remembered and sharing the stories behind their memories. They laughed, cried, and after two hours, Marisol was exhausted.

Kia's phone pinged. "It's Tony. He said you are good. Eric and Sam showed up, and I was going to go in to help too."

"You?"

"Yes, me, and I'm okay with that. It means more Chinese takeout for us," Kia said, squeezing Marisol as she wrapped her arm around her and put her head on her shoulder.

"I'm sorry."

"No. No. No. That's why I didn't want to say anything. Plus, Sam and Eric are doing the most. They beat me to it. But I need to start in a few."

Marisol looked from her mother's things to Kia. She wasn't planning on putting any of it away. She had done what Doña Elvira asked, but she hadn't found anything that might help her understand how to face Salvador. Not yet. Still, the act itself had been cathartic. She wanted to do as Kia said. She wanted to be selfish, sit with her mother's things, and forget about everything else, instead of searching.

Kia stood.

"You can leave some of your stuff here. You don't have to pack it all up," Marisol said.

Kia was nearly at the bedroom door when she stopped, turned, and smirked. "Wait. Are you admitting you want me to stay here like old times?"

Marisol froze. Nothing could really be like old times, not with the feelings tangled inside her now. Still, having Kia near —even while her insides felt chaotic—brought a kind of peace. And that contradiction unsettled her.

"I'll take that as a yes," Kia said lightly. "Okay then. I'll grab my bag and leave my overnighter here for whenever you want me to stay over. Hopefully soon. No pressure, but hopefully soon."

Marisol laughed. "No pressure, ha?"

Kia winked, which kicked the breath out of Marisol's lungs. *God, it won't be Salvador who kills me.*

She heard Kia move about the house. *This was a good choice.* Marisol felt lighter. The entire day had been heavy, a mixture of joy and the sadness that inevitably came when that joy reminded her of the loss. But she knew letting Kia stay over would be good, even if it killed her slowly.

"Don't forget to lock up after me. I'll call you later. Promise I won't hound you," Kia called out.

The sigh left Marisol before she could stop it. She knew as soon as Kia was gone, the pressure of looking through her mother's things would come back. As much as she wanted to be selfish, she couldn't ignore the fact that Salvador held her parents hostage on the hill. Sitting with her mother's things might be cathartic, but it wouldn't bring her the answers she sought. With heavy steps, she followed Kia to the door, standing in the threshold to watch her leave.

It was midday. They had spent the whole morning surrounded by her mother's memory. It was now time to tackle the difficult tasks.

When she waved Kia goodbye and locked the door, Marisol grabbed the pebble from her mother's altar. It made her feel stronger, more secure in herself. It was a part of her mother, something she had seen her hold whenever she was deep in thought. Maybe it could help Marisol, too. After putting the pebble in her pocket, she made a beeline to the kitchen.

Marisol made herself a quick smoothie. She was procrastinating; she knew that, but she was also hungry and needed to eat something. After finishing the drink, Marisol drifted back to her mother's room and sat in front of the neatly arranged things. Pulling a sweater close, she closed her eyes, imagining the fabric was her mother's arms. She grabbed a pair of earrings next—her mother's Halloween skull studs lay cold against her skin.

She tugged another box from the closet. More purses. One she recognized instantly: Her mother's favorite.

Marisol lifted it, surprised by its weight. Something inside shifted with a muted thud. The sound sent a prickle up her arms. She set the purse in her lap, palms damp, and unfastened the clasp.

Her fingers brushed against cracked leather.

"What is this?" she whispered, drawing the object out.

Not a purse accessory. Not something familiar.

A notebook. But this was different from the one she had found in her mother's drawer. This one was older than anything else she had touched. It was more like an old-school, leather-bound journal. The pages yellowed, edges brittle. The ink faded, but legible. The script wasn't Josefina's. These first entries were tight, rushed, and frantic. She flipped forward through the pages.

Some had been torn out.

And just past the tear, the handwriting changed. Her mother's looping script picked up where someone else had stopped.

But it was the last note that made every muscle in her body go taut. Everything around her blurred, leaving only the weight in her hands.

The seal is weakening. The magic trapped for so long is pushing back and waking up the hill. Every day it grows louder. I have to stop this before she sees what I've seen.

20

LA POSESIÓN (THE POSSESSION)

Marisol: I found another journal. I'm probably going to stay up reading it.

Kia: Whatever you find, don't judge too harshly.

If Kia only knew, Marisol shook her head. But it's better she doesn't.

Marisol put her phone away and turned her attention to the journal in front of her. She couldn't stop staring at the name.

Isadora Espinal.

It clung to the edge of the page like it didn't belong. Scribbled in a different pen and a different pressure, as if it was added as an afterthought. But it wasn't. She could feel it. Her mother had circled it. Her mother had known.

So, this was what Doña Elvira meant when she said Mami

had been clearing a path for her. Her mother hadn't been guessing. She had been continuing someone else's work.

Her fingers trembled as she turned the brittle pages back and forth. First the frantic script, then the torn pages, then her mother's neat handwriting picking up right where another had stopped. She could almost see it now: her mother at the kitchen table, journal spread open, the flashlight on her phone illuminating a halo around her, murmuring the names of women who came before.

Was Isadora one of them?

Why hadn't Mami ever said her name aloud?

A rustle in the hallway made her freeze. The air felt too still, like the house was listening.

She snapped the journal shut and rose from the bed, clutching it to her chest. She didn't know what scared her more —what she was remembering or that she was finally ready to see.

Then. Movement.

A shift just behind her.

Her skin prickled. She turned, biting at her lip, but nothing was there.

She sensed someone pressing close behind her. It made her stomach lurch, bile rising.

"You are not getting anywhere," Salvador whispered, cold and cruel. Clammy fingers slid up her arms towards her neck and then closed around her throat. Marisol gasped, her cry strangled before it could leave her lips. She clawed at her neck, desperate to pry the hands away, but there was nothing there. No fingers. No grip. Just pressure. Crushing. Unseen.

"How?" she croaked. She had done the protection ritual. How had Salvador broken through that?

As her vision blurred, a single thought cut through the panic. Did he know she had found more information about her mother? Information that could help her get rid of him?

Her lungs burned. Panic bloomed. Her feet left the ground. She thrashed against the air, choking on nothing, like she was drowning in smoke, every breath stolen before it could reach her chest.

"It's all in your head, brujita."

And then...

Gone.

The grip vanished all at once, like Salvador had held her and just let go.

Marisol collapsed to her knees, dragging in gulps of air so sharp they scraped her throat raw. Her vision blurred. Her hands shook. The phantom ache still lingered across her skin like bruises that hadn't formed yet. Was that what he did? Drew the light out of you until all you wanted was for it to end? Until you stopped fighting?

Marisol seized the courage she didn't know she had. She reached for the counter.

If he's doing this, it means I'm getting close to what he doesn't want me to find out.

Trembling, she pulled herself to her feet and looked out the window. She hadn't realized the day had turned into night and long shadows had spread across her kitchen floor. She spotted a fast movement outside the window. A trickle of cold sweat rolled down her temple. *What now?*

A figure darted across the porch. Too fast. Too quiet. Like it wasn't human. Marisol froze, fingers curling around the handle of the kitchen knife. The steel slipped from the wood with a smooth shing as she moved to the door.

She flung the door open, her hand pulled back, and she nearly stabbed her best friend.

"Buenas noches, Marisol," Kia said, standing still under the flickering porch light.

Marisol's arm trembled at the weight of the knife and adrenaline shooting through her body. In a state of rage, she had almost harmed Doña Elvira, and now, panicking, she nearly killed her best friend. Her fingers went numb. The knife fell, clattering on the floor.

Kia drew near, her smile strange—wide yet unsure, too slow, too settled. It didn't make Marisol's nerves any better.

"You shouldn't be here," Marisol said, breathless.

Kia's head tilted, a smile flickering like a bad signal. "Ay, pero... I thought I was always welcome here. I even left some of my belongings here."

To Marisol, Kia's voice sounded off. Not wrong exactly, but older. Heavier. Tinted with something that didn't belong.

The porch light buzzed again.

Kia flinched, throwing an arm over her eyes.

That was strange. Kia had never flinched from light.

"Must you have that on?" she said stiffly, the cadence of her words too formal. "It is...unpleasant."

"They come on automatically," Marisol replied slowly. "I didn't even realize it was—"

Dark. She was going to say dark. But she stopped herself. She had just seen something move unnaturally quick outside her house, which was what prompted her to grab the knife in the first place. *What had been outside?*

"Do not speak further," Kia cut in, her voice suddenly flat, too even. "I can read it in your face."

Marisol blinked. That didn't sound like Kia. Not even on a bad day.

She tried to smile, but something twisted in her gut. The way Kia moved. It was like someone wearing an outfit that didn't quite fit. Her presence was still. Not calm, but dead and uncomfortable.

"I'm tired," Marisol muttered, inching back. She wanted to break away from whatever this was, but this is Kia. Her Kia. Another part of her pushed back— this may not be her Kia. "You know what? It's been a long day."

Kia tilted her head again, in that too-wide, almost birdlike way. "Siempre con el mismo cuento. Always tired. Always the victim. That's your song, isn't it? Like a whiny bolero."

That landed like a slap. Marisol froze.

Kia stepped forward too quickly. Before Marisol knew what she was doing, Kia grabbed her wrist. "Are you not inviting me in? Let me in, Marisol."

The grip was wrong. Too tight. Too cold.

"Not at all," Marisol said, confused. "Come—"

Kia moved past her inside the house. "Tell me what you found. About the hill. About your mother. About...the journal. Tell me everything."

Marisol nodded, but her gaze sharpened. Something wasn't right.

Kia drifted toward the kitchen, bumping into the table like she didn't remember where it was. She opened the wrong cabinet. Twice.

And Marisol's jaw twitched when she thought—*where did I leave the journal?*

She rushed to her bedroom, checking the bed.

Gone.

She tore open the nightstand drawer. There it was. But she was sure she'd left it on the bed.

The contradictory voices began again.

The push and pull of *"Come back... You don't belong here... Watch Yourself,"* invaded her mind.

She slammed the drawer shut. "Stop it! Just stop it."

A knock jolted her. She spun toward the sound and froze. Kia, or something that looked like her, stood in the doorway.

"Who are you yelling at?" Kia said behind her, voice tinged with malice. But it wasn't just the emotion behind her words that threw off Marisol. Her vowels curled in a Dominican cadence that wasn't hers. Not Kia. Never Kia.

"You usually don't knock," Marisol said, while backing away.

But the sound of the back of her thighs knocking against her nightstand told her she had gone in the wrong direction.

Kia shrugged. "Trying something new."

Her friend stepped forward, swaying. Her smile snapped into place like a rubber band.

"You did not come," she said. "I sent messages. Digital ones. Pero tú no me respondes. ¿Y qué te pasa, Marisol?"

She had still been spinning from the moment Salvador's hands had closed around her throat, shock and adrenaline blurring everything after. At first, she couldn't place it. But now the haze was lifting, she knew. This wasn't Kia. Kia didn't talk like that. She never had.

Marisol moved towards her bathroom. She had scissors there. But what did she plan on doing with them? She couldn't hurt Kia. The body was Kia, but whoever or whatever was inside was not her friend.

Marisol tried to answer as casually as she could, careful not to alert the being standing in front of her. "I think the hill follows me. I keep seeing things. Hearing...him."

"Tell me about the journal," Kia said too eagerly.

"Oh. Nothing important. It's just porquerias. You don't believe in that stuff." Marisol reached the ensuite bathroom. She gripped the doorframe, ready to burst in and lock herself in if she needed to.

Kia's neck jerked slightly—too quick, too sharp. "You'd be surprised. Ahora, soy una persona nueva."

You don't say.

Marisol narrowed her eyes. The pebble warmed in her pocket, reminding her it was there. "Actually, no. You've got deep boundaries around this kind of thing, and I respect them."

Kia smiled tightly. "Then you don't know me at all, ¿verdad? You say you love me. Pero no. Eso no es amor."

She stepped forward, voice trembling with something ancient and bitter. "Love isn't holding onto someone who's already leaving. You use her—me—como los demás. Siempre pidiendo, nunca dando. You break my spirit and call it closeness. Eso no es amor, Marisol. Es control."

That voice wasn't Kia's.

And Kia didn't speak Spanish like that.

"You're not her," Marisol said, trembling. What had that file said about the symbol on the pebble? Could it trap? Bind?

Kia's face twitched with anger and distrust. "I am your best friend, Marisol. ¿Y como tu no me crees?"

Marisol held her breath, letting her expression smooth, careful not to reveal the racing of her pulse. She had to play along, had to keep whatever this was calm. "You are right. I'm still in shock over something else."

A small smile slid onto Kia's face.

"You want to know about the journal, right?" Marisol tried to pretend she was back in sixth grade, sharing a secret with her friend. But the being standing in front of her was making it complicated. "You want to see it?"

The distrust dissipated from Kia's face. She smiled and nodded.

"Okay. Give me a second. First, I need to show you this thing that was in it." She approached Kia, slowly, as one does a rabid animal. But instead of reaching for her nightstand, she reached into her pocket, pulled out the pebble, and pressed it into Kia's palm.

The reaction was immediate.

Kia shrieked, but the sound fractured mid-air, splitting into a distinct voice that didn't belong to her friend. Tar-black smoke poured from her eyes and nose, clawing to stay tethered. The spiral burned brighter, pulling tighter, until the last scream cracked into silence.

The spirit writhed. A final word slipped from its cracking throat, heavy with fury and pain. "Tú no me vas a encerrar. No!"

But it was no use. The spirit fought, but the stone's power

was stronger. With a final slurp of black gum, it was sucked into the spiral. Kia collapsed with a sharp, wet gasp, her body folding like a doll gone slack.

The surrounding air warped, the room bending and snapping back into shape like it had exhaled something foul.

Marisol's eyes darted around the room. The air around her didn't smell like cigars or carry the same bone-deep chill that always came with Salvador. Whatever had been inside Kia hadn't been Salvador. This was different. Colder, slicker—like oil sliding beneath her skin. It was evil, yes, but it moved with something thinner, more erratic, like it didn't quite know its shape.

Whatever it was, it wasn't her manipulative ancestor, but it was something like him.

It served him. She didn't know how she knew that, but everything fit and added up in her mind just right.

Marisol rushed to her friend.

Kia blinked up at her, wide-eyed and terrified. "Mari...I couldn't move. I could hear you, but I couldn't speak. I thought...I thought I was losing my mind."

Marisol held her hand tightly. "It wasn't you. He, or she, or something tried to use you."

Kia shuddered. "Who? What are you talking about?"

She couldn't keep Kia away from all of this. Salvador had found a way to bring her in, and that scared her.

"There's a not-so-nice ancestor that is haunting me, and it seems like someone he commands possessed you. But I'm not sure, Kia. I don't really know for sure." Marisol opened her mouth to say more, but nothing came out. The words scattered before they could take shape. What could she say to make this make sense? To make Kia feel safe again?

So, she said nothing, only gripped her friend's hand tighter, grounding them both.

Salvador didn't just live on the hill.

He followed.

He possessed through others.

This spirit saw it. Saw how much Kia meant to her and tried to twist it into something ugly. That's how they worked, right? He found the tender things and made them bleed.

But the pebble did something. It took in the spirit.

Marisol helped Kia up. Once on her feet, she pulled the protection sachet Doña Elvira had given her and slipped it in Kia's hoodie pocket.

They weren't safe. Not yet.

But they weren't powerless, either.

Marisol pulled her phone from her pocket with trembling fingers and dialed Doña Elvira. A flicker of guilt rushed over her. She'd already called her three times this week, maybe even more. But what else was she supposed to do?

Everything around her was unraveling, and Elvira was the only one who never made her feel crazy for asking questions she couldn't explain. Marisol grabbed everything, packed it, and both Kia and she left for Doña Elvira.

21

THE NON-BELIEVER Y LA BRUJA (LA QUE NO CREE AND THE WITCH)

The yerbería was quiet, save for the low ticking of the clock above the herbs and the occasional creak from the ceiling beams. Marisol sat in the back room on a worn cushion, her body still vibrating from what she'd witnessed.

Kia was across from her, sipping cinnamon tea, trying to pretend like her hands weren't still trembling. Her hoodie was zipped up to her chin, and when Marisol looked at her pocket, she could see the edge of the sachet peeking from it.

Doña Elvira dropped a sprig of ruda onto the hot coals, its bitter scent rising in sharp, curling smoke. The air thickened around them, the smoke threading like invisible guards at the edge of their circle.

"He used her body," Marisol said, voice rough. "Whatever that thing was, it wasn't him. I know how his presence feels. He choked me."

Elvira's eyes went wide. "He did what?"

"He choked me. His presence is sickening, repulsive—and the cigar smoke is always strong when he's near. But this one wasn't that. It was slimy. Slick. Corrupted."

Elvira grabbed Marisol's hand and squeezed hard. "That spirit is dangerous. But it wasn't him. He can't. Your house is protected. You would have had to invite him in."

Marisol frowned. She thought of the spirit that possessed Kia. How it asked her to come in. Kia had never needed an invitation. God, she had been so dumb. Marisol scrubbed her face, letting out a breath. She turned toward Elvira. "What do you mean he can't?"

"What he does—that pressure—it's in your mind, not your flesh. Fear makes it feel real. But to leave bruises, to move a body, to speak with more than an echo, he or any other spirit would have needed a body. Since your instincts told you it was not Salvador, it means he used one of his corrupted ones to do his bidding."

Marisol's hand rose to her throat. "A corrupted soul. So, the suffocating, the...way my feet left the ground—"

"He twisted your thoughts. And the mind of an Espinal woman is powerful. That's why you must be careful. Your great-grandmother buried the power, but she couldn't bury you. You are still what you were born to be—someone who can turn thought into reality."

Marisol shivered. Thought into reality—that was her gift, buried but never gone. Yet all this time she'd doubted herself, allowing others to tell her who she was, even now calling herself dumb. All this time, she'd been her own enemy. She shook her head. Well, now that she knew, it was within her grasp to change.

What she couldn't control was Salvador's power to call and bend corrupted souls. *A corrupted one.*

Her stomach twisted. One person came to mind immediately. Someone who had always wanted more.

"You think my dad was dissatisfied?"

Her dad, with his secret family in the Dominican Republic

and the way he left Mami when his other wife found out, seemed like the perfect soul for Salvador to twist deeper into rot. She couldn't put it past him.

Elvira nodded slowly, voice dipping into something quieter. "I think your dad was fooled. Something or someone brought him here. Perhaps it was you, Mija. But Salvador is clever. Clever enough to trap him on the hill. From what your mom told me about your ancestors, he knew how to get a yes, and not just with charm. He wore people down, twisted their desires into obedience. That was his power. Not brute force but persuasion, convincing people they were missing something, then offering it to them with open arms. You think your dad possessed Kia?"

"What the heck, Mari?" Kia said, almost coughing up tea.

Marisol shrugged. She dreaded even thinking about it.

"Did something seem familiar about the spirit?" Doña Elvira asked.

Marisol swallowed hard. She paused and forced herself to examine the event she had already shoved to the back of her mind. When she found nothing that reminded her of her father, she sighed. "No. Not really."

"Then that's your answer. You must trust your instinct."

Marisol stole a glance at Kia, who shook her head as she bent low over her mug. Steam curled up, brushing her face like a fragile blessing. But Marisol couldn't forget—something had possessed her. So many horrible things could have happened. A tingling spread through Marisol's fingers, the kind that came after being out in the cold too long, thawing back to life. She turned to Doña Elvira.

"Still...someone else possessed her. And that's not right."

"Mari, I was not—"

"Hold up, Kia," Marisol said, her voice cracking sharper than she expected. "This is serious."

Kia clattered the mug onto the table, ceramic ringing sharply in the air. Marisol knew she was upset, but she couldn't let her derail the conversation. Not now. Kia had been in danger, and the shock still hadn't worn off. Once it did, she might start to believe, or at least sense enough to know. And that made her even more vulnerable. The faster Marisol figured out which ancestor's spirit had been twisted, the quicker she could pull Kia out of the danger zone.

But in the back of her mind, a darker fear gnawed. What if it had been her mother? According to Elvira, Josefina had grown increasingly anxious and paranoid toward the end. Marisol hated how she'd brushed off those phone calls, how she'd pulled away instead of listening. What if that hadn't been loneliness? What if Salvador had already been poisoning her mind while she was alive?

"¿Y Mami?" Marisol asked, not wanting to know but needing to.

Something passed across Elvira's face. Grief, yes, but also guilt. Marisol could feel the air shift between them. She opened her mouth to press her for more, but Elvira spoke first.

"Your mom..." she began, her voice low. "I don't think she was fooled. I don't think she gave in. I think she is fighting every day—I also think that maybe...I should've done more. I should've asked her harder questions. Should've stayed when she pushed me away."

Marisol stayed quiet; her throat thickened. She and Elvira carried the same guilt.

Elvira finally met her eyes. "But I didn't. I thought she'd tell me if things got bad. And I was wrong."

Marisol crossed her arms, wishing to draw in warmth. Her chin began to tremble. Her mother had died trying to get rid of this ancestor-turned-monster, and even in death, she still fought, and her dad was being tortured by something he knew nothing about.

"But the longer they stay in this other plane, the more they forget who they once were. So, they are very much at risk."

Marisol rocked back and forth, trying to suppress the scream rising in her throat. She knew she shouldn't feel this way, but she couldn't shake the sense of failure.

And what am I doing? Getting little sachets to protect myself while my only friend gets possessed? Flinch at shadows?

Her mom was out there, somewhere, still fighting for her. And here she was, ducking under blankets, avoiding the truth like it wouldn't find her anyway.

Anger followed closely behind the guilt. Not at her mother, but at herself. At Salvador. At the way everything had turned her grief into a maze.

Marisol wiped her eyes and exhaled shakily. She didn't know whether she was angry or ashamed.

Elvira's voice cut gently through the silence. "Don't get mad, Mija. No one could've predicted this. Like I said, your family is complicated, full of secrets. Not even your mom knew them all. Shoot, not even your Mamá Belén knew most of it."

Marisol nodded as tears rolled down her cheek. She heard steps before feeling Kia's arms around her. She was so cold. *She shouldn't be comforting me. I should be comforting her.* "I'm okay," she said.

Marisol walked her back to the couch and then wrapped a green throw around her shoulders.

Walking back toward Doña Elvira, she asked, "Y Mamá Belén? I haven't seen her on the hill."

And she didn't want to.

Elvira tilted her head. "Maybe she hasn't shown herself. Or maybe she's hiding from Salvador's grasp."

Marisol swallowed hard. "That makes sense, and maybe that's why I can't hear Mami."

She thought about how things had shifted in her house. The familiar warmth that wrapped around her sometimes, even when everything else felt cold. That was her grandmother. A thought occurred to her, and she gasped. *Had Mamá Belén moved the journal to protect it from getting into Salvador's hands?*

"Mamá Belén has been helping. I think she may have hidden the journal when that thing was in my house."

Elvira nodded. "It sounds like your grandmother. But what journal? You mean the notebook?"

A long silence followed, broken only by Kia's slow sip. Marisol pulled the notebook and the journal from her bag.

"No. I told you about the notebook." She put her finger on the faded, spiraled notebook. "But when I was going through Mami's things, in one of her purses, I found this—a journal." Marisol pulled out the journal and handed it to Elvira.

Marisol explained to Elvira the differences in language and script. Her theory was that the notebook had been solely her mother's, while the journal seemed to have been passed down.

"I don't know how Mami got it. But after finding it in her purse, I remember seeing it. She had written on it and been very intense about it. I just don't know when or how she got it."

"Maybe the journal found her. Maybe this journal finds the ones that need to know what's inside." Elvira placed her hand over it. She closed her eyes and, after a moment, snapped them open. "Marisol, this is an heirloom, a weapon. Your mother may be trapped on the hill, but she's talking to you, guiding you through this. It feels old. This—this is what you use to fight back, and it belongs to you."

Marisol sat back on her chair. A week ago, she would have rejected everything Doña Elvira was saying. Still, after everything she'd gone through, this made sense.

"Salvador wants you and wants this journal," Elvira said finally, tapping the journal's hard cover. "And he'll do anything to get what he wants. Even go through her."

Kia pushed her chair away from the table, spilling some of the tea.

"Okay, stop. Please, stop talking about me like I'm some kind of vessel, a thing, and not a person." Kia buried her face in her hands, then pulled off her hoodie as she lifted her head, a low groan slipping out. "Do you hear yourself? You're talking about spirits like they're facts and I'm just...collateral damage."

Kia's gaze locked on Marisol. "You say you care, but you're not listening. I don't believe in this. Whatever this is. And I need space to breathe, not more witchcraft shoved down my throat."

Elvira tilted her head, her gaze soft on Kia, but she stayed silent.

Kia crossed her arms. "I believe in spiritual attacks. I do. But God's bigger than this. He always comes through. That's what I believe."

"How can you say that?" Marisol asked, her voice rising. "You saw what happened! You felt it. How can you still say God's got it?"

"The same way you let people bully you for years and only now decide to fight back," Kia shot back. "Let me come to terms with this at my own pace and believe what I want to believe."

Marisol let out a heavy sigh, her fists clenched tight on her lap. The words stung, but she recognized the tremor beneath them. What Kia had said, she'd spoken it through pain. Still, she needed to make her understand the risk here.

"It used your voice. It looked through your eyes. That wasn't just an attack to test you. Kia. Do you understand that it tried to be you—to erase you."

"But it didn't," Kia said, standing. "Because God covered me. Not your herbs. Not your witchcraft."

Elvira stood, hands raised slightly. "Enough. You don't have to agree. But two people who love and care for one another shouldn't carry anger between them, especially not when malevolent spirits are watching."

Kia looked between them, eyes blazing with anger and

tears. "Well, maybe people who care for one another need space, too. Maybe people who don't believe in this...need space from spirits. It's me, I'm people." She turned and walked off. But just before her hand met the doorknob, Kia looked back. Her grip on the doorknob loosened, her voice dropped. "You want me close because you're scared. I get it. But you're not the only one who's scared, Mari." Her gaze lingered, then cooled, distance sliding back into place. "And we can't be each other's comfort object. Not like this."

Marisol looked down at her hands, as if there was something she should be doing but didn't know what. The bell over the shop door jingled sharply. It wasn't just the sound of someone leaving. It was the sound of something breaking. Marisol didn't say it aloud, but it felt like something sacred had cracked open between them.

Elvira sighed. Marisol watched La Doña get up to go after Kia. She shook her head.

"Let her go," Marisol said. "Déjala."

Elvira turned to her, gently. "Mija, she's not protected."

Marisol said dryly, "I put the sachet in her hoodie. It will protect her. Or maybe the way she'll see it is that God used me to put the sachet in her hoodie. So, maybe it's her God protecting her after all."

Elvira looked relieved. "That's good. It doesn't matter who gets the credit, Mija. What matters is that it's done, and she'll be protected. That may be the only thing that keeps her safe."

They stood in silence, the smoke curling upward between them.

Finally, Elvira spoke again. "You need to keep going through your mother's things. I know it's hard, Mija. But you have to."

Marisol didn't argue. She knew Elvira was right. She couldn't wait to do it slowly, to expose herself to the pain gently. She needed to rip the Band-Aid off.

Elvira re-adjusted the mask over her nose before pouring more tea, and that's when Marisol noticed the tremble in her mother's best friend's fingers. It was small, but it was there.

She opened her mouth to say something, then stopped. She couldn't continue to procrastinate on this.

22

LOS NOMBRES EN LA PIEDRA (THE NAMES ON THE PEBBLE)

The old bed frame creaked as Marisol shifted her weight. A pipe knocked somewhere deep in the wall, rhythmic and hollow, like a far-off heartbeat. She sat with her back against her mother's bed, one leg stretched out, the other bent at the knee. In front of her: a million and one things that had once belonged to her mother. Worn shoeboxes filled with birthday cards, handwritten recipes, and post-it notes with half-thought-out reminders. Scattered perfume bottles still held the faint ghosts of every scent she'd tried before going back to her old faithful, Ralph Lauren Blue. Marisol's back ached, but she didn't stop. Doña Elvira was right. She couldn't be timid about this. She had to rip the Band-Aid.

Hours later, Marisol sat surrounded by her mother's things, having uncovered more about her. Her flaws, her fears, her hopes. In so many ways, they were alike. And in other ways, worlds apart.

She hadn't found any clues, not the kind she was looking for anyway. But getting to know her mother through her belongings was a kind of strength all on its own. A tether she could reach for when everything felt hollow. That alone made the pain of tearing open barely scabbed wounds worth it.

She reached for the final two items she had set aside.

In front of her were the notebook and the journal.

Her mother's faded red notebook sat next to the older journal like a compare-and-contrast lesson—one new, yet marked by time. The other ancient, as if it had been waiting.

The notebook seemed to hold her mother's own thoughts and emotional responses. Her reactions, her doubts, her growing fear. Based on the dates, it looked like she had found the journal later and picked up where someone else had left off.

Where Isadora had left off.

Her mother's notes echoed everything Marisol was facing now. The same spirals. The same warnings. The same pull toward something more profound.

But who was Isadora?

An ancestor, that much was clear. Yet neither Mamá Belén nor her mother had ever mentioned her.

She must have been forgotten.

A cold draft slithered across the floor, lifting the edges of the red notebook. Marisol pressed her hand down on the page to still it, fingertips tingling against the paper. Her mind filled with thoughts and fears identical to the ones Marisol had when she first heard the voices. Together, the two books told a story that was still incomplete.

She needed to put it together.

But what was she even putting together?

Her mother's looping handwriting wound across the pages of the journal. It wasn't just notes. It was a memory. Intention. Warning. The word "La Vega" kept surfacing—always on the edge of context. Scribbled in margins. Underlined without explanation. Sometimes it stood alone at the top of a page, as if it were meant to be a heading for thoughts that never came. Marisol had skimmed past it earlier, unsure what to make of it.

They had family in La Vega. She and her mother had gone there more than once. They visited cousins, attended birthdays, caught up with tíos and tías who demanded gifts from Nueva Yol, and insisted on feeding them until they couldn't walk. But this felt different. The La Vega that showed up in her mother's journal wasn't just the hometown she remembered. It was layered with meaning, threaded through the margins like a secret map, repeated with reverence, never explained. As if her mother had seen something there. Maybe it was more than a place. Perhaps it was a turning point, or a memory too powerful to put into words. Marisol's thoughts snagged on the mystery, but as her eyes drifted back to the page, something else pulled at her focus.

One margin had a faint sketch of what looked like a stone with names carved into it on one side and the spiral on the other. Beneath it, her mother had written:

> She touched it and saw everyone before her, including herself.

The following line was even fainter, written with a shaking hand or almost inkless pen:

> Mamá Belén said it reflects more than just names. It holds the labyrinth that traps the souls stuck on this plane. And the names it reveals? Those aren't just ancestors. They're Las Cerradoras de la familia--the finishers. The ones that must

walk the path alone to finish the story that began with Altagracia.

Then, below that, only half a sentence remained:

If she finds it, she must...

Marisol ran her finger under the words, willing more to appear. Nothing. But she knew her mother wouldn't have written about something she hadn't seen. And if she'd seen it, she had to have left a way back.

The radiator hissed behind her, and a sudden burst of heat touched her back. She gathered the journal and notebook, inhaled sharply, and then sat back against the bed, pulling out the pebble from her coat pocket. It was warm, warmer than it had been before. Her fingers tightened around it as she opened the journal and looked again at the sketch of the spiral. It wasn't a different stone. It was this. This was what her mother meant. What Isadora had written about.

She ran her thumb over the spiral and flinched.

The pebble felt heavier now, like a vacuum that hadn't been empty after many uses. Her eyes widened. It was heavier and warmer now, because it was carrying that additional weight. That thought almost made her drop the stone. But she caught it and, feeling it bounce on her palm, brought back the moment when the stone sucked the black tar oozing out of Kia, trapping it within the ridges of its spiral.

She heard something emitting from it. Marisol put it against her ear.

"*Let me out,*" someone screamed.

She pulled the stone away and wrapped her hand around it until she couldn't hear it. This was odd. She knew the pebble had sucked whatever entity had been inside her friend, but to listen to its voice was something else. She opened her palm. "Who are you?"

"*You don't even know your own family,*" the voice sounded as if it spat those words.

"Then tell me."

"*Ahh, Josefina. Holding on to information, being selfish as always.*"

"If you tell me, I will let you out. As long as you promise not to come back."

A pause ensued.

"Well?" Marisol prompted. She held the pebble closer to her ear.

"*Efigenia. My name is Efigenia Espinal. Now let me out.*" Her words were demanding, violent.

Marisol stared at the pebble in her hand. She was never going to let this spirit out. But now she had a name she could research. A mixture of fear and cringe passed through her as she stared at the pebble in her hand. Here she was, talking to spirits trapped in a rock. "No. You have chosen harm."

Marisol took a steadying breath. She ignored every scream that came from it until she couldn't hear them anymore. She put the pebble under the light to see what else she might have missed. She could almost make out faint markings on the opposite side of the spiral, including curves, loops, and something that could've once been names, now eroded with time. But one stood out.

Her own.

Marisol's pulse spiked. She hadn't seen it. Really, hadn't cared to see it. She had grabbed the pebble, walked around with it, used it to save Kia, but hadn't stopped to inspect it.

She reached out with trembling fingers, letting her hand rest on the center of the stone.

A chill shot up her spine. The room dimmed.

Outside, a sudden gust rattled the window. The journal pages fluttered violently, as if caught in a breeze she couldn't feel.

Then, a shimmer. A mirror surfaced with names inscribed.

But it wasn't a regular mirror because it wasn't made of glass. It was reflective in the same way one can see their reflection on still water. But this was more.

In it, Marisol saw herself at age five, twirling in Mamá Belén's garden. Then, older, curled under the covers, sobbing after Mami's funeral. Then, at the café, her hands shaking as she lied to Kia.

Then, the image changed. She saw herself now. Jaw tight, shoulders slumped. Ordinary. Afraid.

Then, one more reflection.

A version of herself standing tall. Eyes sharp. Hair wild and free. A Bruja going up the hill.

Marisol gritted her teeth against the rise of panic. She wanted to run. To unsee everything. To go back to thinking she was just someone grieving for her mom and making lattes. Not someone tethered to a war that began long before she was born.

This was too much.

She wasn't ready.

"I see you," the image of herself told her.

Marisol broke. Her knees gave out, and she slumped forward, shoulders heaving. Tears poured freely now, not from fear alone, but from the weight of everything she had been holding in—every doubt, every time she told herself she wasn't enough. Every moment, she longed to be more than ordinary and was terrified of what that might mean.

She curled forward until her forehead met the floor, her arms wrapped around herself as if trying to hold all the shattered pieces in. The cold wood pressed against her skin, grounding her. She stayed there, breath stuttering, until the worst of it passed. Slowly, her fingers loosened, and her chest stopped seizing with sobs.

Maybe being ordinary wasn't a curse. Maybe that was the point.

An ordinary girl. An ordinary bruja. Still standing. Still fighting.

A floorboard groaned. The house seemed to be holding its breath. She looked at her reflection, eyes red, body trembling.

"Why me?" she asked. "Why now?"

The mirror version of herself tilted her head. "Because you've always known you were meant for more. You just thought you had to earn it when it was always yours. So, you hid from it because you thought yourself unworthy."

Marisol bit her bottom lip before asking, "What if I fail?"

"You will," the reflection said gently. "And then you'll get back up. Because that's what Las Cerradoras do."

Those words landed heavily on Marisol. She rubbed her sweaty hands on the side of her jeans. The idea of failing, of falling short, of not being enough—it strangled her like a memory too painful to name. She took a step back. She didn't want to hear that she would fail. That she would have to try again. It sounded too much like her life already. Too much like grief. Like guilt. Like every unfinished thing she'd ever buried. Her eyes welled with tears again, and a choked sob built inside of her.

"I don't want to fail," she murmured. "I don't want to mess it up like I always do."

Her reflection didn't flinch. "That fear you feel right now means you care, and care enough to finish. So maybe you won't fail, but only you would know that."

Marisol stepped forward and nodded. She understood what her reflection was saying. She just didn't like it. "Why do I need to carry it alone?"

"Who says you do? I remember Doña Elvira telling us otherwise."

The reflection placed a hand on the glass. Marisol mirrored it. Her palm met its own.

"Own it," the reflection whispered. "Even if it terrifies you."

Marisol moved closer to the mirror, lips quivering. "I'm so scared."

The reflection smiled, warm and knowing. "You're ready."

Her own eyes stared back at her. And slowly, her reflection began to weep. Not out of sorrow, but out of release. Forgiveness.

Marisol hugged herself with one arm and touched the mirror with the other. "I'm sorry, I believed all the bad things they said about us. And the bad things I told myself, too."

The mirror shimmered once, then faded. The names returned, soft as breath, barely visible under the light.

Somewhere in the house, a door slammed, though no one else was home.

The pebble pulsed softly in her palm, as if responding to her acceptance.

A wind howled outside. Inside, the walls rattled. Lights flickered as if the house was convulsing.

A distant hum vibrated through the walls. Even the floor beneath her shifted slightly, like the house exhaled all at once. From somewhere in the distance, but not far enough, a scream erupted. Not human. Not entirely. It was a war cry.

Marisol stumbled back, catching herself with her hands.

The hill felt her acceptance, and so had Salvador.

Marisol scrambled to her feet and rushed to the window. Outside, the sky was still. But she could feel it. Something had shifted.

He knew she had seen her name in the stone and now knew who she truly was.

She backed away slowly and sat on the bed. Her hands still

trembled, but this time it wasn't out of fear. It was out of recognition. The stone hadn't just shown her the past. It had remembered her.

She reached for the journal again, flipping to a blank page. For the first time, she picked up her own pen and wrote in the journal passed down from an ancestor she didn't know. She will be the third one to write in it.

He saw me. But I saw myself too.

She paused, then wrote:

I think Mami knew I'd find it. I think she wanted me to.

At the bottom of the page, she wrote the word that kept surfacing without an explanation, but was persistent. It tugged at her like a half-remembered dream, its presence scattered through her mother's journal like a breadcrumb trail. She didn't know what it meant yet, not entirely. But the way her mother wrote it with reverence made it feel important. Sacred. Like a place not just to go, but to find.

La Vega.
La Vega.

As she capped the pen, a whisper curled through the air, soft and patient.

"*¡Por fin! I knew you'd find it.*"

A smile tugged at her lips. Marisol knew that voice. "Mamá Belén!"

She pressed the journal to her chest, eyes stinging. She thought of Kia. The way she stormed out. The way she'd stood her ground.

"She'll come back. I know it. She just needs space to process," Marisol said to herself. But at least she's protected, she thought.

But something cold whispered back.

"Be careful. He knows she matters now."

23

REFLEJO DE PODER (A REFLECTION OF POWER)

Marisol woke up with the journal still clutched to her chest and the pebble curled in her palm. The morning light seeped through the curtains in soft streaks, but the house felt different, like something had shifted in its bones while she slept.

She sat up slowly, the ache in her muscles catching up to her all at once. Her body felt as if it had crossed through something. Not time, but trial, the kind of passage that leaves you changed. She placed the journal carefully on the nightstand. She set the pebble beside it, letting her fingers linger just a second longer.

In the bathroom, she caught her reflection and didn't look away. The girl in the mirror was still tired. Still scared. But she was no longer hiding.

After getting dressed, she picked up her phone and hesitated before typing. Her thumbs hovered for a moment. She had given Kia a whole day to cool off. Should she give her more? Let her be the one to reach out? But she couldn't. She had to make sure she was okay, even if she was mad at her, and once Marisol decided that, her fingers moved quickly.

She waited. No response.

She stared at the screen, willing it to buzz.

It didn't.

She slid the phone into her pocket and forced herself to keep moving. Maybe Kia was still resting. She didn't know how worn a possession made someone, but just dealing with the accidental exorcism had left Marisol drained.

Downstairs, the house was still. Her mother's favorite mug sat in the sink where she'd left it the night before, and the faint scent of the ruda, albahaca, and rosemary floor wash still lingered from Elvira's last visit. Marisol wrapped her arms around herself, unsure if the chill in the air was from a draft or something more profound.

She needed to see Elvira and share with her everything that had happened.

The walk to the yerbería stretched longer than usual and not just because she'd left the car behind. Each step felt like a test—a test she was giving herself to prove that safety wasn't made of steel and glass. That it was something she held within her body. Each step was a quiet rebellion against her old self.

It felt endless, but at least the distance gave her room to think. To wonder.

Was this the future self she had glimpsed? The one who didn't flinch, didn't fold, didn't run? The one who moved through the world open and unafraid? The thought prickled the back of her neck, but she didn't shrink. If she was going to become that version, she had to start now. She had to walk like she already was.

Hold your head high, she told herself. She lifted it.

Fang-like ice hung from rooftops and power lines, sharp as teeth. The road to Main Street no longer looked darker—just more known. The cracked sidewalk that once felt like a path to judgment now seemed layered with memory. Ghosts lived here. Her mother's steps lived here. Her steps lived here.

She had avoided this path for so long, yet now every house, every flickering porch light, every gnarled branch felt like it had been watching her become who she was meant to be. Was this what it meant to turn thought into reality?

When she arrived, Doña Elvira opened the door before Marisol could knock. "You walked all this way?"

Marisol nodded, still catching her breath.

Elvira pulled her into an appreciative hug. When she let go, her eyes searched Marisol's face. "I heard him scream."

Marisol swallowed and gave another slight nod. "He did."

Elvira stepped aside and gestured for her to come in. "You have that man shaking in his boots. Come. Sit y cuentame todo."

Marisol moved past her into the back room. The space was warmer than the air outside, but the energy inside still felt charged, as if the walls remembered what had been said here the last time. She sat across from Elvira, exhaling slowly, fingers threading together in her lap.

"I saw something," Marisol began quietly. "Or...someone. Myself. A version of me I didn't think I could be."

Elvira raised an eyebrow, settling into her chair. "You touched the pebble again?"

Marisol nodded. "And the journal, my name is on it. So are the others. Isadora. Mami. It showed me everything I hadn't been able to say aloud."

Elvira didn't interrupt. She waited, letting Marisol find her way through the words.

"I wanted to run," Marisol admitted. "I almost did. But I didn't—and I think that's when the hill—when he—reacted. That scream...was angry. It was like I had taken something that didn't belong to me. That belongs to him."

Elvira's eyes narrowed, but her lips curled into something

almost like a smile. "To him? No. You can't take something that was always yours. His only claim was the one he forced."

A shiver traced Marisol's spine, the kind that came when recognition finally caught up with denial. Her mouth opened, but no sound came out. The words felt unreal, too big, too final. Her fingers clenched on her lap. She stared at Elvira as if waiting for her to take it back, to tell her she was mistaken.

"I did..." she whispered, affirmation tinged by fear, as if saying it aloud might make her newfound courage vanish.

"He knows," Elvira said. "You're not running anymore. You're remembering. And that makes you dangerous."

Marisol straightened slightly, then leaned forward with a sudden spark in her eyes, like a thread in her memory had just tugged loose and brought something vital with it. "There's something else. I keep seeing it in the journal—La Vega. My mom wrote it everywhere. In the margins, at the top of pages. As if it were some kind of clue. But what does it mean?"

Elvira's mouth pulled tight. "Your mother's family is from La Vega. That's no secret."

"I know," Marisol said. "We went almost every year. Brought suitcases packed with food, clothes, hair products, purses, and sneakers. It's just...family. I don't know...it doesn't seem like Mami is talking about *that* La Vega."

"Well..." Elvira began. "That place is where the break began. Where your family splintered."

Marisol blinked. "What do you mean, splintered?"

Elvira's tone gentled, though her eyes stayed sharp. She clicked her tongue against the roof of her mouth. "You were a child. No one was going to sit you down and say, *'Your family name used to carry weight, until it shattered.'* But that's where it began. Salvador's wife, María, left him for a U.S. Marine during the invasion. And Salvador wasn't just any man. He was one of Trujillo's. Loyal. Ruthless. That betrayal cut twice. Once, from the woman he'd abandoned his name for—though truth be told, no one thinks it was because of love. He wanted the power she carried, the family she came from. And then again, from his closest friend, who chose the Marines, chose the United States, and left Salvador humiliated."

She paused, letting the words settle. "He left La Vega after that. Took Altagracia and vanished. That was the fracture. That's when the Espinals broke."

Her voice dropped. "The ones who stayed kept their heads down. If their skin was light enough, they made it through. But some of those who stayed grew bitter. Josefina once told me there's still a branch of her family that blames Altagracia for everything that happened. They carry that grudge like an inheritance. Others left, like Salvador. But Salvador didn't leave because he had to. He left because his pride couldn't bear the shame."

Elvira leaned closer, her voice now a near whisper. "People bury their stories until silence becomes habit. Until even they forget. For María, a married woman who defied the island by choosing another man, the shame clung to her family. For Salvador, it was the humiliation of giving up his name for a woman who still left him, and of being abandoned by his friend. And silence? Those who carry it take it to their graves. Maybe your mother was already digging through that silence. Maybe she had started to remember what everyone else had worked so hard to forget."

Marisol sank back into her chair, her mind already spiraling. This was so far beyond anything she had imagined. Her thoughts started to spiral.

Her family had left the Dominican Republic because the worst dictator in Latin America betrayed Salvador, and he couldn't stomach the shame. Was that what forced them here? Was La Vega more than just a place now? A scarred landscape heavy with memories, calling her to remember what she never lived? Was she supposed to go there? Buy a plane ticket, dig through forgotten records in some distant, dust-covered family home? She could barely keep it together in Willowshade. How was she supposed to uproot her entire life in search of answers scattered across an ocean? And even if she did...would anyone there even understand her? Half the time, her mother had to translate for her. Her aunt hadn't called in years. Who would she even turn to?

The thoughts left her hollow.

Everything felt too slow. Too far. And there were people trapped here on this hill, in this house, in this moment. Her mother. Her father. The others. She didn't have the luxury of time.

No. La Vega would have to wait. For now, it was a breadcrumb, something she could circle back to, but not chase just yet. She needed something actionable. Something immediate. Because whatever was holding her mother and everyone else trapped by that hill wasn't waiting for her to buy a plane ticket.

Before she could say anything else to Elvira, her phone buzzed in her pocket.

She pulled it out, expecting to see Kia's name. Hoping to see it. But the message wasn't from Kia.

Unknown: You forgot something.

Marisol frowned. "That's not her number. That's not even a contact."

Elvira leaned forward. "What happened? Let me see."

Marisol held up the screen. Another message came through.

Unknown: You always forget what matters most.

Her blood turned to ice. "That's what the hill said. The voices. That's what they told me."

Doña Elvira handed Marisol her car keys. "Go now. Check on Kia. Now."

Marisol didn't wait. She was already moving, already out the door, her heart slamming against her ribs as her boots hit the pavement. Once in the car, she gripped the steering wheel so tightly her knuckles ached, barely noticing the sting in her eyes as she sped toward Kia's apartment. Roadsigns were nothing but blobs blurred by tears, only identifiable by their color. The trembling in her hands didn't stop, even after she parked in front of Kia's building and bolted from the car.

The apartment was quiet when she got there. Too quiet.

"Kia?" Marisol called, breathless.

No answer.

The floor creaked beneath her feet as she stepped farther in, every sound magnified by the suffocating stillness.

"Kia?" she tried again, louder now, her voice catching on the second syllable.

Still nothing.

She reached Kia's bedroom door and hesitated. Something in her gut told her not to open it, not yet. As if pausing just a second longer might stop whatever truth waited on the other side. But the silence pressed against her back, urging her forward.

She turned the knob slowly and pushed the door open.

The room looked normal. Almost. But there, on the floor, just inside the threshold, was Kia's hoodie. Crumbled. Abandoned.

Marisol's breath hitched. She took a step closer, and then she saw it, the sachet. Or what was left of it.

The herbs were no longer bundled. They were scattered across the hardwood like ashes, as if something had clawed through the protection and spit them out in pieces.

Marisol's legs buckled. She couldn't hold herself upright anymore and collapsed to her knees. She crawled toward the scattered pieces of protection, her hands trembling, and gathered the shreds. Her heart drummed in her ear so loud she couldn't hear anything else.

"No," she whispered. "No, no, no."

She was too late.

The hill had taken Kia.

24

LA VEGA, WHERE ARE YOU? (¿DONDE ESTA LA VEGA?)

Marisol clenched and unclenched her fists. The remnants of the stems from the herbs pricked her palm. She looked around. But her brain was enveloped in a cloud of fog. She couldn't think what to do next. The knock came just as Marisol was about to unravel.

She opened the door, expecting what exactly? She wasn't even sure. Another warning? Another figure in the shape of someone she loved? Kia telling her everything was back to normal? Instead, Doña Elvira stood there in her long coat, a scarf looped twice around her neck and pulled up over her head like a hood, and a matching mask covering the lower half of her face.

Marisol hadn't returned Doña Elvira's car, so the poor lady had taken a Lyft.

I can't get one thing right.

"You came," Marisol said breathlessly, voice barely audible.

"The spirits don't always show what we want to see," Elvira said, stepping inside, her voice low and steady. Her coat still smelled faintly of church incense and the dried rue that always clung to her sleeves. "But they don't stay silent when something or someone is taken."

Marisol said nothing. She closed the door behind her and slumped against it, staring at the floor. The air in the apartment felt heavy, thick with what had just happened, with what hadn't yet been understood.

"Kia's gone. And I don't know how to get her back. I was right there, Elvira. Right there."

"He's grown bolder. Salvador no longer waits for women to come to the hill. He reaches for them now. He sends what he's twisted. Spirits that serve him. Ones that used to belong to us."

Marisol's eyes snapped up. "The ones he turned?"

Elvira nodded solemnly. "Yes. Remember how I told you your family splintered, and some that stayed may not have been very happy about it. When you left, I kept turning Josefina's conversations about your family over and over. You thought it might have been your father whom Salvador turned, but I don't think it was anyone from your immediate family. But your mom had a distant cousin from that part of the family. Her name was Efigenia."

Marisol gasped as she thought of her mother's notebook and the names she had written there, and the one that had been severely scratched, ripping the page, with the curved E still visible.

Doña Elvira continued. "She tried to come through...others. Thinking about her made me remember another conversation with your mom. One I had after clearing your house. It had bad energy. This was not the first time Efigenia tried something.

Altagracia had a sister. A sister who refused to follow her father to the U.S. Some say she had good reason to stay away from him. Pero de eso no se hablaba. Those kinds of things people kept to themselves back then, and even now, too. But she had a daughter named Efigenia.

Altagracia's sister ended up in jail after saying something

Trujillo didn't like, and she died there. Efigenia always blamed Altagracia for that. Back then, when we cleared your house, it was her energy we found. In death, like some spirits do, she had found a way to claim what she thought was hers—a place here. She attached herself to your house, and it seems she's still bulldozing her way in. It would have been easy to turn her. Hate was already in her spirit when she died."

"But it can't be her. She's trapped in the pebble." Marisol began pacing, pulse rising. How many other ancestors could Salvador twist against her? If spirits could cross over from the Dominican Republic, then...this could get bad quickly.

"How do you know?"

"It's a long story. I heard a voice—I started talking to the rock."

Doña Elvira nodded, confused but accepting. "She's probably not the only one Salvador has turned."

The words landed heavily, dragging Marisol's thoughts to her father.

"So, she's like Papi. Didn't die here, but got stuck here? Do you think—" Marisol cut herself off, shame biting at her tongue. She didn't say this aloud, and Elvira had alluded to it before that perhaps her dad had come back because of her. The thought felt foolish, but it gnawed anyway. If Efigenia's longing had dragged her spirit to Willowshade, then had her father wanted to come back too? Had he regretted leaving her? Was that why he lingered? Was he trying to apologize?

She clenched her jaw. No. She couldn't ask. That man had let her down too many times, and her heart couldn't take one more disappointment.

"Spirits have that ability. They don't have the physical boundaries we do. All they need to do is follow an attachment, and they are there. For Efigenia, she thought she deserved to be here, so she found herself in your house. For your father..."

Marisol looked at her hands.

Lowering her voice, Doña Elvira continued, "Maybe. Like I said before, you may have been the reason he came back. Sometimes spirits visit the ones they love to say goodbye or to apologize."

Marisol bit her lip and choked a sob.

"Spirits sometimes do that, and maybe that's when he was trapped." Doña Elvira squeezed Marisol's hand. "I'm sorry, Mija."

Marisol's chest tightened. She shook her head. "It's okay. I guess I'll never know." Marisol straightened her shoulders. She couldn't focus on Papi, even if she wanted to. A spirit had worn her friend like a shirt, and now another spirit had taken her. This had to be her focus. Her mouth went dry, but she had to say this aloud. "This means Salvador has many to do his bidding, and Kia is with him on the hill."

"I'm afraid she is, Mija," Elvira said gently. A solemn look settled on her face. Tears welled in her eyes as she grabbed Marisol's hand.

But Marisol didn't want to be still. Not moving felt too stagnant, as if every thought would pile on top of her and suffocate her. Her fingers found her temples and began kneading them, soothing the tension there. "Then I need to go back. I need to get her—"

"No," Elvira said firmly. "That's what he wants. For you to run back. Unprepared. Guided by panic. You want to save her? Then you need to destroy him."

"Destroy Salvador?" Marisol said through gritted teeth.

"I think that's what your mother was trying to do. If you do it, it will free them."

Marisol let out a bitter laugh, but it didn't feel humorous. It felt like panic wearing a mask. Her heart thudded. She barely knew how to survive her own thoughts most days, let alone take down a centuries-old ghost with a God complex. "Great.

How am I supposed to do that? Where's the instruction manual on exorcising family curses?"

She slumped into a chair, staring at the table in front of her like it might offer clarity. Gosh, she had felt so strong, so put together. Her reflection, the walk through the neighborhood... She should be ready. But was she?

Her thoughts turned to the journal waiting for her back home, pages scattered with her mother's and Isadora's words and warnings. The spiral, sketched so often, had started to feel like a brand. She wished it were here now, something to ground her, to guide her through this unraveling.

Was Mami even ready when she tackled this monster?

Marisol wrung her hands together. Her palms pooled with sweat. She squared her shoulders and looked at Elvira. "Mami was searching for La Vega. She wrote it so many times. Maybe I should just...go there. Book a ticket. Ask around. Someone has to know something."

Elvira paused. "It doesn't sound right. Your mother never left the country while she was researching this. Not once."

Marisol stared at Elvira, her jaw slack. Her shoulders sagged under a sudden weight of confusion. "What?"

"She was here," Elvira said, slowly, like she was just realizing it herself. "Every day, she'd go up that hill from sunup to sundown. She stayed in Willowshade. Always."

"But she kept writing about La Vega."

"Exactly," Elvira said. "But a place doesn't always have to be physical, Marisol. Haven't you ever wished to be anywhere else? Maybe it's a place you don't visit with your feet, but with your grief."

Marisol thought of all the times she'd wished for a cocoon. A hiding place. A world that didn't look at her like she was too much, or not enough.

"What if La Vega isn't where we think it is?" Elvira said.

Marisol's brow furrowed. "You think it isn't the city in the Dominican Republic?"

"I think it's something else. Something older. Maybe, something imagined?"

Marisol nodded slowly. Back when she was little, before she ran from her identity like it was a marathon she didn't remember signing up for, there were days she wished she could curl up in Mami's room, tucked under her blankets, listening to her stories while she did her hair and makeup. Even now, when the world felt too loud and too heavy, she imagined being in that space. How it felt before grief made it hollow.

"Wait a minute," Elvira said suddenly, her brows drawing together. "There was a day—years ago—your mom disappeared."

Marisol perked up. "What do you mean? Like Kia?"

"No, not like that. She didn't vanish as if someone or something had taken her. I just remember...she walked toward the base of the hill, and I lost sight of her. Completely. She didn't answer my texts for hours. When I saw her again, she said something strange. That it was better if I didn't know too much. Promised she'd explain it one day when the time was right." Elvira paused, her voice dripping with regret. "I trusted her. I figured she would. But then COVID hit. I stopped going out. She wouldn't answer my calls. And I thought she was mad at me for not helping. So, I stopped reaching out."

Marisol squeezed Elvira's hand, understanding the weight her mom's friend was carrying. "So, you think it's an imagined place on the hill?"

"At the base of the hill, by where that Ceiba tree is," Doña Elvira corrected her. "Maybe it's a place that brought safety or peace to the Espinal women. It would have given or shown your mom something, or else she wouldn't have gone there so many times."

The silence that followed was charged.

And for the first time, Marisol didn't flinch from it.

She thought about the journal. Kia trapped on the hill, like her mother and father. So, whatever was written in that journal was more crucial than ever. But now she understood what she had missed: the pages about La Vega weren't pointing her to a city. Instead, they were directing her toward something here. If she wanted to find it, to understand what her mother and Isadora had been chasing, she'd need to do what her mother had done—walk toward the base of the hill toward the Ceiba tree and see what was there.

Marisol let out a breath. *I'll finish what Mami started and get Kia.*

25

ISADORA Y YO (ISADORA AND I)

Marisol sat perched on the edge of her bed, the journal lying open across her knees. The mattress dipped slightly beneath her weight, the familiar give of it grounding her more than she wanted to admit. Her fingers hovered over the yellowed pages of the journal, tracing the delicate ink like it might vanish if she pressed too hard.

She had been back from Kia's apartment for only an hour, but it felt like days. The Sun had begun to set. The quiet of the house was different now. It wasn't just the absence of noise. It was awareness. Like the walls had seen what she'd seen and now held their breath alongside her.

Her eyes kept returning to one name:

Isadora Espinal.

The name shimmered with a mix of familiarity and unease. Whoever Isadora was, her handwriting lived in the same notebook as her mother's. But her writing was different—faster, heavier. Like she'd been running away from something as she wrote.

Marisol turned to the entry that had pulled her back before. Her mother's words echoed in her mind:

"The hill is waking up again. It's getting stronger. I feel it watching. I have to stop this before she sees what I've seen."

Before she sees? She means before I see?

Marisol shivered. Her mother had known.

Marisol exhaled and turned back to an older entry, the one signed by Isadora.

"Isadora," she whispered.

Her finger brushed the corner of the page, and the air shifted slightly like the moment before lightning. Her vision blurred, and the edges of her room started to bend, warping like a watercolor left too long in the rain.

Then, the floor beneath her rippled, just once, like the earth itself inhaled. Her stomach flipped, gravity stuttered. Her hands flew out to brace herself, but there was nothing to grab. No edge, no frame of reference.

Then, the floor dropped.

A gasp escaped her before she even felt herself fall.

It wasn't a fall like tripping or dropping into a dream. It was slower, stranger. It was like being pulled through something soft and alive. The light stretched, bent, then broke. The air grew thick, humming with memory. Her skin prickled like it had passed through a threshold she couldn't see.

Marisol clutched the journal, but it blurred in her hands, then dissolved.

And then she landed.

She wasn't in her room anymore.

The air was thick with the scent of old paper. Ink. Time.

Brick-lined walls and exposed wooden beams framed the room. The ceiling was low, and the lighting was dim. Just a single bare bulb hung from a cord, casting a soft yellow light that pulsed ever so slightly. It smelled faintly of old books. The air carried the hush of a place meant for archiving things long forgotten.

It reminded Marisol of the Willowshade Library, but not any part she'd ever seen. This looked like a basement, and she'd never been to the library's basement. And yet something about the room tugged at her memory, like a place remembered from a dream.

At the center of it was a woman hunched over a wide wooden table, scribbling furiously into a journal, as if the words might vanish if she didn't get them down on paper fast enough.

She wasn't writing in just any journal. She was writing in *the* journal. The one passed from this woman to her mom.

Marisol held her breath and inched forward.

The woman paused mid-sentence. Her shoulders tensed. And as if she sensed Marisol's presence, she whirled around on her stool. For a split second, her eyes looked wild, like a cornered animal. That is, until she noticed Marisol.

The woman was small, almost delicate, but there was nothing fragile about her. Her frame was compact and graceful, yet carried a quiet weight, like grief that had worn long enough to settle into her bones. Her skin was soft and brown with a cool undertone, the kind that glowed in candlelight. A patterned scarf held back a thick crown of tightly coiled hair, though a few defiant curls had escaped at her temples.

Behind thick-rimmed glasses, her gaze was all sharp lines and layered silence, like a woman used to holding back everything she wanted to say. Her eyes—God, her eyes—were large and dark, and they looked like they'd already read Marisol's whole life and were slowly judging it. They were like Mami's, only more judgmental.

She wore a muted cardigan stitched with delicate spirals at the cuffs, the thread barely catching the light. Her skirt was earth-toned, her blouse vintage. It was the kind of outfit that looked as if it had been inherited instead of purchased.

Marisol didn't know how she knew, but she knew.

This was Isadora Espinal.

The first Cerradora.

The one who tried before any of them.

And in that moment, Marisol wasn't just looking at an ancestor. She was looking at a mirror that had been sharpened by time.

Realization crossed Isadora's eyes, and then her face drained of color. "No," she murmured. "No, no, no... you're not real."

Marisol held up her hands. "Wait! I'm not a spirit! I'm alive."

Isadora's lips moved, frantic, chanting something Marisol couldn't understand.

"I'm not here to hurt you. I swear," Marisol insisted, holding her hands up.

The light bulb flickered maniacally.

Isadora backed away, knocking her stool over. "You shouldn't be here," she said.

Marisol's chest tightened. She'd heard those words before. The whispers in the dark. The warnings.

"I don't know how I got here," Marisol said honestly. "But I need answers. The hill. It's waking up again. No, it's awake, and it took my friend."

Isadora froze for an instant. When she spoke, it was a frantic whisper. "If it's awake already. If you're here, it means it's already too late."

"Wait. What's too late?"

Isadora stepped forward, clutching Marisol's wrist. Her fingers were ice, but real and solid. "Listen. You have to find what I couldn't."

The cabinet shook. The shadows on the floor lengthened.

Isadora's voice dropped to a whisper. "Just find it before *he* finds you. The hill is only the first doorway."

Marisol's breath hitched. "Isadora. Wait. What am I supposed to find? What's too late?"

Isadora scuffed at Marisol's questions. She began to pull away, but then stopped. Her eyes widened. "He's still there, isn't he?"

Marisol nodded slowly. "He's turning spirits. Those who were part of our family. He's keeping them trapped. But what am I supposed to find? La Vega?"

Isadora's face crumpled, grief and fury warring in her expression. Her lips pressed into a thin line as she shook her head slowly, disappointment radiating from her like a chill. "So, he's found you. And he's growing stronger. You won't last long. I only hope the seal can wait for another Cerradora to be born."

Marisol's eyes narrowed, heat blooming behind them. Her shoulders rolled back, spine straightening as something sharp clicked into place. So, that was the story the ancestors told about her? That she was soft. Breakable. Ordinary. Like she'd been made to shatter.

Let them.

She'd watched, first physically then through glimpses on FaceTime, her mother unravel—quietly, painfully—until there was nothing left but a woman standing on that cursed hill, day after day, trying to carve a path forward for someone else. For her. All the while, Salvador had clawed at her mind until even her memories weren't her own.

And Marisol? She had faced spirits that shouldn't exist. Survived the shame the girlies wrapped around her like a noose. Endured the sting of family silence. The ache of being forgotten by the very people who should've held her close.

And she was still here.

A slow fire built in her chest. Not from rage, but from knowing.

"I'm not fragile," she said, voice even and blade-sharp. "And I'm not done. Not while Kia's still out there. Not while he thinks he can use me or anyone else in this family."

She met Isadora's gaze and didn't flinch. "So, if you think I'm just another Espinal girl who's going to break the moment a man sees her truth, then you weren't paying attention."

"You're the one who's not paying attention. His ways are dangerous, lethal. He can't create, so he twists. He made my mom, Altagracia, bind the power to the land. Ay, Mami," Isadora said, as she put her face in her hands.

And Marisol heard it then: the way Dominicans sing when they speak. The island lived in her voice. She was first-gen and still held the culture close.

Isadora straightened and met Marisol's gaze. Pain still clung to the edges of her expression, but her voice steadied. "I didn't know it at first. Not until I read my mother's instructions, my inheritance." Isadora's voice then sharpened into a warning. "You think you understand? You don't. He pushed her to the brink until she dreamed a place into being. A place that only exists on the hill because it was the only place she ever felt safe. He was a horrible man.

"And when he died, he didn't leave. He anchored himself to it. Not to guard it. To guard against us. To keep us out. To make sure no one could reach that place again. And now he feeds on what still lingers there—the power, yes, but also everything we have left behind—our doubt. Our guilt. The pieces of ourselves we forget to claim."

Marisol's voice rose. "La Vega. Then it *is* an imagined place, like Doña Elvira said."

Isadora gave her a blank stare, one brow inching up. "That's what I just said."

But Marisol wasn't listening. She was pacing. "And it was your mom who created La Vega?"

Isadora sighed, her jaw tightening. "Yes. Must you repeat everything I say?"

Finally, Marisol turned to Isadora. "Then where is it? Is it by the Ceiba Tree?"

"Those don't grow here." Isadora narrowed her eyes before shaking her head and murmuring. "You're more lost than I thought."

Marisol's nose flared as she inched closer to Isadora. "Then tell me where you found it? Where did you find La Vega?"

"I-I don't know." Isadora looked at her hands as if she could find something there. "I couldn't find it."

"Elvíra, my mom's best friend, told me it opened for my mom. She said it was near a Ceiba tree."

Isadora flinched. Her voice dipped into something sharper than disappointment. "Then you must listen to her. Because it didn't open for me. I couldn't find it."

The shame in Isadora's voice was unmistakable. Quiet, but jagged. And beneath it, something else shimmered: jealousy. Marisol saw it clearly. She knew that feeling too well. The way it crept in when she watched las tres mojonas glide through life like it owed them something. Like they'd already won.

"I understand," Marisol said softly. And she did. She wanted to say more, to tell Isadora that the feeling doesn't last forever. That comparison fades if you stop feeding it. That it's hard—shoot, almost impossible—not to measure yourself against people who seem to have it all figured out, especially when your own mother made survival look effortless.

But if you look closely, really look closely, you start to see the cracks. The struggle to hide behind perfect posture and polite smiles. No one has it all together. Not really.

She also knew that just because it hadn't opened for Isadora, it didn't mean it wouldn't open for her. That was Isadora's path. Not a prediction of hers.

And for once, Marisol refused to inherit someone else's ending as if it were her own. She squared her shoulders, the realization settling into place like a bone finally setting. People project.

She inhaled deeply, her feet steady, her jaw set. The flickering light danced across her face, but her resolve held firm.

"I will find it," Marisol said.

Then, a deafening crack.

And Marisol fell.

Fell fast.

Fell back.

Until the mattress caught her again.

Her breath slammed against her chest. The warmth of the room felt jarring. Too still, too bright, too real. The light from the dim cone-shaped light bulb was gone. So was Isadora. But her voice lingered in Marisol's mind, etched deep into the space between one heartbeat and the next.

She blinked.

The journal was still open across her lap. Her hands gripped its pages so tightly they'd started to crinkle.

Isadora's name was gone, and in its place was fresh ink, still glistening:

I'm sorry I doubted you. Walk toward the base of the hill. As long as you don't doubt yourself, the path will open.

Marisol didn't just feel watched.

She felt chosen.

She wasn't just uncovering the past anymore.

She was in it.

And it was far from finished.

26

LA CANCIÓN FALSA DE MADRE (MOTHER'S FAKE SONG)

Her world was still spinning, but Marisol sat motionless. The message was still there, the ink dark and wet as if it had just been written:

I'm sorry I doubted you. Walk toward the base of the hill. As long as you don't doubt yourself, the path will open.

She ran her fingers over the words, half expecting the ink to smear. Instead, the page snagged her skin. "Ouch."

A bead of blood welled and sank into the paper. *Every take carries a give*, Doña Elvira had told her. Marisol turned her finger over. The cut was there, but the blood had stopped. Maybe this was her gift, her way of feeding the thing that had been guiding her.

The journal lay steady across her lap. For the first time, it didn't feel haunted. It felt alive. A companion that had belonged first to her mother, then to Isadora, and now to her.

She exhaled slowly. The air in her room felt different. It was more like waiting, less like watching. Like the house itself had shifted from suspicion to camaraderie.

She looked down at the journal again. The page pulsed faintly beneath her fingers. Just below the new message, a corner curled upward, revealing a sheet she hadn't seen before.

She turned it.

The handwriting had changed.

Her mother's.

~

La entrada no está lejos. Just beneath the slope, where the ground softens, I stood there for hours, waiting for something to change. But I was afraid. So afraid. What if it hurt me? What if it hurts her? What if I die and she's not ready? I don't think I am ready either.

Elvira's eyes were watching me. I knew they were, and I was too ashamed to tell her how much I feared. But I cleared my mind at least for a little while. For a little while, I stopped doubting myself. I stopped doubting what I have learned, and it opened because the path doesn't open for fear. It opens for belief.

But the doubts came back, like a migraine slowly taking over every bit of my head. I couldn't think of anything else. The path began to close in on itself. I stepped back, and before it rejected me, I walked back home. Elvira had already gone.

MARISOL TRACED THE PAGE. "You were right there," she whispered. "And you turned back. You were scared. Like me."

The image of her mother at the base of the hill formed vividly in her mind. Her mom's eyes were full of conflict, her steps hesitant, the wind tugging at her hair like it wanted to pull her forward. She got so close, but then she left this instead.

To Marisol, her mother had always been a rock. A pillar. A cement block, unmoving and unshakeable. But going through her things, touching the clothes she left behind, the notes scribbled in the margins, the lipstick, she had seen something else.

She had seen the woman.

The softness, the doubts, the ache she tried to mask with routines and rosaries.

It was like discovering a secret side of a monument you thought you knew. That moment when the pedestal cracks, and instead of breaking, what's revealed inside is warmer, more human, more real than anything one could imagine.

To realize that her mother had wavered like water in a container rippling from force gave her pause. On one hand, she wanted the journal to lie to her and maintain the image she had always had of her mother. Yet on the other hand, she knew she needed the truth that only the journal knew how to give. Because it was in the pain of the truth that Marisol knew she would find clarity in this chaos.

Marisol sat back. The hill hadn't just been calling her. It had been calling all of them. Isadora. Her mother. Maybe even Mamá Belén. But only Marisol had made it this far, and that didn't make her feel any better.

She swallowed, fighting back every bit of pressure that had suddenly built up in her chest. "I'll go. I'll walk to the base."

She rose from her bed, stretching the stiffness from her

limbs. She felt the journal in her hands. It was now hers to carry.

She crossed to her desk and picked up a pen.

On the next blank page, she wrote:

If this is how it starts, then let me be the one who finishes it. I will finish the story they started. I will write the last page because I am meant to close it.

Marisol hesitated before writing the last line.

Because I am La Cerradora.

She let out a long breath. The ink glistened, then settled.

For a long moment, nothing happened.

Then, a word appeared beneath her writing, curling into existence like smoke:

Altagracia.

Marisol stared at it.

The beginning.

The rebellion.

The inheritance.

Tonight, she would walk to the base of the hill and would undo what Altagracia had been forced to do.

And this time, she would not turn back.

A whisper. Low. Insistent. Found her.

"You're already running out of time."

Marisol shut the journal, hugging it close as she pressed her back against the headboard.

A sharp knock echoed through the house.

She flinched. It came from the front door. But something in her gut told her she wouldn't like what was on the other side.

The air thickened.

Another knock, louder this time.

Marisol forced herself forward, each step dragging in reluctance.

As she reached the front door, her fingers hovered over its handle.

She swallowed hard.

Knock. Knock.

And then.

A voice. Too close. Too wrong.

"Marisol."

She yanked her hand back as if burned.

It was her mother's voice. But her mother was dead.

The voice was gentle. Familiar. Too perfect.

"Mija...por favor. It's me. Open the door."

Marisol's knees buckled slightly.

She wanted to believe it. So badly did she want to believe this. But something in the tone, timing, and exactness of the cadence was off. Manufactured.

Salvador knew how to manipulate. How to imitate. How to twist what was real into something just convincing enough to pass.

A flicker of rage replaced the fear rising in her chest.

"You don't get to wear her voice," she said through gritted teeth.

The door remained shut, but she could feel the cold on the other side deepen.

And somewhere beyond it, she swore she heard it breathing as if it were human. As if it were her mom.

27

OJOS EN LA PUERTA (EYES ON THE DOOR)

The voice was wrong. She knew it was. It wasn't desperate or pleading; it also wasn't begging to be let in. It was patient. Steady.

It was waiting.

Another three raps, precise and deliberate.

"Mari, mi pollita...open the door."

A chill ran down Marisol's spine. Her mother had called her that a thousand times in a thousand different ways: gentle, teasing, exasperated. But this? This was wrong.

Her grip tightened on the doorknob, her palm slick with sweat. Every instinct screamed at her not to open it, not to look at what was waiting for her on the other side, not to listen. Still, the familiarity of that voice pulled at her like a thread unraveling a sweater.

She remembered her mother at the stove, rolos barely held in place by a stretched hair net, her voice competing against the TV in an unspoken battle of who could be louder. Her mother singing "Sana, Sana Colita de Rana" over scraped knees, insisting she had to learn to ride a bike or risk being the only kid who couldn't. She remembered the sign of the cross, the whispered prayer her mother had said outside the college campus before being dropped off—words Mami had uttered only once and never explained.

But she had been too grown. Too grown to acknowledge the tears burning her eyes. Too grown to dry the tears running down her mother's face. She was finally out of Willowshade, on her own, free to do as she pleased. So, she turned away, pretending she was already too grown to care.

She swallowed hard, stepping back from the door.

Mami?

"I forgive you, Mija. I forgive you for not coming back. I forgive you for not being there for me, as I was there for you. I forgive you for it all. All we have is each other. If we don't forgive, then we will be alone. Come, mi pollito. I just want to see you."

Marisol turned around and dragged herself back down the door, feeling the stillness of whatever was behind it. "I can't. I can't."

Those were the exact words Mami had said once after one of their worst fights: *If we don't forgive, then we will be alone.* It was specific. Too specific. Not just mimicry, but real.

The air around her thickened, like the walls were leaning in, like the house itself was bracing itself for something.

Marisol held her head between her hands.

Another knock. More forceful this time. She felt it on her back. Tears poured from her.

What if she was wrong?

What if...what if it was her? What if Mami had escaped Salvador, and this was her only way to be safe?

She stood and turned to face the door.

Her hand hovered above the lock.

Her breath hitched.

A whisper slid through the air. This time, from behind her.

"Don't open it."

Marisol shook her head. Her mother knocked on the door again.

It was Mamá Belén._*"That's not your mother. Ask her something very personal."*

Marisol stepped away from the door. She pressed her fingers together, whispering a quiet thank you to Mamá Belén. Her voice had pulled her back from the edge, just when doubt had begun to creep in. She hadn't realized how close she'd come to opening that door. And now, she didn't want to think about what might've happened if she had. A soft, weak knock interrupted her train of thought.

"Please, mi pollita. Salvador will find me again. All we have is each other."

"What prayer did you whisper to me when I left for college? You made the sign of the cross, but it wasn't just that. What did you say? What did you pray for, Mami?"

She couldn't let herself believe it. But what if this was her mother?

"I prayed you'd stop doubting yourself..."

Marisol reached for the doorknob.

"And finally make me proud."

Marisol jerked her hand away. Those were not the words her mother whispered in her ear. Her mother was dead. No matter how much she wanted to believe otherwise, no matter how desperately she wished to see her walk through that door, she knew the truth. She knew her mother was gone.

She took another step back. Her body shook with disbelief. Whatever dead thing was behind her front door was still there.

"Go away," Marisol said, biting back the rage rushing through her veins. She turned in the direction Mamá Belén's voice had come from. But her grandmother's presence was gone. The space around her felt empty. A cold sweat broke along the back of Marisol's neck.

She pressed a hand to her chest, trying to steady her breathing. Her gaze darted around the dimly lit hallway. The shadows stretched strangely, curling at the edges.

Knock. Knock. BANG.

The door shook violently, the force rattling through the house.

Marisol jumped, her breath catching sharply, a cold prickle crawling down her spine. This wasn't soft. This wasn't patient anymore. Whatever was outside was done waiting.

"Spirits. Good spirits, please protect this house," Marisol murmured, rocking herself back and forth. She envisioned the house being wrapped in white light, a shield surrounding it. "Please."

The whisper came again, this time urgent. *"Good job. You did the right thing."*

She snapped her eyes open. "Mamá, you're back."

When she heard nothing, she arranged herself in front of the door, dragging her knees to her chest, taking a deep breath. The house was different. It shifted around her. The hallway stretched long. The doors to the empty bedrooms stood slightly open, though she hadn't touched them. The air rippled, as if the space between her and the front door was warping, thickening.

Altagracia may have buried their ancestral powers deep in the ground, but Marisol still held to some. *If you believe it, then it's true,* Mami had told her, and she had been right.

She had awakened the house. Or had the house been awakened all along? Was that why the light flickered when Efigenia in Kia's body had come inside? Had it been the house instead of her grandmother that hid the journal when Efigenia had come in?

Either way, the house protects. That is what I believe, Marisol thought, and that made her feel less alone.

The voice of whatever monster pretending to be her mother

came again. This time, right at the door. As if it was speaking through the crack by the deadbolt.

"Mi pollita...por favor."

The handle of the door began to turn. It was no longer waiting patiently.

Marisol didn't think. She bolted for the front door, her body moving before her mind could catch up.

The words thundered in her skull until they burst from her lips, raw and shaking. "Get out. Get out. GET OUT. You are not my mother. You could never be my mother. Get out."

Marisol imagined a gust of wind taking the abhorrent version of her mother that stood outside her door back to the hill where it belonged.

The door stopped rattling.

Then, a familiar, caring whisper curled around her, softer and nurturing. *"Good girl."*

She exhaled.

The house fell silent again.

Marisol stepped back, never taking her eyes off the door until her back hit the wall opposite it. Her heart slammed against her ribs, trying to find a rhythm, one it hadn't known in a long time. *When was the last time I felt peace?* She didn't have an answer.

She slid down the wall, her legs folding beneath her as the tremors of adrenaline finally caught up. Her body sagged, useless and heavy. La Vega. She needed to find it before Salvador got further into her head. She pressed her palms to the floor for leverage, but her limbs refused to obey. A wave of nausea rolled through her.

The being pretending to be her mother was gone. The knocking had stopped.

But something in the air had changed.

Something had lost its patience with her.

She curled forward, pressing her forehead to her knees, trying to calm the spinning sensation and breathe.

Salvador had been counting on her not remembering.

But she did.

"Para que el alma no se pierda..."

The memory cracked open—her mother's voice, low and soft in the dark.

"Lo que es nuestro, en barro encierro..."

She saw it clearly now. Mami's fingers brushing a stray curl behind her ear, like she always did when trying to calm the storm. A kiss to her forehead, warm and lingering. Then her thumb, tracing the sign of the cross right where her lips had been.

"If it can't be me...let it be you."

That was it.

That was what her mother had whispered the day she dropped her off at college. Not whatever that thing outside her door had said.

And just like that, Marisol broke.

The sob ripped free before she could stop it—ugly, full-bodied, the kind that gutted everything. She buried her face in her knees, trembling as the weight of it all crashed down on her.

She wasn't just remembering.

She was being called.

And this time, she was ready to listen.

Because now, without a shred of doubt, she knew she was getting dangerously close to the truth Salvador had spent generations trying to bury.

La Vega.

28

ENTRADA AL LABERINTO (THE LABYRINTH'S ENTRANCE)

The house was quiet now, but not in a way that felt empty. It felt...expectant. It was waiting to see what Marisol would do next.

She listened—really listened—to the creaks in the floorboards, the hum of the refrigerator in the next room, the soft tick of the hallway clock. Normal sounds. Familiar sounds. But layered beneath them was something else. Something she couldn't name.

The house, Mamá Belén herself, had protected her. She was not alone.

Yet, her mind was a tangle of panic and exhaustion, thoughts zigzagging too fast to grasp. She wanted to trust her instincts, to believe the house was on her side. But her nerves were raw, scraped thin. And there was still a part of her that didn't honestly believe. How could she be sure?

The shadows along the hallway seemed to stretch and contract with each breath she took. The air still shifted in strange, subtle ways, like a wind from a door that hadn't opened. She stayed still, barely blinking, afraid that if she moved too soon, she might trigger something.

For a long moment, it felt like the house and she were in sync.

It didn't feel threatening. Or hostile.

It felt protective.

Maybe even...afraid like her.

She slowed her breaths, trying to quiet the storm inside her chest. The static in her head began to soften. Her heartbeat no longer drowned out the world.

And then it changed.

The shadows no longer reached for her. Clarity settled like dust after a storm.

The house, she realized, had never turned against her. It had been fighting alongside her, shielding her the only way it could. It had kept her grounded, even as her mind frayed at the edges.

The house was a witness. A companion. A keeper of memory and warning. And maybe even a guardian.

The danger, at least for now, had passed.

She crept to the front door and placed her hand near the doorknob. Not to open it, but to test. It was cold. There was no pressure from the other side. She pressed her ear against the wood. Nothing.

Whatever had worn her mother's voice had given up, for now.

She whispered, barely louder than breath, "Thank you, Mamá Belén. Thank you...house?"

The journal was already in her bag. The pebble, too.

She crossed the room, each step quiet, reverent. At the door, her coat hung like a sentinel. She reached for it, fingers brushing against the worn fabric.

If the path opened through belief, she would offer all of hers. No matter how frayed it was.

She pulled on her coat, fastened the buttons with trembling hands, and shouldered the bag. The house exhaled behind her.

A final gust found her, soft and warm, like the brush of a grand-mother's palm over the crown.

Then, she turned the knob and stepped outside.

She stood on the porch for a few seconds. The silence of Willowshade pressed in from every side. The streetlights cast long, thin shadows across the pavement. Wind stirred the bare branches overhead, making them click softly against one another like bones tapping in rhythm. The surrounding houses sat tucked beneath the trees, their porches dark and their windows still. But it didn't feel empty.

The town wasn't asleep. It was watching.

As she walked, each house felt like a witness, waiting to see if she'd go through with it.

But she didn't stop.

The hill was waiting.

And this time, she was ready. When she reached the edge of the woods, the moon was high. The hill loomed ahead—taller than it should have been. Its slope was dusted with frost, but still she didn't feel cold. Every trespass influenced by Salvador burned through her mind. It simmered in her bones and boiled in her belly, spreading a sort of heat that kept the frigid Ohio winter air away.

Her feet crunched over brittle leaves as she approached. She didn't know where the entrance to La Vega would be. She looked around. The pit of her stomach squeezed at the thought of turning back. Smoke billowed in front of her as she sighed in frustration.

But then she saw it.

The Ceiba tree, which even during an Ohio winter hadn't lost its leaves, despite not being native to this climate.

This was it.

The ground softened, just like her mother had written. It pulsed faintly beneath her shoes, as if it remembered the others who had come before her: Isadora, her mother, and maybe even Altagracia.

She pulled the journal from her bag. It fluttered open to the page she'd written:

If this is how it starts, then let me be the one who finishes it.

The wind stilled. The trees didn't rustle. Even the air held itself still.

Marisol took a step forward. Isadora hadn't found it. Her mom had had it, but lost it when she doubted herself. Yet, here she was, having seen spirits, felt Salvador, and sensed her grandmother's presence, as well as witnessed her best friend being worn like a coat by one of Salvador's cult followers. She knew Salvador made the land and the home she now lives in a living and breathing hell for his daughter, making her turn toward an imagined place of respite that, like thoughts, manifested into something tangible. So, she knew La Vega was real. She knew it was a place to dream and remember, but most importantly, she knew it was a place where Altagracia felt loved.

Something shifted in her soul. Her spirit. Her mind. This no longer felt like traveling. It felt like coming back to something too important to forget.

And that's when it finally dawned on her—truly dawned on her. This is La Vega. It is a knowing, a piece of Altagracia that survived the silence. It was the memory of resistance. A living record, hidden in the hill, waiting for a Cerradora to remember. Warmth spread through her chest, slow and quiet.

Then came the vision.

Flashes of another time.

A woman kneeling in the dark, a jar clutched tightly to her chest. Altagracia.

She dug into the base of the hill with her bare hands, broken nails, and bloodied knuckles. Behind her came a man's voice. Marisol could tell he was furious. Salvador.

Altagracia struggled to move the jar. It was heavy. Glowing. Buzzing. She whispered something into it before burying it under roots and stones. She kissed her daughter's forehead, then placed her hand over the girl's eyes. The child blinked and forgot.

Forgot the jar. The magic. The rebellion.

The vision ended.

Marisol's breath returned in a rush.

She wasn't just here to unlock the past.

She was here to remember what had been stolen.

"I remember for all of us now," she prayed. And this time, there was no doubt in her voice. Isadora had said the path didn't open for fear or doubt. Her mother had turned back when her doubts returned, and it was then that Marisol realized she was good. She knew fear and grief weighed down her bones. She knew doubt hovered over her like a nimbus cloud. But her doubts and fears were not her. She felt those emotions, lived with them, but they were not part of her spirit. She could step over them, leave them by the side of the road, and so she did, and kept walking.

The earth sighed beneath her feet.

And the hill let her in.

29

BRUJA ENTRE MUNDOS (A WITCH BETWEEN WORLDS)

The ground shifted beneath Marisol's feet.

And then, she wasn't in Willowshade anymore.

The air was warm and filled with unfamiliar and familiar scents: damp earth, sugarcane, and something citrus and bittersweet. The sky above was too bright, the clouds too still. It was like standing inside a memory painted in saturated colors.

Except it wasn't hers.

It belonged to a girl. A girl barefoot beneath a tree, her hair pulled into loose braids, her eyes swollen from crying. She walked in circles, hands clenched, her jaw set tight with grief that had long since passed words.

Altagracia.

Marisol didn't know how she knew it was her, but she did.

She couldn't touch anything. She couldn't speak. But she could feel everything Altagracia felt.

Her homesickness was like a wound left open to bleed out. Her grief, like a shadow she couldn't shake. Her anger, too, because Altagracia hadn't chosen to go. She'd been taken.

Dragged away from a land she still carried in the soles of her feet and the rhythm of her heart.

Marisol watched her whisper into the wind: "La Vega, no me dejes." Her voice cracked on the last words. Don't leave me.

The wind didn't answer.

So, Altagracia walked, each step digging into foreign soil, each whisper a plea the land refused to return. The trees, the sky, even the air were wrong. And still, she kept walking, holding onto what little memory she had, like it might anchor her.

She found the hill—Hallowthorn Hill, but younger, and less scarred, untouched yet by what Salvador would do. She stood at its base and cried so hard she had to kneel. And there, in the dirt, she carved her longing into the land. Not with magic. Not with a spell. But with sheer need.

Marisol watched the world bend.

Not violently. Not suddenly. But gently, like a curtain lifting.

And there it was. A city that did not belong. A memory made solid. La Vega.

Not the one Marisol had visited as a child. This was a version born of memory and built on heartbreak. And it had waited for those who longed to return to their genesis. Because isn't that how one finds the end? By starting from the beginning.

Altagracia stepped through the veil she had made, and La Vega opened for her.

Marisol's heart ached as she watched the scene unfold. It was beautiful, but she could also feel how lonely it was. A home made for one.

The vision shimmered.

Altagracia's voice echoed one last time: "If no one else remembers, I will."

Darkness.

The vision ended, and Marisol was once again standing at

the base of the hill. The frost had melted, and the ground beneath her feet pulsed once, welcoming her. It was as if La Vega had tested her and, having found her worthy, opened the real entrance. She didn't hesitate and stepped forward.

Each footfall landed softly, the earth rising to meet her soles as if remembering her before she could remember herself.

She was still on the hill, but not the one everyone else saw. The world around her was distorted, like memory pressed through fog. The trees were familiar but taller. Older. The path ahead dipped into shadows lined with roots that glowed faintly beneath the ground.

The journal vibrated in her bag.

Marisol pulled it free. It opened on its own. A page flipped. No words came.

"Take what you need." Marisol placed her hand on the page and felt the cut against her skin.

Words formed, appearing like condensation on glass. *"You are close."*

She kept walking. Her breath came steadily now, her body focused even as her nerves hummed. The further she went, the quieter everything became. There were no birds. No breeze. No sound but her own heartbeat.

Then, just ahead, she saw a circle of trees. Twelve trunks, twisted in a perfect ring. In the center was a worn and cracked stone slab. A spiral etched deep into its surface, glowing with faint light.

Marisol stepped into the circle.

ANOTHER VISION BLOOMED.

Altagracia again, but older now. Weary. Hardened. She stood in front of the same stone slab, a jar in her hands. Two

little girls who looked like her stood behind her, their eyes darting, alarmed, as if they were keeping watch.

The ghost of Salvador loomed in the background, hiding.
He hadn't entered La Vega—not fully. His spirit couldn't go
where it had been rejected. But his influence lingered like a
pressure that had settled into their bones—always hovering,
always there. His voice was low and serpentine. *"You can't undo
what's already begun,"* he said.

Altagracia replied. Her voice shook, but she was determined. "But I can keep you from finishing it, Father."

She kneeled and kissed the jar. Then, she traced the spiral
into the stone slab, moving slowly and deliberately, each turn
carved with purpose. Marisol knew with certainty that Altagracia was whispering intentions into this spiral, yet she
couldn't understand what she was saying. The words on her
lips were neither English nor Spanish. Altagracia dug deeper.
She was frantic at this point.

She then plunged the jar deep into the pit she had dug. The
air pressed on Marisol's shoulders as if someone had thrown a
weighted blanket over her. *What are you doing, Altagracia?*

Just then, Altagracia said one phrase, and this time, Marisol
understood it. She raised her hands to the sky, her voice steady
but fierce. "Let this spiral trap those who dare steal what is ours
and send them back to where they belong. Let this spiral call La
Cerradora home, so she may finish what we could not."

From the shadows, Salvador's voice thundered, cold and
righteous. *"You dare defy thy father? You vowed to bind the power.
To bury it, as I had commanded you. You lied to me. A lie to one's
father is a lie to God. A sin such as this is not merely rebellion... It is
heresy. And heresy, child, is an offense most grave in the eyes of the
Lord."*

Altagracia turned, her gaze unshaken.

"You are no father. You are no man of God. You are the devil
cloaked in scripture, and your whole life is an offense."

She looked at her daughters. Light shimmered at the center of their brows, pale and flickering like a flame. Marisol's breath caught.

"As I taught you," she said to them.

They joined their mother, voices rising together—young, clear, and full of power.

"Let this spiral trap those who dare steal what is ours and send them back to where they belong. Let this spiral call La Cerradora home, so she may finish what we could not."

The chant hung in the air—raw, electric, and ancient. Gold flecks spiraled around the younger girl. Her curls were wild and frizzed into a halo that refused to be tamed. Her large, dark eyes, sharp and knowing, looked at the flecks with resignation, as if she knew what it meant to be surrounded by magic. There was strength in her petite frame, something stubborn and sure beneath the fragility. Marisol felt it settle into her skin like truth, desperation, and defiance.

This was Isadora, the first Cerradora.

Then, the vision faded.

Marisol stood alone again. She crouched beside the stone and touched the spiral. It pulsed beneath her fingers.

Altagracia had initially tricked her father, but after he died, his spirit discovered the truth. He threatened his daughter until she had no choice but to do it, but even though she buried it, she refused to give him access to it. She sealed it with the spiral and bound it with a promise. The promise of La Cerradora.

The promise that she or someone like her would come to end all of it. That sent a chill up Marisol's spine. She took a deep breath, willing her heart to stop hammering against her chest. But then a whisper rose from the ground, this time not from Salvador.

"You've come further than any Cerradora."

"I'm not here to finish this story," she said. "I'm here to take him out of the story because he was never meant to be part of it."

The words echoed back to her, not in sound, but in force.

She placed both palms on the slab and leaned in. The spiral glowed brighter. The earth thrummed.

And then she understood. The jar hadn't been buried to protect the magic. It had been buried to keep Salvador from consuming it, from absorbing every last drop.

Altagracia hadn't hidden the power. She had starved him of it.

But now the seal was aging. Weakening.

If Marisol didn't unearth it soon, the rest of the magic might rot beneath the soil, or worse, be found by him first.

As if in response to her realization, the trees groaned.

The ground trembled.

Shadows began to slither in from the edges of the circle, curling like smoke.

Marisol stumbled back, the journal clutched tight to her chest.

A voice crawled into her mind, not from around her, but inside it.

"You're too late."

Salvador.

Then came another voice. Kia's. Desperate. Raw. "Help!"

"Kia?" Marisol called out.

Kia's voice tore through the circle like a scream in the wind. "Mari! Mari! I'm here. Please. Please help me."

Marisol gasped, her heart lurching. It wasn't like the others. It wasn't twisted or manipulated. It was Kia. As herself. Real.

"Kia?" she shouted, eyes darting wildly. "Where are you?"

But only silence followed.

Panic and fury surged through Marisol in equal measure.

Her head throbbed. Her knees buckled. The spiral at the center of the slab began to glow a deep red.

She fell forward, catching herself as her bag swung and the pebble—throbbing and burning—tumbled to the ground. There were two spirals now. One on the slab. One on the pebble. And then she saw it. If she brought the two together, they formed a complete circle. A seal. A signal. Completion.

She gasped, falling to her knees. Her fingers shook as she placed the pebble against the etched spiral until the lines fused seamlessly.

The moment it clicked into place, the ground exhaled beneath her, and Marisol's chest tightened with something ancient and undeniable.

The voices stopped.

The spiral glowed.

She wasn't just finishing something.

She was activating it.

And from within the pebble, there came a crack, and a voice slipped through the stone, too quiet at first to understand. Then sharper. Wet. Splintered. *"Tú crees que puedes sellarme otra vez, muchachita?"* You think you can trap me again, little girl?

Efigenia.

The spiral pulsed violently, and a sharp hum tore through the silence. A burst of dark mist flared upward, twisting into the shape of a woman, her face obscured, hair wild, and mouth open in a silent scream.

Marisol stumbled back, but the figure didn't come for her.

It hovered, hissing, and then vanished into the rising dark.

The ground gave way beneath her.

And Marisol fell.

30

RAÍCES CON NOMBRES (ROOTS WITH NAMES)

This time, falling was a matter of pure pressure. Dense and crushing, like the world had collapsed inward and taken her with it. Everything felt heavy, like the weight of everyone's shame and guilt resided on her chest.

Then stillness.

Marisol landed hard, the wind knocked out of her. She gasped as the cold floor met her back, damp and pulsing like it was alive. Her fingers splayed against mossy stone, rough and warm in places, impossibly cold in others. It took her a moment to sit up.

Wherever she was, it was not the hill.

It was beneath it.

She rose slowly, every muscle aching. Her bag, slung across her shoulder, still held the journal. The pebble, the one with the spiral that had opened the way, was gone, left behind at the entrance. She could feel its absence like a door propped open behind her. She was underground, but it wasn't like any underground cave she'd ever seen. The surrounding space was woven from roots, walls of gnarled wood and stone streaked with veins of glowing amber. The ceiling arched impossibly high, held up by tangled branches that glowed faintly from within.

The air shimmered.

This was La Vega, but not as Altagracia had dreamed it.

This was what happened when something sacred was sealed away.

When longing hardened into survival.

When love was forced to hide in the dark and call it safety.

Marisol thought of Kia, and dread curled tight in her stomach. She didn't know what Salvador would do. She didn't know if she would survive this. Or if they would come out scarred in ways that couldn't be undone.

But this she knew: If they made it out—when they made it out—she would tell Kia the truth.

Even if it wasn't returned.

Even if it made things awkward.

Because some truths didn't belong in the shadows.

They deserved to be spoken. To be seen.

With that resolution grounding her heart, Marisol took a step forward. Her balance faltered, and she caught herself on the wall—then jerked her hand back. Something slimy had pressed against her palm.

She glanced down. A bloated root, the size of her forearm, ran along the wall. Its tan-brown surface was slick with condensation, like sweat, like rot. The texture clung to her skin. She wiped her hand on her jeans, grimacing.

Tracing the root with her eyes, she saw how it stretched back into the dark. It wasn't alive, not entirely. It looked sick. Poisoned.

Disgusted by it, she turned the other way. But what she saw made her pause. The color shifted as it went on—brown to tan to pale cream. And etched into those roots, she saw something that stole her breath.

Names.

Hundreds of them, carved into the wood. Some she recognized. Others had been scratched out, erased mid-letter. One glowed faintly: *Isadora.*

She brushed her fingers near it. The root it was carved into flinched.

Marisol's heart pounded. Something moved deeper inside the spiral chamber. Light flickered ahead.

She followed it.

The glow led her to a chamber encircled by twelve curved trunks, like the circle from the surface, but inverted. At the center stood a stone pedestal. And atop it was the jar.

The jar vibrated with light. Cracks webbed its surface, but they weren't just structural; they buzzed with speckle-like atoms pushing against the glass. The wax that once sealed the jar clung to its mouth, brittle and fractured, the imprint of the spiral still faintly visible. It looked like the magic inside had long grown restless, too powerful to be confined for much longer.

"You are about to burst, aren't you?" Marisol said to it.

She inched closer. Dust coated the jar's exterior. Cobwebs cradled its base, as if the world itself had tried to wrap it in forgetfulness. Two spiders, frozen in place, shriveled, lay beside it, like they had ventured too close to something they shouldn't have.

The spiral symbol on its side was jagged, incomplete. The spiral was there, but it wasn't whole. It lacked the hum she'd felt from the pebble and the other places she'd seen the symbol inscribed.

Marisol frowned. Doña Elvira told her that Altagracia had not only been magical but strategic. What if this wasn't the jar's final resting place? What if this wasn't it? A false jar in a real place, just convincing enough to keep Salvador clawing at a dead end. Marisol stepped closer. In the dull reflection, the jar still held, she thought she saw someone. Or was it only wishful thinking?

"Kia?" The name slipped out before she realized she'd spoken it. And as if Kia had heard, a sound echoed through the space—soft, broken, but unmistakably hers. Her voice was lilting and low, but unsteady, like pain and distress had warped its melody mid-breath

Marisol turned.

A figure hovered above the chamber, barely formed. It was Kia's shadow, suspended in the air, threaded from mist and prayer. She wasn't truly there. Not physically. She was being projected into the space. A warning from Salvador of what was really at stake if she remembered what she shouldn't.

Marisol looked. Kia's presence pulsed with life, resisting yet fading. Her eyes glowed faintly, but they weren't focused on anything in particular. Her mouth moved as if she were singing, but Marisol couldn't hear the melody.

"Kia?" Marisol stepped toward her. "It's me. I'm here."

The figure turned, but her pupils were gone.

"Kia, what did he do to you?"

With tears stinging her eyes, Marisol drew closer.

Kia's lips began to move, but Marisol still could not hear her voice. She pressed her ear closer to the suspended figure. She heard a voice, quiet but confident, as if it was breaking through the fog and distance.

"I prayed for you," she said. "For a long time. I thought I'd forgotten how. But I remembered."

"I'm here," Marisol said.

Kia's suspended image flickered, but her voice, barely a whisper, held steady. "He told me if I touched the jar, it would all stop. That I'd be free. But something in me screamed not to. I can't explain it. So, I prayed. Not like before. Not with fear, but with my gut—and something answered. It told me to wait. To trust you. So, I did. I've been praying for you ever since. And now...here you are."

Marisol's breath hitched, and tears began to spill from her eyes. What had she done? "I'm going to get you out of here, Kia."

Kia hadn't reached for the jar. Not because she couldn't, but because someone had whispered to her not to. The girl who didn't believe in the supernatural had stood her ground against her manipulative ancestor. She didn't deserve this. Marisol reached towards Kia's figure. But before she could get her, a voice slithered into her mind.

"She's only here because of you."

Salvador.

Marisol's knees buckled. She pressed a hand to her head as his voice crawled behind her eyes.

"You brought her to my attention. You wanted me to see this abomination. These unnatural feelings contradict both God and humanity. This, Brujita, is your doing. You wanted this. I am only doing your bidding now."

"No," Marisol whispered. "An abomination? Unnatural feelings? Your entire existence is an abomination. All you do is twist, manipulate, and hurt. You hurt innocent humans who have to carry the weight of that pain for the rest of their lives. You hurt your own daughters. Kia and I are not the problem here. You are."

The jar pulsed.

A different whisper rose. This one, not from Salvador._*"He shouldn't be here."*

The voice trembled like wind through dry leaves. It came from the walls, the roots, the space itself.

"And neither should the jars."

The hill was not just a vessel; it was a symbol. It was a keeper. A guardian that had been burdened with something it was never meant to hold. As the seal weakened, the weight of that magic began to suffocate its roots. It was like an animal shelter overcrowded with animals no one came back for.

Every day, it held onto what did not belong to it, and in doing so, it lost access to its own natural rhythm. Its blessings, its breath, had been paused, held hostage until someone came to claim what was theirs.

The seal was fading. It had heard Marisol's sobs. It had felt her footsteps. And now, it was calling. Not out of rage, but recognition. She was back, and the hill needed her to take back what belonged to her.

Marisol's breath caught. That meant something. He wasn't supposed to reach this place. The hill didn't want him. But the cracks in the jar were a representation of the fading strength of whatever spell Altagracia had placed on it, and Salvador was exploiting that weakness.

"Break the seal, and he goes away."

She stepped forward, her heart thudding against her ribs. The spiral etched into the jar vibrated as if waiting for her. Around the chamber, the shadows moved, circling like vultures scenting decomposition.

Sweat slicked Marisol's palm.

What if she was wrong?

What if breaking the seal didn't banish him, but instead fed him? And polluted the hill? If the magic was in the jar, then unleashing it could make everything worse. He'd gorge on it, devour it, grow even stronger.

Her fingers trembled as she reached for it, then pulled back.

"It has to be you. It couldn't have been your beloved. From your hands, it would know what to do," the unfamiliar voice said.

What if that was the trick? What if this voice was actually him, manipulating her to do what Kia wouldn't do for him?

She closed her eyes.

He'd thrived on the sealed magic. Because it was still—trapped and stagnant. Magic like the Espinal's magic was never meant to be caged. If she had learned anything from Salvador's antics, it was that he thrived on secrets and doubts. He could feed on it because it had nowhere else to go.

Her eyes flew open.

But what if, once you open it, it could move again? What if magic could choose? Is that what that voice was trying to say? *From my hand, it will know what to do.*

She stepped forward, reaching for the jar.

The whispers grew louder, overlapping in a rising hum that prickled beneath her skin. Not all of them sounded like Salvador, at least not at first. Some had the slick cadence of fast-talking salesmen, too eager, too polished, promising safety in one breath and betrayal with the next. Others wept or pleaded, their voices breaking like people being dragged into unmarked cars for being undocumented on stolen land.

It was a cacophony of desperation, deception, and noise. And that was the problem. Salvador didn't need to speak in his own voice to twist the truth. He could wear any voice.

Marisol's chest tightened. It was impossible to tell which voices were real—which, if any, had escaped his influence. That was how he worked. He didn't just silence people. He made them echo him.

"You don't know what you're doing."

"He'll make you one of us."

"It's better to be forgotten than to burn."

Marisol faltered, but then she remembered Kia's voice: "I prayed for you. And now here you are."

Kia believes in me. Mami believes in me. Mamá Belén, Doña Elvira...and me. I believe in myself.

For the first time, she believed in herself not because others needed her to, but because she now understood what she carried and what she could awaken.

Salvador had always twisted choice. He forced others to bend to him. But this magic was older than him. It came from Espinal women who remembered what he wanted forgotten. It wasn't his.

It never was.

That one voice was right. What if magic could choose? If she set it free, it wouldn't run to him. It would run from him. It would return to its rightful owner.

To her.

To all the Espinal women.

She stepped forward and placed her hand on the spiral.

"I'm not sealing it away," she whispered. "I'm letting it come home."

The spiral glowed brighter as she inched closer. The roots above her rattled and stretched, like a net tightening. The jar's cracks spread, trembling in response.

She pressed her fingertips on the jar's fractured edge. The cracks were sharp, pulsing with energy that the glass could no longer contain. It vibrated beneath her skin, alive and furious.

The jar had tried to hold it all in. But it wasn't built for this.

Not for the weight of generations.

Not for the grief.

Not for the power that refused to stay buried.

A shard sliced her finger. She hissed but didn't pull back. Warm blood spilled from her cut, trailing down the glass, slipping into the cracks like it belonged there. It pooled at her feet, soaking into the earth as if answering a call.

And then she felt it. What had been locked away wasn't just magic. It was memory. Pain. Truth. It was the fury of every Espinal woman who had been silenced, their voices braided into raw, pulsing energy.

It could burn down worlds.

The blood kept dripping. Marisol gritted her teeth.

"Then let it burn."

The air exploded around her. Roots lashed out from the floor, the walls, the ceiling. Shadows shrieked.

Kia's scream tore through the chamber. "Maaariii!"

Marisol lunged, holding on to the imploding jar, and then everything went white.

31

______

HERENCIA Y MALDICION
(INHERITANCE AND A CURSE)

They were running away.

Altagracia, Isadora, and a young Belén. Their curls bouncing wildly, they raced through the thick woods surrounding the base of Hallowthorn Hill. Stars still clung to Isadora's skin, luminous and stubborn, as if refusing to let go of their first Cerradora. This was after they'd sealed the jar, Marisol realized. The ritual had ended, but the danger had not.

"Mami, is it me? Am I a Cerradora now?" Isadora's voice cracked.

"Ahora no. There's no time for that," Altagracia said, lifting her skirts to lengthen her stride.

"Tag. You're it!" Belén called, grinning as she matched her mother's pace. "But, Mami, how come it's not me?"

Altagracia stopped so abruptly that both girls stumbled. Her chest heaved, but her voice remained steady.

"We can't do this right now, girls." Her gaze landed on Isadora. "Yes, it's you. Unless the fates change their mind."

Then, she turned to Belén. "And you should be grateful you don't have this burden."

Both girls quieted. Belén looked down, guilt flashing in her eyes. Isadora's fists were clenched tightly at her sides.

"Let's go," Altagracia urged. "I need to wake the house. I need to make it our protector. With your grandfather's ghost loose, his limitations are no longer tethered to the physical world. When he realizes I tricked him again, he'll react. And violently."

"Like Joseph in school when he lost at kickball?" Isadora asked.

"You're so dumb," Belén muttered.

"Uh uh," Altagracia warned, not breaking stride. "We do not use that kind of language with ourselves or each other. Especially not family. Words like that twist in the mind. They become curses of their own."

She looked at Isadora again. "Some men never outgrow their tantrums. But their size, their strength, their influence turn those tantrums into a dangerous thing. Yes, your grandfather's behavior is a bit like Joseph's."

Belén laughed, a little too loud for Altagracia's liking. "So, grandpa is not only a bad guy, but he's a crybaby like Joseph from school?"

Isadora managed a small, uncertain smile.

Altagracia's hand shot out, gripping Belén's arm. "Did he do something to you?"

Belén's eyes dropped to the floor. She shook her head quickly.

Altagracia's grip tightened around her daughter's arm. "You can't keep secrets from me. Do you understand?"

"We know Abuelo is bad." Isadora shrugged. "I didn't cry when he died."

"I didn't either," Belén whispered.

Altagracia's hand trembled as she pulled a handkerchief from her pocket. She let out a long, exhausted breath as she dabbed at her eyes, but her voice was steady. "Neither did I.

That man never deserved our tears. But listen—if anyone is ever doing something they shouldn't, you must tell me. At once. Do you hear me?"

"Yes, Mami," both girls echoed.

Altagracia straightened her spine, as if to shake off the weight that had suddenly pressed on her. "Come. We're going home. Now."

Time shifted. A new memory emerged.

Isadora's dress had changed. While the stars were gone from her skin, their shimmer remained. Her eyes, wide and searching, were also the same.

She was walking alone now, her steps hesitant. She approached the edge of a clearing.

Marisol followed.

And then she stopped cold.

A body lay sprawled beneath the tree, limbs bent at angles they shouldn't bend. The soil puckered and split around him, like lips peeled back, as if the earth itself had spit him out. The skin had gone waxy, the face bloated and mottled. A cigar lay tucked in the breast pocket of his suit jacket, as if he meant to reach for it again someday and light it like always.

Salvador.

Isadora's face went pale.

She turned and ran. "Mami! Mami!"

Altagracia emerged from the house, hair tangled, incense smoke clinging to her like a cloud of grief and resistance. The scent was sharp, with notes of pine resin, rosemary, and thyme.

"What's going on?"

"Grandpa... He's over there. Dead."

Altagracia wrapped Isadora in her arms, swaying her gently, whispering words into her daughter's hair—words not meant to fix, but to ground, to soften the horror of what had been seen.

"He was so still," Isadora murmured.

"Juanita!" Altagracia called.

A girl barely in her teens emerged, her dress prim, her posture composed.

"Si, Mami."

"English," Altagracia snapped. "We're on our own now."

Juanita bit her lip. "Yes, Mami."

"Take your sister. Make her the tea I taught you."

"I will."

Altagracia kissed Isadora's temple. "I'll be back."

She turned and walked away.

Marisol followed Altagracia.

The body hadn't moved, but now someone else was there. A man kneeled beside Salvador, carefully arranging his limbs, muttering something under his breath.

Altagracia grabbed the man's arm. "You have no idea what you're doing."

The man flinched, then straightened. The scent around him was acrid—sulfur, leather, musk. A thick, old cologne that tried to mask rot. "Ma'am," he said, his voice sharp, "you need to unhand me before I call the police. You folks aren't exactly beloved around here."

Altagracia stepped back, instinctively.

"I'm his daughter," she said, softer now. "So, it should be me taking care of my father."

The man raised a doubting brow. "He told me specifically not to let you near him. Paid me good money before he died. Told me to ensure he was buried on ancestral land, and that's exactly what I'm going to do."

"Ancestral land?" Altagracia repeated, baffled.

The man smirked. "You know exactly what I said. Now don't you try to thwart me. Your daddy told me you'd come and try to meddle. Said the women in his family always try to take what ain't theirs, and...he was not wrong."

Altagracia's lips curled with distaste. "The hill spat him out. It doesn't want him."

She leaned closer to her father's body.

"That's why I'm moving him somewhere else—somewhere fitting." He narrowed his eyes before putting his body between her and Salvador's corpse. "You women have better things to do. Like minding your daughters while your husband is away. It would be a shame if something happened to them."

His smile turned Altagracia cold. She took a step back, looking inward, seeing what she could do. The magic in her bones stirred, but it was thin and weak. She had given it up, locked it in a jar.

She stepped back some more, slowly and deliberately. She could always wish. She could always imagine.

"Then may misery cling to your soul," she whispered, "just like his clung to ours."

The vision fractured.

32

EL CAMINO DE DOLOR (THE PATH FILLED WITH PAIN)

After the vision faded, Marisol saw nothing but a white void. Not light. Not warmth. Just blank nothing.

Then, the world unfroze. Marisol blinked, but the whiteness didn't fade. Her body felt weightless, suspended in something too still to be air. Then came the pull. Gentle at first, then steady.

Her feet hit solid ground, but she wasn't back beneath the spiral.

She was standing in a field, lush and green with wildflowers bending against a wind she couldn't feel. The sky was cloudless, with an impossibly blue hue. But there was no sun. No sound.

And then the landscape rippled. The flowers twisted into patterns, curves, and loops.

A spiral.

She gasped. La Vega wasn't just a hidden city. It was a spiral-shaped labyrinth.

She reached for the journal in her messenger bag. It opened without resistance, pages fluttering until they stopped on a page with a familiar diagram: a hand-sketched spiral flanked by notes in her mother's handwriting.

Marisol traced it with her finger. The spiral wasn't a symbol. It was a map.

"This place is a maze," she whispered, the realization sharp in her voice. "And a trap."

The spiral had grown out of Altagracia's grief, but then she'd twisted it into something else. Something to survive Salvador.

Had she known what he would become?

Had she seen the future? Or simply knew what a narcissist could do, even in death?

The flowers shifted again, flattening into a path.

Marisol inhaled sharply, her mind racing. If this were the spiral, then walking it wasn't just a matter of movement. It was a test of what she could remember.

She took the first step.

The ground pulsed beneath her foot. The spiral path shifted slightly, drawing her forward. She ambled, carefully, and the further she went, the more the world bent around her.

Then came a voice.

"Mari?"

Marisol froze.

It was her mother's voice. Not warped like before.

The world flickered.

The spiral peeled open, revealing a room that didn't belong here. A room that had once been hers, but not really hers. A space she had slept in, studied in, smiled in, but never belonged to. Stone countertops, buttery soft bedding, and floor-to-ceiling windows that framed a view Marisol hadn't earned. It was too clean, too cold, like wealth trying to impersonate comfort. A phone lay buzzing on the desk. Her phone. She remembered this.

Marisol was back in the home that belonged to her college

roommate. The one who had ghosted her after Mami died. The one with skin untouched by melanated undertones, hair that wasn't shaped by the ocean's waves that tie us to our homeland, or the spirals and swells that shaped centuries of crossing, longing, and return. Hair that didn't echo the stories written in tide patterns or the memory of salt air. She was the kind of girl who could afford a self-care day and never think twice about money.

Marisol watched herself sitting cross-legged on the bed, scrolling on her phone, her mother's voice crackling over the speaker.

"Mari, did I ever tell you the story about the night your tatarabuela—"

"Mami," her past self interrupted, a little too sharply. "Can we talk about this another time? I'm tired."

She hadn't meant it cruelly. She was just tired and overwhelmed. Mami had been calling more than usual, and Marisol knew she was anxious about her being away and COVID killing so many people. But it seemed that no matter how many times she told her she was as safe as she could be, Mami would continue to call. And she had been young, dumb, and determined to hide.

But watching it now, Marisol felt the words land like a slap. She saw the way her mother's mouth tightened at the corners. She could see how her eyes, always so full of stories, dimmed just slightly.

On the screen, her mother had nodded and said, "Okay." But it hadn't been neutral, okay. It had been a quiet, resigned okay. The kind of OK that was a sacrifice, a small offering placed gently at the feet of a daughter still trying to disappear. Mami folded the story back into herself without a complaint, like she had done so many times before.

Marisol's eyes burned watching the memory.

Back then, she used to bristle at her mother's timing. At her voice. At her accent that curved each English word with the rhythm of another country. It embarrassed her, though she never would've said that aloud. That lilt was a mark, a sound that betrayed lineage, that hinted at questions Marisol didn't want to answer. It wasn't her mother's fault, but it was her voice. And at the time, that was enough.

Marisol had once wished her mother would speak like other moms—the ones whose words didn't carry a map, whose syllables didn't reveal history. She used to think the accent was a burden that clung too tightly to their family, a curse that refused to be diluted no matter how many generations had been born on U.S. soil.

But now? Now she knew better.

That had been the last full conversation they'd ever had, and Marisol had used it to shut her down.

She watched her younger self's head turn away, shoulders slouched in the selfish posture of someone who hadn't yet lost what mattered most, and her throat closed with guilt.

Her mother had been trying to give her something. Not just a story but a warning. A key.

And Marisol had looked away.

Now, all she could do was remember.

And carry it forward.

The memory rippled, changing beat. Her past self laughed at something her roommate said from the bathroom. She never picked up the next call. Or the one after that. She remembered this time clearly. Before she found out her mother had died, she had felt light. Luxe. Cocooned in borrowed comfort and proximity to someone who came from old money and a long-ago immigrant lineage that had been embraced by whiteness instead of pushed to the margins.

Marisol had thought this was how it was supposed to work. That if she just got close enough to that kind of life, all the inadequacies she carried would fall away. That adjacency would cleanse her.

But when her mother died, her roommate had become uncomfortable with the weight of Marisol's grief. Her friend didn't come to the service. Didn't send flowers. She just slowly disappeared like Marisol's grief was a contagion she didn't want to catch.

The spiral whispered: *"You chose them."*

Marisol dropped to her knees. "I didn't know. I didn't know it would be the last time."

The air thickened.

"You didn't want to know," the spiral hissed.

Her chest ached. Her hand clenched around the journal. The voice was right. She hadn't wanted to know. She hadn't wanted to acknowledge it. She had hidden from the truth.

She forced herself to her feet.

"You're right, I didn't," she said, her voice low and rough. "Yet, part of me knew. Part of me knew I had to acknowledge the truth I didn't want to see, and that part of me dragged me here to confront it." She breathed in sharply. "And I'm still here."

The room faded. The spiral pulsed.

The path opened again.

She stepped forward, her breath shaky but even. Her cheeks were still wet, but her spine was straight. She wasn't the girl in that borrowed room anymore. She wasn't a shadow of someone else's comfort.

The spiral twisted ahead of her, narrower now, its edges sharper. She walked forward anyway.

Then, another shift. The air turned colder. The sky—if it was a sky—dimmed to a blue-gray haze. Her ears popped. The silence cracked.

This time, she was in a hallway she didn't recognize. It looked like her house, but it wasn't. The walls stretched too tall. The doorframes leaned inward. And at the end of the hall, there was a hospital bed.

Her mother lay in it. Eyes open. Still. Staring at her. "Why didn't you come home sooner?" the dream-version of her mother asked, not with cruelty, but with a sadness that seemed to come from every version of her mother Marisol had ever known.

"That's not what you said back then, Mami. You told me it was okay. You told me to stay at school and not quit."

"But you knew I was sick," this dream-version whispered. "Didn't you?"

Marisol shook her head. The walls pressed in. Her pulse pounded.

She hadn't known.

Not because no one told her.

But because she hadn't asked.

She had been so wrapped up in her own preservation, survival masquerading as strength, that she ignored what her intuition had screamed at her all along. She'd let it rot. She'd turned away willfully.

Marisol backed up, her throat tight. "No," she said, her voice sharp. "You don't get to twist her words. That's not what she meant." Her voice trembled but didn't falter. "I know she wanted me to stay at school. I know she didn't want me to quit. But I also knew something was wrong. I felt it. And I ignored it, not because I didn't care, but because I was scared. Because I thought that if I knew for sure, the pressure would crush me, and I'd come back home as a failure. And guess what?" Her hands curled tighter around the journal, knuckles white. "That still happened. I still came home. And my ignorance didn't save me. It only made me feel worse."

The spiral snarled. The hallway twisted inward.

"She was waiting for you," it hissed. *"And you never came."*

Marisol's voice cracked. "Didn't you hear me? I was scared."

"Not scared," it said. *"Ashamed."*

Tears slid down her cheeks, but she didn't fall.

"I was scared and ashamed," she said, steadier now. "I tried so hard to erase the parts of me that stood out, that marked me as other. I thought if I could just blend in, if I could bury the pieces that came from her, from this place, I'd finally make it."

She wiped her face with the back of her sleeve.

"So yeah, when Mami talked about brujerías, I pushed it away. It felt like another reminder that I didn't belong anywhere. But I was wrong. I was wrong to deny her. Wrong to deny myself. Wrong to run."

She stepped forward.

"And I'm allowed to change. I'm allowed to grieve for her, for the choices I didn't make, for the silence I carried like a shield."

Another step.

"And I'm allowed to try again."

The spiral shrieked.

"This time," Marisol said, her voice unshakable, "I'll get it right."

The hallway cracked.

And then it shattered.

And Marisol stepped into the next turn of the spiral.

The light shifted again. It was warmer now—softer. She stood in a forest clearing, and at the center, she saw a figure hunched over.

Altagracia.

Her shoulders slumped. Her hair was loose and gray. Her eyes were resigned and bitter all at once, like someone who had given it their all and still lost. She looked up straight at Marisol.

"I tried," she said. "But he took everything. And you will too."

The words hit like a punch.

"I'm not him," Marisol said.

"You carry his blood."

Marisol stepped forward. "So did you."

Altagracia stared at her. Her fingers twitched slightly, and her eyes flickered, not with malice but with something like sorrow. Or hope. Marisol couldn't quite place what she saw on her ancestor's face, but she wanted to tell her something. She wanted to say, respectfully, that she was wrong. She wanted to say that just because Salvador is part of her lineage and her blood, it doesn't mean he was part of her path because she gets to choose her own path.

Her mouth opened slightly, then closed again. She mulled over her words before speaking them.

"I'm not here to repeat your story," Marisol finally said, her voice steady and sure. "I'm here to finish our story."

Altagracia lifted her chin and nodded, slow and sure. One hand drifted to her chest, fingers resting lightly over her heart. She closed her eyes, not for long, but long enough for Marisol to witness it: the release.

The grief that had clung to her like a second skin, etched into the lines of her face like a birthmark, finally let go.

Altagracia's shoulders eased. Her posture softened.

And then, so quietly it might have gone unnoticed, a breath escaped her lips. A breath she had been holding for decades.

When she opened her eyes again, Marisol saw it.

Not sorrow.

Pride.

The clearing shivered. The spiral straightened.

Ahead, there was a chamber. And at the center of the chamber, there was a stone platform that cradled the real jar. Not the echo. Not the decoy buried higher on the hill, the one meant to distract, to mislead, to keep anyone who followed from reaching the truth.

That was why Salvador haunted the hilltop like a starving dog at a butcher's door. Josefina hadn't just buried a fake. She braided it with a sympathy-tether that copied the jar's "song" at a low, constant hum. As long as the decoy sang, it masked the real chamber beneath the roots and bled off a trickle of power, just enough for him to feed on, but not sufficient to free him.

For years, he and his spirits had fed on its power, but now the enchantment was thinning. The illusion was beginning to crack. Not because the real jar weakened, but because the lure had been doing its job for years, and its charge was finally running thin.

This jar. This one pulsed with power.

With intention.

With purpose.

Still whole.

Still glowing.

Waiting.

33

LA TRAICÍON DE EFIGENIA
(EFIGENIA'S TREASON)

The chamber was quiet.

Marisol stepped in, the spiral closing behind her. The air was thick with the weight of everything she'd just experienced. The jar rested on a stone pedestal, its glow casting a warm light against the surrounding roots. It was smaller than she expected, no larger than a cantaloupe, but it buzzed with a pressure that made her chest tighten.

The spiral etched across its surface was faded, as if it were reaching an expiration date that Marisol knew nothing about.

It was wounded.

She took another step. The journal in her hand grew warm,

Around the chamber, she saw the names again. Espinal names etched into roots, woven in the chamber. Some glowed gently, others were scratched out entirely.

A whisper slid through the air, slow and serpentine: *"We chose peace."*

Then came another, softer: *"We chose him."*

Marisol gasped. The names—unreadable, scratched, dismembered. Her stomach twisted, and she stumbled back.

These ancestors had surrendered their names. They weren't

long-forgotten women. They had surrendered their identity for the false sense of peace Salvador had promised them.

She swallowed against the nausea rising in her throat. "But what are your names, then?" she asked, her voice barely above a whisper, testing a theory she didn't want to believe.

"We don't have one. We are his. He brought us peace. We chose him," they said in unison.

Marisol covered her mouth to keep a gasp from slipping out. The names weren't lost to time. They had been erased by choice.

The journal quivered in her hands, and a page flipped on its own. A name that had once been scratched out began to reappear, stroke by stroke, bold and sure, like someone trying to reclaim it quickly.

Marisol's breath caught.

This wasn't random.

One of them wanted back in.

A low hum filled the chamber, vibrating through stone and marrow.

Efigenia Espinal.

The spirit that had torn through Kia like wind through shattered glass. Ruthless, invasive, wearing her skin without care for her boundaries, her choices, her freedom. The spirit she had trapped on the pebble who then escaped when the spiral opened to latch onto the decoy jar.

This was the spirit Doña Elvira and her mother had found in their home. The one who had been trying to bulldoze her way while stepping over others.

Altagracia's niece.

Fooled by her own misplaced hate.

Claimed by Salvador.

Marisol's breath caught.

It was her.

"You will not trap me," she had said, and now, here she was,

clawing her way back into a place she'd forfeited when she aligned with Salvador.

Marisol's chest tightened. "You took Salvador's side."

The spirit materialized in front of her. Being close to their magic gave Efigenia some strength, but not much, because Marisol could still see through her corporeal body. *"He gave me something no one else could. Not even your mother."*

Marisol's fists clenched. "You could've helped her. You could have helped my mother."

"She was never meant to reach it," the woman said, her voice cold. *"Just like you weren't."*

Marisol stepped forward. "So, instead, you turned your back on the women in our family?"

Eerie silence followed, swollen with rot and shame.

But Marisol didn't stop. Her voice sharpened, cracking at the edges. "You think that makes you powerful? That siding with him gave you purpose?"

Her breath hitched, but the fire inside her roared louder. "You came back through him. Not through truth, not through healing."

Her throat burned now, and her hands shook. "You didn't walk any sacred path. You corrupted it."

A sob nearly broke her words, but she pushed through. "You tried to steal Kia's body, her life, because you refused to face your own. Altagracia didn't take anything from you. Your mother chose to stay, and she had a good reason for doing so. But you went and aligned yourself with a monster? With someone who hurt so many? You are mad at the wrong person, Efigenia. All these years. All that time wasted, hating someone who did nothing to you."

That last line tore from her like a wound ripped open. Raw. Furious. Unforgiving.

The air buzzed harder. The chamber shook. She had hated all the parts that make her, her and pushed it away. She could have been like Efigenia, lost in misplaced hate. The magic around her pulsed angrily, unsure but determined. That was no longer her path. She had chosen differently, and it was time to guide Efigenia in another direction.

Marisol squared her shoulders. She wasn't done. "You haven't changed. You think you can just take because someone did you wrong. You think being wronged gives you permission to do wrong unto others. You have not learned. Instead, you tainted the family name."

Her voice trembled with anger, but instead of slowing, it fueled her. "You don't get to come back into this family by forcing your way in. You come back by doing the work. By facing what you ran away from. You don't get to hurt the person I love and still ask to be named."

Silence surged.

Marisol took a breath, a long, steadying breath. Then she spoke the words that mattered most. "Efigenia Espinal...you are not ready to have your name written in the roots of this spiral. Not yet."

She slammed the journal shut. A gust of wind whipped around her, taking Efigenia away. Her ancestor's screams echoed until silence filled the space again.

Marisol stepped closer to the jar.

The air rippled.

This wasn't the same jar.

The spiral here was whole, etched with clarity and purpose. Not brittle. Not dulled. Not a trap. But like the one above, it was fading, expiring. Still, it pulsed with the weight of truth, and that let Marisol know this was the one.

And just like that, Marisol knew—Altagracia had outsmarted Salvador.

The jar in La Vega had been a decoy. A delay. A false climax for a man who always thought he was the center. For a man who took and damaged without feeling any remorse. But this... was the heart of it all.

A voice unfurled behind her eyes. *"Break the seal and you break yourself."*

Salvador. He had followed her here.

When the decoy collapsed, the sympathy tether recoiled— veil first, then scent. For a heartbeat, the real chamber's trail must have flashed bright inside the spiral, and he latched on. The implosion of the decoy had given away the real jar's location, and he'd followed the scent like a dog, relentless and hungry until he found it.

The chamber darkened. The spiral etched on the jar continued to fade. The roots trembled. The spiral had always been the blueprint—not just a symbol, but a spell. Etched into story, carved into stone. It mapped where the magic was sealed, and how it could be found again.

The pebble was its key: A portable seal-breaker, a spirit trap. But it was never meant to hold what lived inside the jar.

That burden belonged to this chamber in the hill, and it was ready to let go of that weight.

The jar—the real one—held more than magic. It carried every memory, every grief, every power the Espinal women held. The same power Altagracia had called back to her and buried. Now Marisol could see the cracks weren't only in the glass. They split through the family's past and their future. If the magic remained bound—or worse, if Salvador stole it—the souls of their ancestors would never rest, and those yet to be born would be only shadows of who they were meant to be.

She strained picking it up.

"You need not do this," Salvador said, his voice turning coaxing. *"Let it end here. Let the past rest."*

She felt him reach—thin, cold.

He's scared, Marisol thought.

The spiral glowed as she lifted the jar, as if asking: Are you ready to release what was never meant to be caged?

An image flickered in Marisol's mind. Kia, suspended in the roots, her skin ashen, her eyes distant. I'm so ready.

"Would you squander such power for a girl who will never forgive you? Who will never love you?" Salvador asked.

Marisol shook her head. "You don't get to influence me anymore, Salvador. I can see through your lies now. Every pain, every violation you caused to others became a crack in your spirit. You noticed that, didn't you? But you chose to look away, pretend as if it hadn't happened, and it started stacking up on you. It's heavy, isn't it? That's the weight of every sin you committed and haven't atoned for. So, when you died, you wanted others to feel the same filth that covered your heart. You wanted us to feel that same shame and guilt."

Her voice strengthened with every word. "But I know Kia. I know myself. And we can forgive. We can move forward. We can love one another. But to do that—really do that—I have to be free."

The words rose from somewhere deeper than fear, deeper than anger. They were Marisol's truth—laid bare and unrelenting. "And none of us—not me, not them—can be free while you keep feeding on the pieces we were forced to leave behind."

Salvador's voice grew cold again. *"You presume to know what freedom is. But you are a child playing in ruins. This was never meant for you."*

"But it was. It is meant for me. I am meant to be here. Your own daughter called for me."

Salvador's voice slithered through the chamber, thick with contempt. *"You speak of loyalty as if it were your right to define."* He stepped closer, his presence coiling through the shadows like smoke. *"She is nothing but a traitor to me, to her blood."*

He sneered, his eyes cold and gleaming. *"She's not like the others. They offered me their silence, like daughters should."*

His voice lowered, almost reverently now, as if remembering a twisted kind of devotion. *"What you call betrayal, they called peace."*

Marisol didn't flinch.

"There can be no peace in the absence of freedom, Salvador. You know that. But you've lied to yourself for so long, you carried those lies with you into death. And now you believe them."

She looked down at the journal in her hands.

She remembered Altagracia's whisper.

Isadora's fear.

Her mother's guilt.

Kia's screams.

And herself, lying in a room that didn't belong to her, hoping adjacency would make her whole.

Not anymore.

She dropped to her knees beside the pedestal, the journal —her weapon, her heirloom—open in her lap. Its pages trembled with memory, ink-stained and time-worn. It was more than paper now. It was the voice of two women who had walked this path before her.

It had brought her this far. It could carry her the rest of the way.

She placed both hands on the journal, her heart pounding. "Please," she whispered first. Then louder, "If there's anything left. If you ever believed I could do this, show me how."

Her voice broke. "Mami...Isadora... I'm here. Help me."

The pages stirred, and the sting of a cut broke through her skin. Take it all, she thought. Take all the blood you need to help me get through this. A page flipped, then another. And then it stopped. A symbol she had never seen before—spiral-shaped, but folded inward, like a seed waiting to bloom— glowed faintly.

Marisol ran her fingers over it. On the page, the ink shimmered, then it lifted and sank into her skin. Guided by a knowl-edge she didn't know she had, she moved her finger to the pedestal.

The ink crawled from her finger to the stone filling the spiral at the base.

The pedestal lit up as if awakening. She laid her palm flat against it, feeling its warmth surge through her.

The jar began to glow brighter.

Salvador screamed.

Marisol pressed her hand against the pedestal harder. A jolt of energy vibrated through her. Light surged. Magic burst through the room, angry, old, and holy. It clawed through every crevice, every scar left by silence and shame.

The pedestal split.

The roots recoiled.

For one breathless second, everything stilled. The chamber seemed to exhale, deep and slow, as if it were bracing for what was about to be born.

Then, the jar shattered. Not with a crack. Not with an implosion. But with silence.

A silent explosion, like fireworks blooming without sound, like stars tearing through the sky with nothing but brilliance to announce them.

Magic burst outward in all directions, shimmering and weightless.

But it wasn't stars that fell. It was them—the weight of every Espinal woman who had waited, aching, whispering, watching for this very moment to happen.

One by one, they fell into her.

Not to crush her.

To become her.

Her mother.

Isadora.

Altagracia.

Even the names history had buried.

Their sorrow.

Their strength.

Their stories.

All of it collapsed into Marisol's chest, settling like breath returned to lungs that had waited generations to be filled.

And in that final, blinding moment, Marisol vanished in the light.

34

UNA BRUJA CON CORAJE (A WITCH WITH COURAGE)

There was no falling this time. No crashing light. No bone-rattling impact. Just breath.

Marisol exhaled into the silence, and the spirits that had mounted her body came out. She curled her body on the chamber floor at their release. The scent of damp earth was thick in her nose. The ground beneath her was warm now. No longer was it trembling—no longer angry—it pulsed gently, like a living heartbeat, a steady rhythm beneath her ribs.

She opened her eyes.

The roots above glowed faintly, like veins beneath translucent skin. The jagged pedestal where the jar had once sat was split in two, its edges blackened, no longer radiating that terrible hum.

Marisol sat up slowly. Her legs trembled, but they held. The journal lay beside her, closed yet warm, its cover rising and falling like it breathed. She longed to ask where Kia was—to hold her, to know she was safe.

But something in the chamber caught her eye. A figure.

"¿Papi?"

He stood at the edge of the light, half-shadowed, like a guest unsure if he was welcome. He had been trapped here like the others, but when she reclaimed their magic and stripped Salvador of his power, she'd released her father too.

Marisol froze. Would he vanish before she could say anything?

He met her gaze. And for the first time in years, there was no shame. No lies. Just raw honesty.

Tears shimmered in his eyes. *I'm sorry,* he mouthed.

Marisol nodded. That was enough. He had come back to say goodbye, to apologize and had gotten trapped here.

"I forgive you." And with one final glance, he faded, the air rippling softly where he'd stood.

Marisol exhaled into the sudden quiet. Only then did she realize how constant Salvador's whispers had been—always slithering through Willowshade, twisting fears, bending thoughts. In the chambers where the decoy and the true jar once pulsed, he had used their leaking magic to project Kia's image and lure her deeper. But now, with both jars gone and no body left to anchor him, Salvador was nothing but silence.

"Kia," Marisol whispered.

She had to do something, and she knew where to start. Frantically, she reached for the journal that had fallen to the floor, but stopped. The ground beneath her was alive with light. Spirals etched themselves into the earth, glowing faintly, spreading outward like breath.

She reached out, brushing her fingers across it. A shiver crawled up her spine, and they began to glow.

The symbols etched on the ground lit the room, and Marisol saw names carved into the wall of the chamber— Isadora, Josefina, Marisol—Las Cerradoras. But now, other names began to appear. Names with Taíno, African, Portuguese, and Spanish roots. Each one carried the legacy of a magic first grown by the Ciguapa, who lured colonizers to their deaths in a desperate bid to free her people. That vengeful magic had bloomed into something enduring, passed down from woman to woman, strengthening their belief in themselves, killing doubt just as they had once killed their invaders.

A breath of wind stirred the roots above her. She looked up to see eyes staring down at her.

And then the whispers came, faint and reverent: *"She broke it. And we remember."*

The spirals beneath her pulsed, and something inside her chest responded; it wasn't her heartbeat but something older and more profound.

She pressed her palm to the journal, and it flipped open on its own. Pages fluttered, then stopped on the last one. Ink bloomed like steam across the page, rising in soot-dark letters:

I know it feels cruel to carry this alone, but that is the way of a Cerradora. Each of us must face the hill by ourselves, and each of us takes the path farther than the one before. You have reclaimed our magic, and you have carried it further than any of us. I am proud of you.

—Altagracia

A sob caught in Marisol's throat.

Beneath the message, a new drawing unfurled: a spiral blooming into the roots of the Ceiba tree by the entrance of La Vega.

Marisol traced it slowly, reverently, her eyes burning. If only Kia were here. She had to find her.

"Kia? Please come to me." She closed her eyes, imagining the sharp lines of her jaw, the way her eyes seemed to spark when she laughed, her arms when they wrap around her, her smell that seeps into Marisol's clothes, and even her own skin when she's near.

"Kia," she called to her. Marisol opened her eyes and watched the shimmer glow more boldly at the chamber's edge. *What was that?* She rose, turned unsteadily but resolutely, and walked toward it. The roots there pulsed and parted, curling away like they recognized her.

And there, hovering inches above the ground, was Kia. Not suspended. Not trapped. Just...there.

Her eyes fluttered before opening slowly, unfocused. Her skin was ashen, her lips dry, but she was breathing.

Marisol's breath hitched. "Kia?"

Kia blinked. Her voice came thin and raspy. "Mari...?"

Marisol rushed towards her, grabbing her hand. It was cold but not lifeless.

"You came back to me," Marisol whispered.

Kia's gaze wandered, her brow creasing. "I heard you, and then something pulled me. But he didn't want to let me go. I remember...screaming. Then, nothing. Just...dark."

"You're safe now. We're okay. We're going home."

Kia nodded faintly, but her legs buckled. Marisol caught her, one arm around her back, lowering her gently to the floor.

"Hold up, let me put this away." The journal trembled in her free hand. It had saved her. It had saved Kia.

And then his voice came.

"You may have broken the jar," Salvador rasped, each word fractured and clinging to the corners of the room like smoke. *"But you still doubt yourself. And that is enough. You cling to a friend who doesn't believe in the magic you now call your own. That contradiction, your tether to the nonbeliever, will rot you from the inside, niña. Just as it did for those who came before you. Leave her here. She's no good to you."*

Marisol turned toward the voice. A shadow twitched near the broken pedestal. Long. Thin. Wrong. She stood tall, shoulders squared. "You got me fucked up. It's called boundaries, Salvador. And yeah, Kia doesn't believe in this magic, but she believes in me. What I've always needed—what Kia has always given me—is respect and support. She may not believe in magic, but she's never stopped believing in me. That's what makes her different. And that's what makes me strong. I know who I am now."

The shadow convulsed.

"You talking to him?" Kia asked feebly from the ground.

"Yes," Marisol said, still watching the convulsing shadow. "He's trying me. But no. No more."

Kia's eyes widened slightly. "Jesus. He won't give up, huh? But God. I tell you. But God."

And then the shadow collapsed into dust.

The silence that followed felt earned, like the chamber itself had heard and was relieved to see Salvador gone.

Behind her, Kia stirred. "He's gone, isn't he? It's like the air is smoother now."

Marisol nodded.

A soft golden light pulsed near the far wall. Roots curled into an archway; a doorway of light. It was their way out.

Marisol helped Kia to her feet, bracing her with one arm. It felt different being the strong one, not in the muscle-and-might kind of way, but in the unshakable kind that came from finally seeing herself clearly. Kia didn't believe in magic, but she believed in Marisol—had always believed in her, even when Marisol couldn't believe in herself. That had never changed. And maybe that kind of unwavering loyalty was its own kind of magic. Her bag hummed gently, as if the journal agreed.

Behind her, the chamber, the names, the spiral, the roots, glowed. She wasn't escaping the hill. She was bringing them all home.

She stepped through the threshold of light, with Kia beside

her, the weight of generations around her, and the spiral, at last, whole beneath her feet.

35

YOUR GIFTS ARE NOT EVIL (TU DONES NO SON MALOS)

The house was quiet when they returned. It wasn't the silence of peace, but of pause, like everything inside it had exhaled and settled for a bit.

Marisol closed the front door softly behind her, her free hand still clutching the strap of her bag. The journal inside pulsed faintly, as if sensing they'd crossed a threshold.

Kia leaned heavily against her. "I'm fine," she muttered, though her legs buckled the second they passed through the doorway. Marisol caught her without hesitation.

"You're not fine," Marisol said gently, guiding her to the couch. "You were trapped and subjected to Salvador. Sit. Breathe. Let your body catch up."

Kia flopped onto the cushions and groaned. "Okay, yeah. Maybe I need five minutes. Or ten."

Marisol grabbed the throw blanket, folded it over the back of the couch, and draped it across her. "Start with ten."

She moved to the kitchen and began making tea, the kind her mother used to make when her nerves were bad and the nights were worse. Manzanilla y hierbabuena. Her fingers moved automatically. She could almost hear her mother humming as she worked, moving with the same grace and care. The kettle hissed softly as it came to a boil.

While the tea steeped, Marisol braced her hands against the counter. Her body felt like it had been turned inside out and re-stitched. She was exhausted, but there was a clarity in her bones she hadn't felt in years. Not since before the funeral. Not since before the world fell quiet.

When she returned, Kia was sitting upright, color just barely returning to her cheeks. Her curls were a bit frizzy, her hoodie twisted, but she was still Kia. Her anchor, the girl who made her stomach do flips.

"So…" Kia took the mug Marisol offered. "I need to know… Was I hallucinating, or were you actually…glowing?"

Marisol settled beside her, pulling her knees to her chest. "You weren't hallucinating."

Kia let out a low whistle. "Dang. That was a lot. The glowing, the roots, the voices, the ancestral ghost man. And the way that spiral lit up at the end? Holy glow stick from heck, it felt like…we walked out of someone's dream."

Marisol nodded. "It did. Or a memory." She hesitated. "But it wasn't a dream. It was real. All of it."

Kia went quiet. She sipped her tea, then stared into the steam. "I still don't know if I believe in witchcraft, Mari. Not like that. Not the way you do."

Marisol didn't respond right away. She just waited.

Then, Kia added, quietly, "But I've been thinking about something lately. Maybe…God gives different people different gifts. Maybe that's what this is. A gift. Your gift."

Marisol looked at her, eyes wide with something unspoken. Gratitude. Relief. The kind of recognition she hadn't known she'd been starving for. "You don't have to call it what I call it," Marisol said softly. "But thank you. For seeing me."

Kia shrugged, but her voice cracked a little. "You've always seen me, Mari. Even when no one else did. I'm just trying to return the favor."

Marisol blinked back the sting behind her eyes. "You never made me feel like I had to earn your love. Even when I didn't love myself. Even when I was falling apart."

Kia let out a soft snort and gave Marisol a playful shove, but the shimmer in her eyes betrayed the tears she was fighting back. The shove was gentler than usual, as if her strength hadn't fully returned. Her hand lingered on Marisol's arm a moment too long before she finally let go.

Emotions swept through Marisol so fast that it left her dizzy. She looked toward Kia, and their eyes met. Something warm and charged passed between them. There go the flips again. "So, you don't think I am evil because of my...gift?"

Kia scrunched her brows. "What? No. What made you think that?"

Marisol scratched the back of her neck. "Nothing. Just a random thought."

Kia rested her head on Marisol's shoulder. Her voice was quieter than usual, raspier, like it had been scraped raw. "We've both been a mess," she said. "But that's the thing, right? That's why we work."

Marisol's heart thudded.

Kia lifted her head, her gaze holding Marisol's. "We keep showing up for each other."

The words settled between them, fragile and unspoken. Marisol's throat tightened. She wanted to reach out and say more. She'd promised herself she would tell her everything after all of this. But now was the wrong time. Kia needed to recover. She needed space, not more emotional baggage to sort out. So, Marisol managed a slight nod.

But the look in Kia's eyes didn't go away. They sat there for a while, drinking tea in silence, the kind of silence that came from understanding.

Eventually, Marisol pulled out her phone. Kia had dozed off beside her, steam still rolling off the mug in front of her. Marisol headed to her mother's room. She hesitated for a moment, then dialed. Doña Elvira picked up on the first ring. "¿Marisol?"

"Hey, Doña Elvira," she said, her voice scratchy. "We're okay. Kia's here with me."

A pause. Then a breath of relief. "Gracias a Dios."

Marisol nodded. "It's done. I'll fill you in later, I promise. But for now...the hill is quiet."

Another pause. Then Elvira's voice came through, soft but knowing. "Be careful with quiet, Mija. Sometimes silence is nothing more than the moment that gathers before the scream."

Marisol didn't flinch. "I know."

There was a rustle, like paper sliding over paper. Then Elvira's voice again. "Do you have the journal still?"

"Yes, it's with me."

"Then write down what you remember before it fades. Dreams and visions have a way of unraveling in daylight."

"I will."

They hung up.

Marisol slid the phone in her back pocket. She let her gaze drift toward her mother's room. It was her room now, though she still couldn't think of it that way. She hadn't changed a single thing since Mami died. The door remained cracked slightly, just as it had been the night she passed. Not because Marisol was afraid to close it, but because keeping it open felt like a way to keep her mother near.

She closed her eyes. Let her chest rise, then fall.

Before she headed back to the kitchen, she stopped and looked down. At the threshold of her mother's bedroom door lay a spiral, etched in ash.

Her heart stopped. She blinked and crouched down. The

ash looked fresh. It wasn't soot from a candle or dust from neglect. It was deliberately and carefully drawn. It was a message.

Marisol reached her finger out to touch it, but when she did, it vanished. The ash dispersed into nothing.

Marisol stood there a long moment, her hand hovering over where the spiral had been, the warmth from her hands already fading from her palms.

The hill may be quiet. But it wasn't done.

36

SIN MIEDO (WITHOUT FEAR)

Marisol hadn't slept. Not really, though she'd tried, curled beneath the quilt in her mother's bed. Her body buzzed with a kind of restless charge, like something inside her had been left open. Like she'd stepped through one door, only to find another one waiting.

The journal on the nightstand hummed faintly. Its presence was both comforting and unsettling at the same time. Marisol hadn't opened it again since last night. She didn't need to. Not yet. It wasn't done speaking. She knew that. But she wasn't ready to listen—though she knew she had to.

She slid out of bed carefully. Kia slept next to her soundly like a toddler who hogged the entire bed. One of her legs lay on top of Marisol, making her creep out of bed so slowly as if any sudden shift might wake the feelings she hadn't dared name out loud and wake up Kia. Suddenly, Marisol was too aware of the space between them. Too afraid to close the distance there. She grabbed the journal from the nightstand before crossing the room quietly, skipping the creaky floorboard like second nature. At the door, she paused to look back.

Kia was still asleep, arms wrapped around a pillow like it

owed her rent, one foot dangling off the edge on Marisol's side. Her bonnet was crooked and half-slipped, like it had been fighting sleep too. Marisol's chest ached. She looked peaceful. Uncomplicated. Exactly what Marisol couldn't risk ruining.

She tiptoed down the hallway. The floor was cold beneath her feet. A faint breeze moved through the house, though no windows were open. It was the kind of breeze that didn't shift curtains but still knew how to crawl into one's bones.

In the kitchen, she poured water into the kettle again, her movements slow and familiar. As it heated, she allowed her spirit to calm before turning to the journal she'd laid on the dining room table. Its leather cover was still warm. The pages curled slightly like they'd been touched by moisture.

She flipped to the end. A gentle breeze stirred the room, bringing a familiar and soothing sensation.

You saw Altagracia bless the stone, didn't you? She called you La Cerradora.

Her mother's handwriting appeared on the page.

Marisol smiled. She was free now. She could talk to her. Her hands shook as she pulled a pen from her bag and wrote beneath it. There were so many things she wanted to say, like I'm sorry. I love you. I take it all back. But she needed to tell Mami she was part of this too. That she'd always been. That she didn't fail. If anything, like Doña Elvira had said, she opened a path for her. If it weren't for what she did, she wouldn't have been able to get this far or rescue Kia.

She didn't just call me, Mami. She called both of us.

A pause. Then, her mother responded.

Yes…but like Isadora, I couldn't finish.

Marisol closed her eyes, feeling the truth of it, but without grief this time.

You didn't have to. You and Isadora. You both cleared the path for me.

Her mother responded

I'm sorry I couldn't help.

Marisol wrote:

You were trapped, and I know the rule. I read it. We must walk this path alone, but we can call on the community for assist like Doña Elvira said.

Josefina wrote back:

That's right, mi pollita. You are so wise. ooh, I miss my friend. Tell her I'm sorry for those last few days. I'm sure I scared her. But it wasn't me. I know she knows that. Give her a hug from me.

But look, I want you to listen to Isadora. She's right. It's not the hill. The hill is only the first doorway, and he's angry. Very angry, and he's holding on beneath the roots where the roots have rotted.

Marisol sat down hard.

He's holding on beneath the roots...

A movement came from behind her. Marisol whirled around. She closed the journal. It was Kia.

She groaned. "Why are you up? You're not supposed to function before tea. It's a law. Like gravity."

Marisol smirked. Hearing Kia's sass made everything feel kind of normal. "Couldn't sleep."

Kia had the blanket draped over her bonnet, which was now straight on her head. She rubbed her face and straightened up slowly, groaning like an old door. "Dang. You look like someone who got answers and hated all of them."

Marisol held up the journal and grunted. "You're not wrong."

Kia pulled the blanket tighter around herself and perched on a high chair at the kitchen island. Across from her, Marisol sat at the dining table. "Is this where you tell me we're going back to the hill? Because I'm still emotionally allergic to whatever was in those roots."

"No," Marisol said quickly. Then, softer, "Not yet."

Kia studied her for a long second. "You found something, though, right?"

Marisol hesitated. "Yeah. And I'm still trying to figure out what it means."

Kia nodded slowly. "Well, whatever it is, I support you. From my couch. At a safe distance. With snacks."

Marisol laughed, but it caught in her throat. "And I am fully supportive of that. Plus, I was going to say that I gotta do this alone again."

Kia tilted her head. "Why does that feel like a 'it's not you, it's me' line? Are you ghosting me? Don't tell me you are leaving because you want me to be safe. Is this the part where you say something cryptic only for me to never see you again?"

Marisol could tell Kia was fully awake now. She'd let go of the blanket, which fell over her shoulders. Her eyes were wide open, examining Marisol. God, she felt so vulnerable. She hated that these were the vibes she was giving off. Kia was partly right, but not about the ghosting part. She was being kind of cryptic, yes. But that was because, while Kia now truly understood how bad it was out there when it came to things she couldn't see, there were still some things Marisol had to keep close. How could she explain to Kia that she needed to kill a ghost? First, locate them and then kill him for good.

"It's not," Marisol said quickly, feeling her stomach do a flip. "It's just—this next part, I think it's meant for me alone. And I need to know you're safe."

Kia stepped over the blanket pooled at her feet. She pointed an accusatory finger at Marisol. "I knew it!"

Marisol raised her hand in defense. "But I am not ghosting you. You can even stay here if you want."

At that, Kia stepped back.

Marisol smiled faintly at Kia. "You believe in me, right?"

Kia held her gaze. "Always. But you worry about me like that?"

Marisol didn't know what "like that" meant, but her stomach did a somersault before settling. "Always."

"I like that," Kia said, grabbing the blanket from the floor and putting it over her shoulders again. She sat down beside Marisol, lowered her head to the table, and caught Marisol's hand in both of hers, holding it near her lips as though it were something to cling to.

Kia's breath warmed Marisol's fingers. She itched to touch her lips. To grab her chin, raise it, and kiss her.

"Look, Mari," Kia began to say, breaking Marisol's reckless train of thought. "I understand, but I don't understand. Or I understand it in my own way."

"I just need you to believe in me."

"I do. I always have."

And that made Marisol's stomach squeeze. Marisol took her hand away, pretending she needed to cover her mouth to cough. But the truth was that everything was too intense. The feeling of danger and the love that had been blooming deep within her for this girl she had known for most of her life collided, creating what seemed like chaos in her mind. "Then you know, I can and will stop Salvador, and whatever else is still out there trying to manipulate me and my family's legacy, right?"

A silence settled between them, not awkward but filled with everything unspoken.

Kia sat up and held Marisol's gaze. She whispered, "Yes. Yes, I do."

Marisol nodded and turned back to the journal. She needed to focus. There would be time to tell Kia. She'd find the words, the courage. But not now. Not while Salvador still poisoned the hill, still threatened her sanity. If she didn't end this, he'd come back stronger, crueler, hungrier. He'd take everything from her—Kia, Doña Elvira, the fragile world she'd barely begun to rebuild. He'd rot it all from the inside out.

The ink in the journal shimmered again, like it knew the clock was running out.

Kia leaned down and pressed a kiss to Marisol's cheek before turning back toward the room. Marisol watched her go, the blanket trailing behind her like the train of a wedding dress. She sighed. *After this, I will tell her how I feel. No more procrastinating.*

Marisol dragged her gaze off Kia as she disappeared into the bedroom. She placed her full focus on the journal in front of her and flipped through it further.

"Tell me what I need to know. How do I find Salvador's true form?"

But the paper stayed stubbornly blank.

Marisol pressed both palms to it, grounding herself against the table's wood grain. She closed her eyes, not picturing blood this time, but clarity—the fire of challenge, the surge of energy in her veins.

When she opened them, the page bore a spiral in a circle, a sharp line inside pointing south. She had seen it carved into the chamber stone. This was the path she hadn't explored.

Her breath hitched. *This is where I'll find him.* She knew it in her bones.

For a flicker, she wondered: Why not imagine him destroyed and be done with it? And it was tempting. But the answer came sharp and certain. That would make her no better than the curse he left behind. Her ancestors hadn't passed down their magic for her to avoid the fight. They had trusted her to face it.

She was scared, but she wasn't going to let fear stop her.

In the bathroom mirror, her reflection stared back. This time, she didn't look away, and what she saw was resolve.

37

RAICES PODRIDAS (ROTTEN ROOTS)

Marisol walked.

Outside, the sun was beginning to bleed into dusk. The light was thinner. The hill in the distance stood like a forgotten monument.

South of Hallowthorn Hill, the terrain flattened. The trees grew sparse, but the silence grew louder. There was no trail, no clear marker like the Ceiba Tree that marked La Vega. This was all instinct and whispers from our ancestors.

He's still holding on beneath the roots.

Marisol's stomach turned. The burial site wasn't symbolic. It was literal. Salvador hadn't just clung to power—he had tethered himself to the Espinal women by infecting the very land they walked on.

Where the roots have rotted.

She thought of mold, of infestation, of disease. Marisol remembered cutting across the bald patch near the hill to get to school faster, the sudden nausea that hit her every time. She used to blame the wind or a skipped breakfast. Now she knew better. She'd walked over his grave.

Her phone buzzed. Doña Elvira.

She answered. "Doña?"

"I've been sitting here waiting and realized that I could just reach out myself." Elvira sounded sheepish.

"I'm sorry. I've been meaning to call, but I am glad you did," Marisol said, hoping Elvira didn't feel as if she was ignoring her. Ever since they started talking, she'd been nothing but helpful. "I need to ask you something. Did you know his burial site?"

A long silence.

"Your mother told me pieces. But by the time I started asking questions, it was too late. She wasn't remembering things, her mood had changed..."

Marisol continued. She loved Doña Elvira. The lady was like a tía, maybe even a second mother at one point. She had been one of the two people, besides Kia, whom she could trust. But still...how could she have left her best friend alone when she needed her most? Every Cerradora had to find their own way. She understood that now. But it was she who told her about community. Why hadn't Elvira supported her mother the same way she was helping her now?

"I don't understand," Marisol finally said, her voice sharp with something hotter than confusion. "Why didn't you go with her?"

There was a moment of silence on the other end. Not long, but long enough for Marisol to hear the discomfort in it. Even through the phone, she could feel Elvira shift like she was squirming under the weight of a truth she'd kept to herself. Doña Elvira let out a long breath, almost like an apology, before the words came.

"Because I couldn't," Elvira said quietly. "I was immuno-compromised during COVID. The chemo treatments had wrecked me. Your mother didn't tell me much. I think she didn't want me to risk it. You know, to go outside and get sick. She went alone because she had to. And I let her."

Marisol froze, unable to walk. She brought her hands to her mouth to keep the audible gasp from being heard. After a few seconds, she managed, "Is that why...the masks? I just thought—"

She had assumed Elvira was being cautious. Polite. Respectful, like Mami had always been. But now, she understood better. Both of them had carried something invisible—one haunted by a ghost, the other battling a disease—and both had changed.

Marisol shook her head. "I'm so sorry. I didn't know."

Elvira exhaled. "I didn't want you to know, Mija."

Guilt slammed into her. Tears welled as she realized how much she had missed, how much comfort they could've given each other. If only they hadn't both been drowning. This woman had been so close to her once. And they had grieved side by side, alone.

"She changed after that," Elvira added, voice softer now. "There was something in her eyes the last time we spoke. Not just grief. Something darker. Like a shadow had moved in and started speaking in her voice."

Marisol remembered those final months. Her mother had seemed more paranoid, more distant. But she'd chalked it up to her mom adjusting to life without her.

"I think," Elvira said, "the closer you get to Salvador, the more toxic your soul becomes."

Marisol inspected the space surrounding her. "Then I'll have to be careful."

"Be careful, yes," Elvira said. "But don't be afraid. You carry your mother's strength, but you are not walking her path. And you're not alone."

"I know," Marisol said resolutely. "And I will undo this, so he won't come after us ever again."

The line was quiet for a beat.

"I believe you," Elvira said. "And so do the women who came before you."

They ended the call without saying goodbye. Just a knowing that while Marisol had broken the magic free, Salvador was still out there, willing and able to get in her head and rot her from within.

At least I freed our power and the ancestors, Marisol thought.

But your legacy is still undone, another part of her whispered back.

Marisol took a deep breath. She was ready. She began walking again until she found herself in a familiar place. The bald patch spread before her like a scar, bare earth crusted with brittle ice. Nothing could grow here.

Marisol stepped gently. The ground gave slightly, as if it had been waiting for her.

She closed her eyes and pictured the roots beneath the surface—rotted, swollen, slick with the same poison she had once touched. Not just one, but many, twisting deeper, blackening the further they sank.

When she opened her eyes, they were all around her. Roots split and weeping, veins of decay threading through the soil. She had found the burial site.

38

NOMBRAR EL MONSTRUO (NAME THE MONSTER)

Marisol crouched low, her palms braced against the damp soil as she moved forward. She pulled the candle Mamá Belén had given her. She'd said that it would always show the way.

Marisol looked at the candle. "Show me."

A soft wind passed by her, touched the wick, and lit it. Its flame bent against the flow of air as if showing her where to go. Marisol looked in its direction. Black rotted roots coiled like twisted veins, pulsing faintly with a sickly light. The deeper she went, the more the air thickened, not just with dirt and decay, but with something else. Something wrong.

Her breath fogged in front of her. The damp air clung to her skin, curling around her ears like murmurs.

"You shouldn't be here."

The voice wasn't hers. It came from behind her, from inside her. She pressed forward.

The tunnel narrowed. She had to crawl now, roots dragging across her back like skeletal fingers. Every inch downward became heavier, like gravity was trying to pull her into something she couldn't yet see.

And then it opened into a lower chamber.

She dropped into it and looked around. The space was carved from earth and rot. The roots here weren't just alive—they were wrong. Bloated. Fungal. Decayed. The stench of death filled the air. The roots stretched across the space like ribs and veins, feeding into something at the center.

A mound.

Marisol put the candle down. She reached out to the mound and touched it, feeling a beat underneath it.

It's a body.

Salvador's. He's buried here, but he's not at rest.

"Stay away." Salvador's voice slithered into her mind, coiled and controlled, trying too hard to sound menacing. But beneath the sharpness, there was a tremble. He couldn't do anything but influence and poison someone's mind. His body was nothing but a trembling heart, barely clinging to what remained of life, festering in the soil like rot, and he knew that.

Marisol stood firm. "What are you going to do?"

She envisioned a coif like those worn by knights, protecting her head from any manipulation he may sway her way. But she realized then that his true power lay in her doubt. If she believed in herself, Salvador couldn't get to her.

Somewhere along this path, she had stopped believing his lies, las tres mojonas, and that voice inside her head that second-guessed, and she had started to believe in herself.

Marisol began to claw through the mound. She imagined claws instead of nails. Claws like knives, sharp enough to cut through roots that cocooned him. She was a beast, and this time, she had a purpose. Not to harm but to stop someone from harming.

The roots were thick and gnarled, as if the earth itself had tried to consume him but couldn't finish the job. They wove through his chest, coiled around his limbs, and burrowed into the hollow of his skull, fusing flesh with bark until it was impossible to tell where the man ended and the rot began.

His form pulsed beneath the twisted wood, not with life, but with something else—something slow and unnatural. A heartbeat that thudded out of rhythm, like it didn't belong to him. Like it had been stolen.

She grew fangs and began to claw and bite at anything that held on to him.

The air stank of mildew. The taste of old blood spread on her taste buds. Every breath felt like it clung to the back of Marisol's throat, heavy with decay. There were so many roots like armor that made a gurgling sound as if they were feeding on something. Even with claws and fangs, it was too much.

Marisol fell back at the sight, and the moment she did, the chamber shifted and the whispers sharpened. "Look at you, an animal," a voice rasped, "pretending you're not afraid. But you know you are."

The shadows around her darkened. The roots on the wall pulsed harder.

"You think memory is enough?" Salvador's voice slithered from every direction. "You think naming yourself changes what's inside of you?"

Marisol's fists clenched. Her heart thundered. "I know what's inside of me. And I know what's not."

The laughter that followed was jagged and low. It was everywhere, as if Salvador was everywhere, and he was mocking her. "You parade their names like armor. You change into something fierce. But beneath it all, you are still a frightened little girl with no other legacy but loss."

His presence filled the space, making the air even thicker. The roots shifted, and a figure began to morph.

Kia appeared first, her eyes wide. Terrified. "Mari, please. Don't do this. He's too strong."

Then her mother, her voice thin and her face pale. "You

were never meant to fix this. You're going to ruin everything I held together."

Mamá Belén appeared next, turning away. "You should've stayed small. So no one could see who you are. That would have surely kept you safe."

Marisol dropped to her knees. Tears burned her eyes. Her breath came shallow. The voices tore through her like blades.

"You failed them," Salvador whispered. "You failed me. That's why the power never belonged to you or them. It is also why you would not be able to wield it. Look at you. Just look at you. You are shaken and afraid. You are nothing but a child."

Tears stung her eyes at the pain his words caused. But then the journal in her bag pulsed.

Soft.

Warm.

Real.

She reached for it and pulled it free. As soon as she touched it, the illusions cracked. The visions froze.

I no longer believe his lies.

The visions flickered before coming alive again.

Kia's eyes now filled with encouragement and pride. "You're stronger than him, Mari."

Her mother smiled. "You are more than I ever dared to be."

Mamá Belén turned back her gaze, sharp and unwavering. "Miralo bien, mi amor. Look at him. And end it."

Marisol stood. This was what was real: her mother, grandmother, Kia, and Doña Elvira believing in her as she believed in herself.

"I name you," she said, her voice louder than the tremble in her bones. "Salvador Garcia. That is your real name, not the one you took to take our magic from us."

The chamber howled.

"You were never ours to begin with," she said, stepping forward. "And we were never yours to claim."

The roots pulsed harder, as if trying to pull back into the earth. Salvador's buried body groaned beneath them, like it had heard its own name and couldn't bear the weight of it. His name, once spoken in reverence and fear, now buckled under its own decay.

Marisol leaned forward and knelt once again beside the body. The smell was unbearable now—earth mixed with rot and fungal spores clinging to her lungs, trying to make a home in her body like they had in her family. She gagged but didn't back away. Her claws hovered over the center of Salvador's chest, where the roots met in a jagged knot of bark and sinew and old, corrupted magic.

She lowered her palms there, and the knot vibrated beneath her fingers like something trying to breathe through its last lie.

"You tried to root yourself in fear," she whispered. "But fear is not our inheritance. It's an infection."

Her voice grew steadier. "You are the fungus that grew in the cracks of our legacy. You fed on our doubt. You taught our mothers to hide their brilliance. You twisted our magic into shame."

Light spilled from her hands, colliding with the candle's light, not in a burst, but in a slow, steady unraveling, filling the space, as if it knew that decay took time, and so did healing.

The roots shuddered.

Marisol clenched her jaw and dug her claws into the knots. She pulled and ripped. The bark splintered under her hands. One by one, she tore the roots, first from the ribs, then from the spine, then from the skull. Each one released with a groan, as though the land itself resisted letting go of what had festered in it for so long.

"You made us doubt ourselves," she said, her voice cracking. "Generation after generation, we shrank. We apologized for our knowing. We contorted ourselves into versions that fit someone else's fear. But we were never the problem. You were."

With each root she cast aside, her arms trembled more. The skin on her hands split. Her sleeves tore. But she didn't stop. "You're not our ancestor," she whispered. "You're our parasite. And I'm pulling you out."

She yanked the final root from Salvador's chest with a snap like wet wood breaking. His form collapsed inward, and with it, the fungal bloom curled and hissed as it shriveled. There was no treasure beneath it. No artifact of power. Just rot and lies.

Salvador had not become immortal. He had become an infestation.

Marisol stayed kneeling for a moment longer, letting the silence settle. Her body shook with the aftershocks and the weight of what she had undone. She felt the soil press against her knees, the earth no longer resisting her. It felt soft, almost warm.

She understood now. This wasn't just about reclaiming her family's power. This was about uprooting the disease that had kept them small. The denial of the whole self. The rejection of their own gifts. The self-loathing passed down like an inheritance, and the end of what should have never begun.

That was the fungus. And she had just cut it out. She breathed, allowing her body to become her once again, and once it did, she reached into her bag and pulled out the journal, thumbing through the last blank page.

> I saw him.
> I named him.
> I returned him to the earth, not as an ancestor,
> but as a warning.
> We are not his anymore. We never were.

I pulled the rot from the roots. I cleared the way.

Now we grow. Not in his shadow. But in our light.

I am the last Cerradora, and this is the end of Salvador's story.

Marisol Espinal.

The page shimmered, then it stilled. The glow faded slowly, leaving behind a faint warmth that clung to her fingers. Marisol pressed the cover closed, her chest tight.

A final gust of wind swept through the chamber. The soil beneath her feet shifted.

A path opened upward and into a slope carved in soft roots, glowing faintly. Inviting.

She grabbed the candle and her things and climbed up. Her hands were dirty. Her legs shook. But her spine was straight.

She emerged into daylight. The sky was pale pink and gold. The morning had arrived.

Marisol stood at the top of Hallowthorn Hill, breathless, but whole.

She didn't escape the hill.

She freed it.

39

EL RECUERDO DE ALTAGRACIA
(ALTAGRACIA'S REMEMBRANCE)

The town looked the same. But it didn't feel the same.

Marisol strolled through the early morning quiet, past shuttered stores and freshly watered flowerbeds, past the mural she'd passed a hundred times without really seeing it.

This time, though, she stopped in front of it.

The mural stretched across the side of the visitor's center, its colors still bright, its brushstrokes still clean. Children played beneath an Ohio Buckeye tree, its branches heavy with the distinctive non-edible nut. A line of settlers smiled as they held baskets of grain and proudly displayed the tools of their success: plows, pressed uniforms, and folded flags. The town's "first families," all light-skinned and lovingly rendered, looked out with the calm assurance of those who'd been allowed to write history.

And near the edge, as always, was the woman with the broom. Brown-skinned. Head bowed. Caught mid-sweep like she was tidying up after someone else's celebration. She wasn't part of the story. Not really. But Marisol couldn't stop looking at her now. Something drew Marisol to her, and she realized the woman had a strong resemblance to her ancestor, Altagracia.

Marisol smiled. Here was her tatarabuela, a woman worth remembering.

Altagracia's binding had not been a surrender. It had been survival. She had chosen the only path she could see. A path born out of love for her daughters.

And that was her legacy. That even in fear, Altagracia kept going.

As if in a trance, Marisol imagined a new mural.

Altagracia, with her broom, stood at the center because Marisol saw her. She was known, not forgotten. She had a smile. A trail of roots waited for her. Not feeding off her but upholding her.

The colors of the mural brightened. The breeze carried a warmth she hadn't noticed before, like the town itself was breathing easier now that the truth had been unearthed. The sidewalk seemed less a path for leaving and more like one for returning.

The hill no longer loomed behind her.

It rested.

She passed Sabia on the street, put together, tote bag over her shoulder, brimming with things to do, eyes flickering up with surprise. Their gazes met. Sabia opened her mouth like she might say something, but Marisol didn't stop. Instead, she offered a smile. Not smug. Not sweet. Just...done.

Sabia looked confused. And that was enough.

Marisol turned onto the street, her heart quickening as Kia's building came into view. She felt eyes behind her, as if Sabia was staring at her. She looked back, but Sabia was already on her phone, almost out of sight. Not seeing anything, Marisol kept walking, and as she neared the building's entrance, she spotted Kia at the mailboxes just inside the glass vestibule, barefoot and in Marisol's hoodie, hair loose like a crown on her head, eyes puffy.

The door swung open before Marisol could knock.

"You ever leave for that long," Kia said, worried. She pointed a finger at her, "I swear if something happens, I will drag your spirit back myself."

Marisol barely had time to laugh before Kia pulled her into her arms so hard it knocked the breath out of her.

Should I tell her?

The question rose, sharp and immediate. *No. Not now. Not like this.*

But then she thought, what if there was no next time?

She didn't want to keep holding her feelings hostage, assuming there would always be a better moment. What if something happened tomorrow, and she never said it?

She closed her eyes, pressing her forehead against Kia's shoulder.

Now wasn't the right time. But the time was coming. And when it did, she wouldn't let it pass her by.

"You're okay," Kia whispered. "You're okay."

"I am."

Kia's apartment was small but inviting. Sunlight filtered through sheer curtains. Books and plants crowded a corner shelf, mugs dried on a rack above the sink. The couch faced the kitchen rather than the TV, and books lay scattered across every surface, as if she might pluck one up mid-thought and forget where she set it down.

When they finally sat down, Kia wiped at her eyes and said, "Alright. What happened? I want all of it. No skimming. No, it's complicated.' And definitely no 'you wouldn't understand.' Even if it's magical, I'd rather know than live with the holes."

Marisol opened her mouth but hesitated.

Kia saw it. "Look. Magic still makes me twitchy. But I know

your heart. And whatever this gift is...It had to come from God. I'm sure of that now. So, don't hold back. Just tell me."

And so Marisol did. Not every detail. Not yet. But enough.

And Kia didn't interrupt. Not once.

After they sat in the quiet for a while, Kia declared that there was absolutely no way Marisol was going back to her place. At least not until Kia was convinced she wouldn't wake up with her stomach on the floor, thinking something had happened to her. So, they walked over to Marisol's house together to pack a quick weekender for Marisol.

At her house, Marisol moved through the space with care, pulling a few clean clothes and tucking the journal and her mother's notebook like sacred objects into her duffel bag. When she veered toward the living room, she reached for a candle and a bundle of herbs. She felt eyes on her and looked back to see Kia lifting a brow.

Marisol paused, her hand on a small tin of herbs. "Look—I need this. I'm tethered to this now."

Kia crossed her arms but didn't argue. "Fine. Go ahead. I get it. You've got...mystical attachment issues."

Marisol grinned. "I'll take that."

They returned to Kia's apartment together, arms full of memories and quiet understanding between them, like a newly patched quilt.

That night, after Kia had gone to bed, Marisol sat at the kitchen table. A candle burned low in its center, the same one Mamá Belén used to light on rainy mornings.

She opened the journal.

One final page had appeared.

The handwriting was different. Softer. Maybe it was another ancestor.

The root remembers the one who tended it. Leave your own seed.

She picked up her pen.

I am here. I remember. I will not forget.

She closed the journal.

The next morning, Marisol made tea. She lit a candle. She stood at the window and looked out at the world that had never really changed, only deepened.

On a scrap of paper, she wrote down three things she wanted to grow:

Courage. Rest. Wonder.

Marisol looked down at the ink seeping onto the page. This was magic.

But then she looked around and realized that no matter how much she had run from it, she had always been surrounded by it.

It was in the way the steam curled from her mug.

In the way Kia's laugh echoed from the other room.

In the breath she took, knowing she was still here.

In the way, the hill had quieted, but she hadn't.

And knowing that was powerful.

Because magic wasn't some inheritance she had to earn. It was life itself. And it had always been hers.

40

___

EL FIN ES MIO (THE ENDING IS MINE)

The sun poured into the apartment like honey, slow and golden, unbothered. Marisol stirred the tea in her cup, watching the steam rise into shapes that reminded her of the spiral. Two weeks had passed since everything, and she still hadn't gone back home. She missed it, though. She missed the Espinal house, the ghosts that lingered in its corners like familiar company, the way every memory seemed pressed into the walls like wallpaper. Yet here, in Kia's apartment, the air felt gentler. Less watchful. Almost as if the ghosts had agreed to give her space here.

Behind her, Kia groaned from the couch. "If that's not coffee, I'm filing for a new girlfriend."

Marisol smirked. "It's tea. For grounding."

"Ugh," Kia muffled into a pillow. "You and your leafy therapy."

"You love it."

"I love you," Kia grumbled. "That's different."

Marisol placed a mug on the coffee table and sat beside her. She leaned over and kissed her. The morning was soft in all the right ways, lighting Kia from the inside out. They didn't need words; the truth had already passed between them, spoken in confessions and held back by timing until a week ago. Kiar rested her head on Marisol's shoulder.

"I was thinking." Kia lifted her head. "You should do something with all of this."

Marisol looked at Kia, pointing and swirling her finger at her. She raised a brow. "With what? The trauma? The supernatural infestation? My new brand as the resident town bruja?"

"Yes," Kia said, grinning. "And the hair. You've got powerful curls, and now you've got the resume to back it up."

They laughed together, the sound light and long. This is what she loved. They can be both light and intense at the same time.

"I should," Marisol relented once they stopped laughing.

By midday, she walked to Doña Elvira's shop.

The herb shop looked the same: sun-dried bundles hung in the windows, wind chimes clinked, and the painted sign was still crooked. But Elvira stood just outside the door, as if waiting.

"I was wondering when you'd show," she said.

"I needed one last nap and two servings of toast," Marisol replied, feeling refreshed. "It was the right call."

Inside, the air smelled like ruda and something citrusy. Marisol helped stack dried bundles, ground some fresh rue, and listened as Elvira hummed to a playlist that mixed old-school merengue and R&B.

Elvira gestured her toward a place in the shop. "Come on. I spruced up your corner."

Marisol looked at a desk she had seen in the back of the shop that was now free of dust and held a box on top. It was made of dark and solemn wood, with scratches and mug rings that give it a unique personality.

"What's this?" Marisol asked.

"Yours," Elvira said. "It's time your magic had a place."

Inside the box was a blank journal. A clean sachet. A sprig of rosemary. And a key.

Marisol turned the key over in her palm, then stopped to look at Elvira, drawing up a questioning eyebrow.

"For the drawer." Elvira pointed at it with her lips. "For your notes... For what comes next."

Marisol nodded, unsure if her throat could handle a thank you just yet.

After giving Doña Elvira a hug, she returned to work until they closed, then went for a walk.

Not to chase ghosts. Not to test her power.

Just to walk.

She passed the café. Passed the mural. Passed the hill in the distance.

And then, without planning to, she walked to its base.

Not to climb. Not to enter. But to sit.

She laid her hand on the earth, fingers pressing gently into the grass and soil. It was calm.

"Thank you," she whispered. "I'll keep watch now."

The wind moved through the trees above. As if acknowledging her.

Back at the Espinal home, she opened her new journal and began anew.

> This is not a story about the hill. It's a story about the girl who came back from it.
>
> My name is Marisol Espinal.
>
> I fought for our magic. Found it, and now I walk with it.

She closed the journal, poured herself another cup of tea, lit the candle on the altar, and finally watered the plants she had ignored for the past two weeks.

Then, she stepped outside and let the sun hit her face.

A little girl across the street dropped her doll, and it rolled toward Marisol's foot. She bent down to pick it up, noticing how one of the doll's arms dangled oddly and the button on her right eye was chipped.

"Oh no, my doll!" the girl cried, rushing over.

Marisol held it gently, thinking of the butter cookie tin under her sink. The one with spare thread, old buttons, and a thimble she never admitted she used. She could fix the arm. The eye, too.

"Do you want me to fix her?" Marisol asked.

The girl shook her head and took the doll back. "I'm a healer, you know."

Marisol nodded, fully believing in the girl's trust in herself.

The girl examined the doll carefully. "I'll heal her arm because it broke," she said matter-of-factly. "But her eye has always been like this. It's perfect just the way it is."

She turned the doll so Marisol could see.

And Marisol couldn't help but agree.

Changing the doll's eye—what made her unique—would take away its magic. The arm needed mending, yes. But the rest? The rest should remain exactly as it was.

"I completely agree," Marisol said. "She's perfect, besides the arm. The right thing is to heal what hurts."

She watched the girl sit on a nearby bench and begin a tiny, focused surgery with a shoelace and a hairpin.

"May she always be blessed with the ability to believe in herself. May she always see the magic within," Marisol whispered into the wind.

The wind swirled around her, picking up her prayer and taking it away into the heavens.

EPILOGUE
EL HILL DESCANSA (THE HILL RESTS)

Thank you for being a witness. I knew she would come back! Esa es mi pollita, igualita a su mamá. Pin pun. She climbed the hill just like I once did. Only this time, she finished Salvador's story, and now the hill wasn't murmuring in fear. It was listening to her walk.

What can I say? The hill calls you when you're ready, when you're willing to see who you are beneath the noise of the world. And mi Mari, la pollita querida de su madre, she always heard more than she let on. I knew it. She just needed time to believe it for herself.

I watched her walk that hill. I felt every tremble in her chest, every pull of doubt when her heart asked, Am I enough? The world told her she wasn't. But I knew better.

And she was.

Even when she didn't believe it, she was.

I tried to tell her once, back when her curls still framed a rounder face and her hands clung to mine like lifelines. I told her stories. I braided truths into her hair. I whispered legends into her dreams. I prayed that one day, she'd remember. Not just for me, but for herself too. That she'd look in the mirror and see the history in her eyes. That she'd stop shrinking and start reaching.

And she did.

She remembered when it mattered.

And when she lit the candle in our home and whispered thank you into the air, I was there. I saw her. Not just as my daughter, but as a woman standing in the fullness of her power. No longer hiding. No longer small. She didn't just carry the Espinal name; she reclaimed it.

I'm so proud of her.

But since she untied Salvador from our legacy, Marisol hasn't always gotten it right. She'd gotten messy. Emotional. Stubborn. But she's an Espinal. And she'd earned the right to carry that name con gusto y emocion.

Mamá Belén judged from the afterlife, telling me, "Mira. Le diste mucha cuerda a esa muchacha."

But I don't think so. She's good. She's good. I know she is.

Jejeje. She went in one of Blanca's videos the way she always wanted to. You know, bold, unbothered, and dropped a whole dissertation in there. Then Kia tagged on. Esas dos muchachas. They are so good for one another. I've been watching it build up for years.

And yes, in the comments, she and Kia get a little roughed up, pero they hold their own. They write their truths. They stir the pot. They make a great team, and that's what matters.

And you know what? That's my real pollita. She's a little unhinged. Takes after me.

And now the hill is quiet, not because it has nothing left to say, but because it trusts her to speak for it. She became what I had known her to be. She doesn't whisper anymore. She speaks with her whole chest. For all of us.

And the hill listens.

Oh, my daughter.
Oh, my pride.
Oh, my ordinary bruja.

AFTERWORD

The Ordinary Bruja began as a question I couldn't stop asking:

What happens when we forget who we are?

The story that unfolded became more than just Marisol's—it became a reflection of so many of us who were taught to shrink, to blend, to survive instead of thrive. Marisol's journey is one of grief, reclamation, and the radical magic of remembering. It's for the girls who were called too much and not enough in the same breath. For the ones who carry ancestral wounds and still dare to heal.

If you've made it to this page, thank you. You've witnessed Marisol rise. You've followed her through smoke and shadow, fear and doubt, and watched her reclaim what was nearly lost: her power, her voice, and her place in a legacy that tried to erase her.

But Marisol is not the beginning.

She's the continuation of a story that started long before her—and now, it's time to go back.

The next book in the *Cerradora* series is **Isadora: The First Cerradora.**

Set decades before *The Ordinary Bruja*, this book follows Isadora Espinal—the quiet librarian who once believed she could hide from her bloodline, only to be chosen by the hill when she least expected it. Isadora's story is one of forbidden love, broken lineage, and the first spark of resistance that paved the way for Josefina and, eventually, Marisol.

Con Cariño
  — Joa

ACKNOWLEDGMENTS

Books may be written alone, but they are never made alone. The Ordinary Bruja exists because a lot of people showed up for me in ways big and small, and I will never forget it.

To my beta readers—Kendra Dawn, Gisselle Nicole Gouveia, and Page Grey—thank you for your time, honesty, and care. You helped make this book stronger, sharper, and more whole. You saw what I was trying to do and gently pushed me to do it better.

To my early reader, Witchy Lily (code name, LOL), and Lorna, you both made me feel seen in the early stages, when this story was still tangled in doubt and drafts. Your belief mattered more than you know. To Lorna, thank you for not only being an early reader but an ARC reader. Knowing that readers like you are not afraid to face uncomfortable facts made all the long hours behind the computer worth it.

To everyone who preordered this book: thank you for trusting me with your time, your dollars, and your curiosity. That kind of faith is rare. I hope this story was worth it.

To my TikTok Live family: thank you for being with me on the hard days, for listening when I didn't know what I was saying, and for reminding me that I'm not alone in this journey.

To Amy Lisane for providing thoughtful feedback and sharp insight while maintaining my voice. You helped elevate Marisol's story without ever asking her to become someone she's not. Your notes were a gift.

To my husband—my ride or die, the man who always asks

"What's next?"—thank you for your endless support, for letting me talk about these characters like they pay rent, and for standing beside me even when I wasn't sure where I was going. For commenting on every YouTube video I post. I love you.

And finally, to every bruja, spiritual misfit, cultural question mark, or reluctant magic-maker out there—thank you for reading this book. For letting it sit with you. For walking with Marisol. May you always find your way back to yourself.

THE ORDINARY BRUJA
SOUNDTRACK
SONGS THAT ECHO MARISOL ESPINAL'S JOURNEY.

Prologue – Donde Todo Comenzó
   MALAMENTE (Cap. 1: Augurio) – ROSALÍA

Ch. 1 – Bruja en el Café
   Brujas – Princess Nokia

Ch. 2 – Mean Girls, Spanglish Edition
   Soy Yo – Bomba Estéreo

Ch. 3 – Shhh, El Hill is Speaking
   Lo Que Construimos – Natalia Lafourcade

Ch. 4 – Calor de Memoria
   Cucurrucucú Paloma – Natalia Lafourcade

Mystery of Love – Sufjan Stevens
   Ch. 5 – Huérfana con Wi-Fi

Ch. 6 – Mira Bien, Mari
   Miedo – Pablo Alborán

Ch. 7 – Lattes con Fantasmas
bury a friend – Billie Eilish

Ch. 9 – El Peligro Te Sigue
Haunted – Beyoncé

Ch. 10 – Brava Aunque Temblando
Fata Morgana (feat. Oxxxymiron) – Markul

Ch. 11 – La Duda Que Crece en la Oscuridad
Unstoppable – Sia

Ch. 13 – Grief y Resentimiento
Women – Anderson Rocio

Ch. 18 – El Apagón de Willowshade
Latinoamérica (feat. Totó la Momposina, Susana Baca, María Rita) – Calle 13

Ch. 14 – You Were Chosen, Mija
I Am Light – India.Arie

Ch. 15 – Protección con Sal y Fe
Rise Up – Andra Day

Ch. 20 – La Posesión
Don't Go Yet – Camila Cabello

Ch. 22 – Los Nombres en la Piedra
VOID – Melanie Martinez

Ch. 23 – Reflejo de Poder
Jericho – Iniko

Ch. 25 – Isadora y Yo
LATINA FOREVA – Karol G

Ch. 30 – Raíces con Nombres
Entra en Mi Vida – Sin Bandera

Ch. 33 – La Traición de Efigenia
Messy – Lola Young

Ch. 37 – Raíces Podridas
Little Girl Gone – CHINCHILLA

Ch. 38 – Nombrar el Monstruo
Chitty Bang – Leikeli47

Ch. 39 – El Recuerdo de Altagracia
I Like It – Cardi B, Bad Bunny, J Balvin

Epilogue – El Hill Descansa
Lo Que Construimos (Reprise) – Natalia Lafourcade

SCAN
ME
Spotify

ABOUT THE AUTHOR

Johanny Ortega is a Dominican-American author, literacy advocate, and founder of Have a Cup of Johanny Press. She writes fiction rooted in Dominican identity, ancestral memory, and the generational trauma we're too often told to silence. Her stories center complex Latine characters navigating shame, magic, and self-acceptance. She also hosts the Have a Cup of Johanny podcast and uses her platform to champion diverse voices in publishing. The Ordinary Bruja is the first book in her new Cerradora series.